Acknowledgemen

CW01500378

Nanny Dinah Veryard
Who, when I was seven, had me believe I could be a successful writer and
made me promise I'd write under the ancestral name of de-Veryard

Mr. Essex
An English teacher who constantly stated: 'Wendy, you have a brilliant
imagination and if you keep writing like this, one day you will certainly
have books published'

My mum, husband Richard & children Jo, John & David
For their continual support, humor, faith & encouragement…

Michelle Dudbridge,
May our friendship continue another forty-three years!

All my friends in batb fandom
Keep the Dream Alive!

* * *

And finally for the success of this story, my grateful thanks to:

James Devin, actor (South Carolina)
Goldie Jones, editor (Nebraska)

Nancy Richardson, proofreader (Long Island)
Dawn Yzaguirre, proofreader (Texas)
Donald Harver, Acquisitions (PublishAmerica)

Without you five this story would not be where it is today

Sincerely,
Wendy Christina Tunnard de-Veryard

Star-Dappled Night Mare

By
Wendy Tunnard de-Veryard

Wendy Tunnard de-Veryard

PublishAmerica
Baltimore

© 2005 by Wendy Tunnard de-Veryard.
All rights reserved. No part of this book may be reproduced, stored in a retrieval system or transmitted in any form or by any means without the prior written permission of the publishers, except by a reviewer who may quote brief passages in a review to be printed in a newspaper, magazine or journal.

First printing

At the specific preference of the author, PublishAmerica allowed this work to remain exactly as the author intended, verbatim, without editorial input.

ISBN: 1-4241-0841-1
PUBLISHED BY PUBLISHAMERICA, LLLP
www.publishamerica.com
Baltimore

Printed in the United States of America

For Pop…

Stephen James Veryard

(December 18th 1922 – May 22nd 2005)

My Love Forever…

Star-Dappled Night Mare

Foreword

Premonitions.

He'd had them all his life, pictures of future events.
This one was different.
This one was horrifying.

Twanging, the definite sound of metal over metal.
Accompanying scenes of long thin wires pulled taut and snapping.
Ricochet one after the other... shrill ear piercing sound.

Suspended from a rooftop, the dangling wires were swirling around and around and
around
Sending slices of human flesh flailing across the clearing...
Red and squishy, a definite sight of bone... vertebrae... running through the center.

A man in a giant cheese cutter...
When the premonition ended,
that had been the only way Jack could describe it.

Chapter One

"Will you come away from the window, Jack? What's so fascinating out there anyway?" When he did not reply Sherri touched his arm and prompted, "Jack?"

"Sorry. I was miles away."

"Did you have another premonition?"

"Yes," he replied quietly.

"Want to talk about it?"

Jack shook his head. "Not this time."

"Okay. Well, if you change your mind, I'm here for you okay? I might not be able to make sense of them, but sometimes it helps to talk."

"I know that. Thank you."

Sherri sighed. "So what do you want to do now, Jack?"

The table was littered with board games, the floor with videos. They'd spent the night watching films, playing games, not the sort of night she'd hoped for. Jack could see the disappointment in her eyes.

"I should go."

"Perhaps you should. I'll get your jacket," Sherri replied, irritably.

When Devin had rung to say he was sending Jack over to stay the night, she'd hoped for so much from the evening. His reluctance had been visible from the moment he had stepped into her apartment eight hours earlier. Candles…wine… roses…the room had screamed romance. Jack hadn't even kissed her.

Taking the offered jacket, Jack slipped it on.

"Will I see you tonight, Jack?"

Infinitely sad, he had no words. It was like reaching the end of an arduous journey. He was weary and jubilant at the same time. It saddened him to know that he felt that way about their relationship.

"Maybe," he replied opening the door. She knew he wouldn't. They'd reached the end of the road of a journey that had never begun.

Stepping from the warmth of her apartment building, the air outside was frigid. Jack pulled the collar of his jacket higher, bunching his shoulders, pulling his hat down over his ears. A sliver of neck left exposed to the elements caused him to shiver. Yet…it wasn't just that… Across the road Isaac Park loomed ominously, the cottage Jack shared with his Grandfather was in its center. Mist eerily concealed the yellow light of lamps adorning the walkways. In the hour that was darkest before dawn, Jack was terrified.

* * *

The luminous hands of his watch told Devin it was four twenty in the morning. Begrudgingly he kicked back the coverlet. A half hour from now, his Grandfather's alarm would go off, breakfast needed to be started by then.

Fumbling in the darkness for the jeans he had discarded the night before, he found them, and slipped them on. Standing he pulled and fastened them up over his hips and searched the end of the bed for his shirt. It wasn't there. Sometime in the night it had slid to the floor. He left it there and collected a clean one from the closet.

Dressed, Devin made his way to the door, yanked it open stepped into the kitchen and grimaced when the cold stone tiles met warm skin through holes in his socks.

"Coffee!" He muttered, making his way to the stove. Striking a match beneath the kettle, he turned on the gas, and headed to the counter for a mug. Passing the window he lifted the curtains and looked out at the view beyond. Jack was due home, hopefully before their Grandfather was up.

"Unless he sleeps in," Devin chuckled, thinking of his brother. Thinking of the fact that for the first time since he'd met Sherri, Jack had stayed out all night at her apartment. Still Devin had a definite idea that his brother would be home before their Grandfather rose. Neither wanted their Grandfather to know Jack had been out all night.

Letting the curtain drop Devin switched on the light. Steam was coming from the kettle. He lifted it before its shrill whistle awoke his Grandfather, filled his mug, added the granules, and sipped appreciatively. Slowly he came to life.

Leaning on the counter, Devin eyed the kitchen noticing nothing had changed since he was last there ten months previously. The décor never changed, chipped tiles, peeling paint and three small squares of ruffled wallpaper left behind when cabinets had been removed from the wall. As chief horticulturist, Jack spent all the hours that God sent working in the park, or looking after their Grandfather… he had no time for decorating. That was why, when last evening Devin had arrived for an unexpected visit, he'd given his brother a night off. Leaving Jack no time to argue, Devin had bundled his brother out of the door with strict instructions to enjoy himself. Over the rim of his mug Devin's brown eyes were bright with mischief, no prizes for guessing how his brother should have spent a night with the woman that he loved.

"About time too!" Devin raised his mug in salute, "only thirty year old virgin I know." He shook his head wondrously. "Well he won't win a medal for that now," Devin chuckled. A grin spread across his face as he started preparing breakfast.

* * *

Head bowed, hands deep in pockets, Jack crossed Isaac Park. All was quiet but Jack was acutely aware of his vulnerability as one of his Grandfather's oft-repeated warnings filled his mind.

'Careful, Jack they might be watching…' Breathing rapidly Jack checked his watch, four twenty. He needed to hurry if he wanted to be home and in bed before his Grandfather woke at five. He started to run then cursed the sound his shoes made on the wet grass and he stopped, his heart racing. Slowing to a walk, Jack was agitated, expecting someone to step through the mist, a gun in hand. He'd broken their law. He would have to pay the penalty. It was as simple as that.

Passing beneath a pergola flanked by tall copper beech Jack breathed easily until the pergola gave way to a twisting gravel path beneath a canopy of trees. Here contemplating the final leg of his journey, sweat drenched Jack's armpits and gathered on his brow. He decided to forego the path, and walk through the wooded area, the lesser of two evils. Usually it was delightful there. By sunlight, the wooded area was achingly beautiful. Red squirrels and a multitude of birds nested in the canopies. Large pinecones littered the ground. When the park was open, children climbed the trees, played hide and seek in the woods. Families were drawn by the wildlife and the coolness beneath the branches. Yet, at this time of day, the woodland became more frightening than anywhere else in the park, a*nyone could be there…waiting…* Even so Jack dared not chance the sound his shoes would make on the graveled path. That would be ludicrous. Drawing a deep breath, Jack closed his eyes, opened them again, and resolutely forged ahead. With his first step, he wished he hadn't stayed out all night.

Twigs snapped beneath his feet and his heart hammered painfully, nausea was only the half of it. Stomach cramps doubled him. Jack found it almost impossible to put one foot in front of the other as his Grandfather's warnings raced to mind. *'Baxter said he'd be watching, Jack… Always…always…"* Fear brought Jack to his knees. He was a thirty-year old man reduced to a sniveling child afraid of his own shadow. Jack knew he had to get a grip. Truly, living would be the death of him. In all his life he had never been out after dark, getting through each day was enough for him.

Realizing that a moving target would be harder to shoot, Jack positioned himself and launched into action. He sped through the wooded area, mindless of the noise he was making. When he saw the cottage loom through the mist in front of him, he ran faster still, breaking from the woodland out across the lawn, sprinting for his life. He jumped over the garden gate and didn't stop running till he reached the cottage door. Here, he doubled, catching his breath, hands on knees, composing himself. No one must see him like this. He waited till he could breathe easily and then with one hand on the latch and his shoulder to the door, Jack heaved hoping to lift the door open. When it caught on the stone kitchen floor as he had surmised it might, he winced. There was no denying that sound.

"Who's that?" Grandfather Jack bellowed from his bedroom.

"Only me, Granddad." Jack called as cheerfully as he could. He grimaced at his brother who was carrying a tray of sizzling pancakes to the table.

Standing in the doorway of his bedroom the Grandfather glared accusingly at Jack. "Where the hell have you been?"

"I told you, Granddad. Jack went out for a walk."

Relieved by his brother's casual remark, Jack nodded. "Yes, Grandfather. I went for a walk. That's all."

"At this time of day! And in this weather! You got a death wish or something?" The older man snapped, "what if something had happened to you out there? What would become of me then, huh? I'll tell you, shall I? Just so the two of you know what's what. If anything happens to Jack, I'll be damned if I will go live in the mountains with Devin. Anybody can take a crack at you there. Say they were hunting, have an alibi, get away with it, just like they got away with killing poor Horace. So you listen to me. When you don't have to, you don't go out. Is that clear?"

On his way to the sink, Devin saluted and the sudden sound of his Grandfather rasping forced Devin to look around. "You all right, Grandfather?"

"As if you'd care!" the old man spluttered, "you never visit, never call, you should be here, living with us, not on some goddamned mountain half a world away!"

Devin shrugged, attempting to change the subject. "Have your breakfast, Granddad, before it gets cold."

"You expect to pacify me with pancakes?" his Grandfather seethed.

Devin shook his head. "I have no wish to argue with you, Grandfather. I apologize for not coming home before now. I've been busy."

"Busy, busy...you're always too busy...Take a look at your brother. He works from dawn to dusk. Still he looks after me. Is he too busy?"

"Yes, he's too busy to visit me just the same as I'm too busy to visit him. What do you think I do up there all the time, Granddad? Twiddle my thumbs? I do work you know! Damn hard too!"

"Work, huh!" Grandfather scoffed, "and what do you do? You have no trade, no qualifications you drift from one thing to another. That's not work!"

"Just because Jack stayed here and went to university, doesn't make him the brainy one. Work experience accounts for much, and true, I have done several things. So what? It gives me a wage, and I'm happy."

"You're a drifter, like your father was a drifter...going nowhere."

"Yeah, well when it comes down to it, Granddad, I have more in the bank than Jack does, and at the end of the day that's what matters the most. A nice little nest egg to fall back on, something to give me some security when it's needed."

"Mm, strange how you have all that money yet you can't afford a telephone." Grandfather reminded him.

"It wasn't that I needed to particularly use your telephone, Granddad. I'd left my address book here the last time I stayed and a telephone number I needed was written in it."

"So, you came here only to retrieve the number, and your visit has

16

nothing to do with coming to see me or your brother!"

Heavily, Devin sighed. "Not exactly. If I'd have wanted to go to the trouble of doing so, I could have located the telephone number another way. Would have taken considerable time, but I'd have got it in the end. It seemed to me to be easier to come back here for it, and see you guys at the same time."

"I'm honored, I'm sure." Grandfather was unconvinced, "so tell me, how long are you planning on staying this time?"

"A couple of days. Like I said before, Granddad, I'm busy. I'm involved with several ventures right now, and they're all time consuming in their own right. But while I'm here if there's anything I can do around the place, I'll be only too happy to do them. Just say the word."

"You think your brother incapable? Is that it?"

"Not at all. But like you pointed out, he works in the park from dawn till dusk and he takes care of your needs. So with an extra pair of hands available for a couple of days maybe you'd both like to take advantage of them. Anyway, are you going to eat your breakfast, or what? The pancakes will be getting cold."

The Grandfather sniffed, reaching for his first pancake that was amazingly still hot enough to burn, and with a cry, withdrew his hand and blew on his fingers.

"Here, Granddad let me." Devin used a fork and spoon to transfer the pancake from the serving dish to his Grandfather's plate, and lifted a china jug from the table. "Do you want any more lemon juice?"

His Grandfather waved the offer aside, and Jack went to his room as they ate breakfast in silence.

* * *

Finishing first, Devin looked idly around the kitchen, and spoke his thoughts aloud. "Ever thought of moving, Granddad?"

Staring at his grandson with disbelief, the Grandfather replied stonily, "Move away from here? Never!"

"But, Granddad…" Devin sighed heavily. He couldn't find the words needed to continue. The problem was all so complex.

"But nothing! All my memories are here. Where would you have me go? I'll tell you now, Boy you'll not get me up on those mountains!"

"What's wrong with them?" Devin retorted angrily. Every chance his Grandfather got he made a dig at the place where Devin chose to live and he was getting fed up with it.

"Dangerous place, mountains. Too many places to hide, to watch, to creep up on a man not to mention guns."

"It's not like that," Devin insisted. "It's a great place to live. Fresh air, fruit, berries, nuts and water. No neighbors!" he emphasized, "only living thing you'll see up there are the critters."

"This is my home," his Grandfather reminded him, "I'm too old to make changes. Even if I wanted to, which I don't so don't say another word on the subject, Boy. You'll be wasting your breath."

"A vacation then," Devin ventured.

Askance, his Grandfather stared at him. "A vacation?"

"Yes. To the mountains, to my home, come on, Granddad… it's time you got out more…"

The sound of his Grandfather slamming his hands flat against the table made Devin wince.

"Have you no brains at all!" Grandfather glared at Devin, "have you not understood anything? Horace is dead. DEAD! I was threatened— you and your brother were threatened! The moment you walked out of here and took up residence in the godforsaken Appalachians you risked our lives. Read my lips, Boy! THEY ARE WATCHING US! THEY WILL ALWAYS BE WATCHING US!"

"No, Grandfather…"

"YES!"

"NO! All that happened a long time ago. They threatened us sure, but…Grandfather! Listen to me!" Devin stilled his Grandfather's hand as he leaned forward to switch on the radio. "I'm sorry if you don't want to hear this, but it's the truth. You think a bunch of thugs are still gonna be bothered about you, Jack and I thirty years on?"

"Twenty-eight."

"Twenty, thirty...whatever...a span of time that means nothing anymore. Grandfather, you've got to let it go. Believe me!"

"Never! Always means always! Don't you know anything?" Grandfather glared at his grandson.

"It was just an expression, Grandfather, not literal. The Chas Baxter's of this world come and go...they forget...why on earth should Baxter be bothered with an old man and a couple of guys who have never set eyes on him?"

"It's not that simple." Grandfather's voice shuddered to a whisper. He seemed suddenly older than his eighty-four years, ancient, haggard, worn out. Devin worried about him. He so wanted to change things, to give his Grandfather his life back...to make things right for his brother.

"It can be, Grandfather. You just have to want it badly enough. I did."

Grandfather stared ahead, he would say no more. The subject was closed. His attitude incensed Devin. The old man and his brother didn't even try. They just plodded through life with the problem haunting them, not even bothering to stop and wonder if it was applicable anymore.

Thirty years...okay...twenty-eight...it was still a long time to be afraid of nothing... Eating his breakfast in silence Devin knew he wouldn't give up trying. Changing the lives of his family was the whole purpose of his visit. If he'd done it so could they...they just needed someone to push them a little and...Devin grinned, he was just the one to do it.

Chapter Two

When Jack entered the kitchen an hour later, his brother was seated at the table, absentmindedly doodling.

"Penny for them," Jack asked, "tea?"

"What? Oh…no thanks Jack. By the way there are some pancakes for you in that dish on the stove."

"Great. I'm starved." Returning to the table with a cup of tea and a plate of warm pancakes, Jack asked, "You never did say why you are visiting us at this time of year, apart from having to make a phone call. Don't they have phones in the mountains?"

A wisp of a smile touched the corners of Devin's mouth, a smile that did not extend to his eyes.

"So what's her name?" Jack whispered.

"That perception of yours will get you into trouble one day, Bro." Devin replied. He fell silent and Jack waited patiently, a small smile playing around his mouth, he anticipated his brother's reply any second.

"Her name is Cheryl."

"Want to talk about it?"

"There's nothing to tell. We, brother are in a similar boat. You're seeing a woman you won't love and I'm with a woman who's not mine to love."

"Ah, she's married?"

"Yes."

"She's gorgeous, Jack. And we get along so well together."

Jack opened his mouth to speak, hoping to say something to ease his brother's pain but nothing would come out. It was hard knowing what to say, he was hardly an expert in matters of the heart.

"She isn't happy though. Except when she's with me."

"You spend time together?" Jack was stunned; he had assumed marriage would have been sufficient reason for Devin to keep away.

"I love her," Devin stated flatly. "And she loves me."

"But she's married." Jack was obviously shocked.

"What century do you live in, Jack?" Devin flared angrily, "Cheryl's unhappily married. Isn't that a good enough reason?"

"No, it doesn't make it right, Devin. She isn't free to love you."

"Not yet, but she will be. She's filing for divorce. When she's free, I will marry her."

"Does her husband know?"

"About me?"

"Yes."

Devin shook his head. "No, we've been careful. If he'd known do you think I'd be sitting here now? He'd have killed us!"

"What about children? Do they have any?"

"No. Just as well, he's a real bully. God, Jack, you should see the bruises he's given her!" Devin's eyes filled with tears compelling Jack to hug his brother. "I'm so sorry, Devin. No wonder you want to protect her."

"I just want to get her out of there, Jack and away from that monster, but it's not that simple. Cheryl is so afraid James will come after us she insists we go through the proper channels. It terrifies me to think what he'll do when he knows she intends to divorce him."

"Sounds like a tricky situation. I can understand how nerve wracking it must be for the both of you."

"Yes. But I'm optimistic that things will work out eventually. I'm a great believer in 'All good things come to those who wait'… if only they can wait patiently enough." He finished with a deep sigh, and then felt a sudden urge to do something, anything… that might take his mind off his problems. Seeing Jack's dirty plate and utensils Devin carried them to the sink, where he vigorously began scrubbing them.

Jack watched and remained silent, having nothing substantial to impart on the technique of love and romance. All he knew, and this from his Grandfather, was once a man and woman were brought together before God, they should allow nothing to come between them. But what were the rules when one or the other of those persons became a bully? How did God view the marriage then? How could a woman honor her husband if he abused her?

"Hey you in there?"

Startled, Jack looked up when Devin flicked some water over him. Devin grinned, revealing no trace of his earlier sorrow. "Thinking about the delectable Sherri again were we? So how'd it go last night?"

Jack had no idea what to say, but by his silence Devin seemed to know.

"You didn't do anything, did you?" Devin's tone was flat.

Guiltily, Jack shook his head.

"Oh, Jack! You idiot! You had the perfect opportunity!"

"It's not that easy!" Jack began, "you don't know how it is! It's not that simple!"

"Oh I could strangle you!" Hands covered in bubbles, Devin turned from the sink to face his brother. "Listen…you and Sherri have been together for what… five years?"

"Six."

"Six, good Lord, Jack! You should apply for the Oldest Virgin in the World Award!"

Jack cringed.

"For God's sake, Jack! Don't you know how much the woman loves you?"

Jack shrugged. "I guess."

"You guess?" Wiping his hands on a tea towel Devin moved back to the table and sat beside his brother. "Jack," Devin shook his head in despair, "it's a wonder Sherri hasn't got fed up with you and found someone else."

"Maybe it would be better if she did." Jack replied resigning himself to what seemed inevitable.

"You don't mean that?" Wringing the life from the tea towel, Devin gazed at his brother. Jack's mouth was grim and set, and Devin felt a ripple of apprehension run through him.

"I think I do." Jack's voice was deathly quiet, and with grim determination mounting in his green eyes, he turned to his brother and said, "It's unfair of me to keep stringing her along, Devin. You know how it is. Sherri is a..." Jack peered over his shoulder and added quietly, "journalist. If Grandfather should ever find out...Come to that...if Baxter should ever find out that I'm dating her..."

"You can't help what the woman you love does for a living, Jack." Devin reminded him.

"I know, but because of it, she places all our lives in danger."

Tossing the tea towel aside, Devin sighed heavily. "You're wrong, Jack. I think you've allowed Grandfather to discourage you from having any kind of relationship with anyone. He doesn't realize how selfish he's been all these years...No. Let me finish... No matter how you look at it, Jack, Grandfather's paranoia over something that happened almost thirty years ago has prevented us from having the sort of life most kids take for granted. We've been denied certain rights, Jack. I saw that years ago, Dad saw that before me and if we hadn't gotten out when we did, we'd still be here, like you, afraid of anything and everything. Even our own shadows."

"So you're saying what, exactly?" Jack asked, barely controlling his anger.

"What am I saying? Oh Lord Jack, I don't know." Devin passed a hand wearily through his hair, "You just can't see it, can you?" he asked with exasperation, "you know I'm beginning to seriously believe that you and Grandfather…well you're like two peas in a pod. But that's not your fault and that's the whole damn shame of it! Grandfather has made you like him and you've been too gullible to prevent it from happening."

Jack looked askance at his brother, and Devin sighed raggedly. "Look, forget I said anything, okay? You're either not ready to hear these home truths or too stupid to understand them."

"I am not stupid!" Jack shouted, before lowering his voice to continue, "I know exactly what you are saying regarding Sherri but things are not so black and white. Life isn't just about sex! You might think so, but it isn't. What Sherri and I have between us is more than enough for any relationship to survive. It's only you waltzing in here with all your ideas that stir things up. How did you come to be such an expert on what Sherri needs, how she feels, what she thinks? Are the two of you in cahoots or something?" Jack didn't give Devin a chance to answer as he raged on, "in fact, since you know so much about her perhaps you'd be the one to go and tell her that I think it best that we terminate this relationship, such as you think it is, and give us all some peace!"

Open mouthed, Devin stared at his brother. "You're not serious?"

Jack glared back, his expression shifting from utter annoyance to shock and disbelief…and then, strangely to calm, pure, relief. "Yes, I think I am." Jack nodded slowly. "On reflection, it's probably the best thing to do. If Baxter finds out I'm romantically involved with Sherri… Just dating her breaks the rules, Devin! It's a wonder we're not dead already!"

"That's probably because he gave up on this decades ago. Just like Grandfather should have done. He's carried this garbage around so long now, he can't live any other way. But you don't have to stand for it. And you're stupid if you can't see what it's doing to you!"

"What do you care? I wonder sometimes if you ever think of us, way up there on that mountain. Must be nice all that space, all that fresh air, no one to bother you. Not having to look over your shoulder every moment of every day. So why don't you just sod off back to that damn mountain and bury your head in the sand again and stop trying to give advice on things you left behind long ago?"

Furious, Devin scraped back his chair, grabbed the mangled tea towel, and strode back toward the sink too angry to speak. Very soon the sound of plates being manhandled made Jack feel contrite and he reminded his brother, "Careful, some of ma's best dishes are in there." At the mention of his mother, Devin calmed down. He washed in silence, handling the dishes carefully as he stacked them on the draining board at his left. Jack rose, picked up the tea towel and began drying the dishes. The two worked in silence.

Devin was the first to speak. "You asked why I was visiting at this time of year?" When Jack nodded, he continued, "two reasons. One, I'm moving out of the cabin and buying a house at the foot of the mountain, and two, I'd intended to invite you and Sherri to come to stay for a weekend after I move in. That invitation is still open to you, Jack."

Jack groaned, "you're asking the impossible, Dev. I can't leave Grandfather."

Devin transferred his mother's china to the appropriate cabinets under the counter before he replied, "Anything is possible, Jack. Depends on how badly you want it. And you'll love it there, Jack. Believe me."

Jack shook his head. "Forget it, Devin. It's never going to happen."

"Never say never, Jack." Devin squeezed his brother's shoulder as he passed by heading for the door and his jacket that hung nearby. "Look, I will go see Sherri, but not to tell her the relationship is over. It's for you to break her heart, not me. Although I strongly advise you against it."

Jack looked skeptical. "Then why are you going?"

"Because dear, Brother, when the pair of you visit my new home, there'll be a surprise awaiting you." Devin grinned mischievously, knowing his brother was a sucker for surprises.

Jack gasped, "A surprise? For me? What is it?"

Devin laughed. "If I told you that it wouldn't be a surprise would it?" He told him gleefully as he reached for a bunch of keys that hung near the door. "I'll unlock the park gates for you, shall I?"

Jack replied by pitching the scrunched up tea towel at the door as it closed behind his brother's back.

Chapter Three

"Star Spangled Night Mares? Whatever is that?" Sherri asked over coffee after Devin had arrived on her doorstep an hour earlier.

Laying a newspaper before her, he replied, "read this. You'll see."

Picking it up, Sherri could not fail to notice the large bold advertisement spread across the whole page, and she began to read out loud:

Star Spangled Night Mares

Looking for the perfect entertainment?
Then look no further
We can provide you with an evening that you won't find anywhere else
Just select a date that corresponds with a moonlit night
Then ring us and we'll do the rest
So call now
And book your Night Mare
We guarantee, you will not be disappointed

Silently reading through the small print of further details, terms and conditions, Sherri's eyes lit up and she finally exclaimed, "What a marvelous idea!"

"It is, isn't it?"

"Yes. I think it's wonderful. I've never heard of it before. Is it something new?"

"Yes. It all began when I told a stupid joke that went down like a lead balloon. It's been a huge success, Sherri. How else do you think I could afford the house I just bought?"

"You get a cut of the profits?"

"Yes, a very big cut of the profits. Thirty-five percent in fact."

"Cool."

"So what do you think, Sherri? Would you like to give it a go?"

"Me!" She squeaked, "are you serious?"

Devin nodded enthusiastically. "I've never been more serious in my life. And it goes without saying that the nightmares will be complimentary, a gift from yours truly. I really think a weekend away like this would be perfect for you and Jack. You'd enjoy it so much."

Dreamily, Sherri replied, "Yes, I would." Then her face fell as she added, "but Jack would never come."

"You leave Jack to me. If he'll go, all I want to know is that you'll go also? We could hold it at my new place." He watched the varying expressions cross her face as a trillion thoughts dashed through her mind.

"You won't know this." She confessed at length, "but before your arrival I had pretty much made up my mind to finish with Jack. It's been six years, Devin."

He nodded sympathetically. "I know."

"I'm not quite sure what this thing is with your Grandfather, but Jack acts like some kid around him. I want a man, Devin. If I'd intended to be celibate all my life, I'd have become a nun. But it's not just that..." Sherri grimaced, "it's having someone to be with. A companion. Jack is seldom here and when he is, it's like his mind is elsewhere. He's never relaxed long enough to stay. I don't know whether the problem lies with me or him..."

"Neither," Devin told her sincerely, "it rests with our Grandfather. I doubt I need to ask whether you have wondered about Jack's loyalty to the old man?"

"I have wondered many things."

"Well, there's something that Jack won't have told you and that's partly because of him and partly because of your job. Many years ago our Grandfather witnessed a murder and due to the media, his best friend was murdered. After that his own life and ours was threatened. Since then, Grandfather has been very suspicious of all media and their intentions. Jack has told him about you but he has not enlightened him as to your career."

Sherri's face registered stunned surprise and she assured him, "I would respect his wishes, Devin, I promise. Anything I heard would stay confidential."

Devin nodded. "Yes, I'm sure it would. But Grandfather wouldn't have any faith in your promises. He's paranoid you see. Doesn't trust a soul. He believes the same people who murdered his friend would murder him, too. Grandfather's fears are very real to him. He frets for our safety and that of the wife of his murdered friend. He frets about the whole wide world and what it's coming to. And in turn he allows a lot of those fears to rub off on Jack, who'd rather say nothing than upset Grandfather's feelings."

"Ah, I am beginning to understand now. I wish Jack could have felt he trusted me enough to share all of this." Her eyes were sad at the thought and Devin quickly reassured her, "It wasn't that. I'm sure Jack knows he can trust you. It's just his loyalty to our Grandfather, and the promise he made not to tell a soul would have prevented him from disclosing these facts. My brother, I'm afraid, has been caught between the two of you. Unfortunately, he has decided for his own sanity he should honor our Grandfather's feelings. Sherri, I'm sorry to have to tell you this, but Jack wanted me to come here and tell you that the relationship is over. However, don't worry, I know he doesn't really want that. And I aim to do everything in my power to keep you two together."

"Really? Thank you, Devin."

"You're welcome. I happen to think you and Jack are made for each other. However, I've taken a risk telling you about Grandfather's secret. You will promise not to dig over old ground won't you?"

"I promise."

"Thank you. So you'll come to my place? We'll hire the night mares and the pair of you can have a fantastic weekend." He looked at her optimistically.

Sherri laughed and nodded. "Yes, I'll come. I don't think much to your chances of getting Jack to agree though, not without your Grandfather..." She paused and surprised Devin when she exclaimed, "hey, maybe he'll come too."

"Grandfather?" Devin asked shaking his head, "oh, I don't think so Sherri. He hasn't stepped outside the park for thirty years. I can't see him allowing us to whisk him off to the mountains as nice as that would be. Mind you, that is the eventual plan. But it's gonna take time, lots and lots of time, to influence him. If ever."

"On May thirteenth Jack and I will have known one another for exactly six years. It's our anniversary. It might be as good a time as any to start sealing the relationship..." Sherri's gray eyes twinkled merrily.

"So you'll do it?"

Sherri's eyes sparkled with enthusiasm. "Yes, Devin. I'd love to!"

Chapter Four

Fresh from her shower the following morning, Sherri walked into the dining room and caught sight of the advertisement Devin had left for her, on the table. Vigorously rubbing her wet hair with a towel she surveyed the contents again, draped the towel over her shoulders and picked up the newspaper cutting.

"May as well do it now," she murmured padding barefoot across the thick carpeting to the telephone on the other side of the room to make the call. It was answered after the third ring.

"Good morning...Star Spangles...may I help you?"

"Good morning. I'd like to hire three Night Mares please. Do you have May thirteenth free?"

"Just a second please." There was a moment's silence then, "yes we do. Have you hired a Night Mare before?"

"No. And actually I should have said earlier, the occasion is by courtesy of Devin Richardson."

Laughter came from the other end. "Devin Richardson? Are you telling me he's finally going to have a go at his own brainchild?"

Sherri laughed. "He is. But he doesn't know that yet. He showed me the advertisement and expects that his brother and I will be hiring the Night Mares. I thought it would be nice for him to join us."

"That's wonderful. We've been trying to get him to have a go for ages. Any chance you'll see him before May thirteenth?"

"It's possible. Why? Something wrong?"

"No, quite the contrary. He's just so hard to pin down. We have some things we would like to discuss with him. It's nothing to worry about. If you get a chance to mention it will you have him call us? Or maybe pop over?"

"Certainly."

"Thank you. So that's three complimentary Night Mares for May thirteenth. Where would you like them delivered?"

"At Devin's new address. I trust he's forwarded it to you?"

"Barrington Estate? Yes, he has. Someone will have to be there to take charge of the Night Mares from around two pm on the thirteenth. Will that be a problem?"

"Not at all. I'm sure Devin will do it."

"Great. Even better. If he hasn't been in touch by that time I'll have my husband deliver them personally so he can talk to Devin at the estate. All I need now is your name and that of Devin's brother. Though I take it that would be Jack?"

"Yes, Jack. And I'm Sherilyn Scott."

"Well that's settled then, Miss Scott. Three night mares, Barrington Estate, May thirteenth. I hope you have a wonderful evening. Any questions?"

"Nothing I can think of. The advertisement tells me everything I need to know, even as far as what we should wear."

"Yes, safety is most important. And if there's anything you need just call. We can have it all delivered with the Night Mares. I'll just need to know all your sizes in advance."

"Thank you. I'll find that out and get back to you in a couple of days. So that's it then?"

"Yes, I have everything I need for now. If I'm not on duty when you ring, oh and I'm Jill Staniwell by the way, just leave a message with whomever is on duty and they'll match it to your file."

"Great. Thank you."

"You're welcome, Miss Scott. Goodbye."

"Goodbye."

Sherri replaced the receiver and smiled. As far as she was concerned, May thirteenth couldn't come round fast enough.

* * *

Three days later and armed with a bouquet of his loveliest roses, Jack arrived at Sherri's apartment and rang the bell. His brother had convinced him that going away for the weekend with Sherri was a good idea. His Grandfather was another matter, but right now Jack didn't want to dwell on that.

Peeping through the spy hole, Sherri tugged open the door when she saw who was visiting, exclaiming, "Jack! Come in. I didn't expect to see you today. I thought you told me you had those beds to tend to this week?"

"I have. I wanted to see you. Happy Birthday, Sherri, these are for you." He handed her the roses before removing his jacket and draping it over the arm of a chair.

"It's not till next week, Jack! You know that!" Sherri chuckled and taking the offered blooms she buried her face in the petals inhaling deeply. "Thank you, Jack. Mm, they smell divine. Did you grow these?"

"Yes, in the glasshouse." Jack replied as he moved into the sunny room heading for the dining table. "Shall I sit here?"

"Yes, Jack of course. Just move those paper cuttings to one side, while I put these flowers in a vase. I'll be right back."

Watching her walk toward the kitchen Jack reminisced on the first time he had seen those legs. Long and shapely and back then dressed in black stockings as Sherri had walked ahead of him through the horticultural college. He'd been a student, and she, new in her own field of journalism, was there to write a thesis.

"I've been reading through some reports on that thug Chas Baxter," her voice carried from the kitchen as she continued to tell him, "someone's gotta know how he does it, Jack. A guy can't be in two places at one time can he?"

"No."

They'd discussed this often and Jack was reluctant to get into it again. He found the fact of Chas Baxter being the thug behind his Grandfather's problems difficult to keep quiet. It was the only secret he kept from Sherri.

While Sherri was in the kitchen, Jack looked around the neatly furnished apartment. He loved her taste. A rich deep peach colored carpet ran from wall to wall, complemented by upholstery in soft peach. There were two alcoves where in each a glass and ornate table stood with pots of tall leafy plants that to Jack's trained eye were revealed to be coconut and date palms. And against one peaches and cream papered wall, Sherri had pinned a kangaroo vine that framed some prints hanging there.

Hearing the sound of running water Jack anticipated Sherri's return and looked back toward the kitchen in time to see her peering over the top of a rose-filled vase. Placing it just off center on the table she told him happily, "Until I met you, I'd never received so many flowers. They're beautiful, Jack. Thank you." she told him sincerely, "and they look lovely here in front of the sunniest window. Don't you think?"

Jack nodded. Now that he was here, with his gift given, he was lost for words.

Sherri, however, soon put him at ease. "I expect you're fretting over your brother coming to see me, aren't you?" Before he could reply, she went on, "don't be. It's okay, Jack. Really it is. I understand how it is with your Grandfather. Devin explained everything to me."

"Did he?" Jack was shocked.

"Yes, and not a moment too soon either. I was beginning to wonder why you were so loyal to your Grandfather and now I know. Don't worry, his secret is safe with me, however..."

Still reeling from the shock of his brother revealing the family secret, Jack expected Sherri to ask for the finer details of the story. Instead she surprised him by saying, "One day I'd like to meet your Grandfather. I promise not to mention what I do for a living."

"I'd appreciate that." Jack replied dryly.

"Well, naturally the journalist in me is curious, Jack. Devin told me bits and I'd love to know all. More importantly, I'd love to be able to help your Grandfather get over his paranoia towards journalists. I suppose that will only happen if I don't exploit his story. And since doing so would only alienate you from me that will be the last thing I'd want to do."

"He's very important to me, Sherri," Jack sighed, relieved that she understood, and loving her all the more for doing so. "When our mother died Grandfather took us in. Then Dad left us. Grandfather's fear is very real. He truly believes his life would be in peril if he should step outside of his home and..."

"Devin mentioned this. But wait, do you mean he never goes outside?"

Jack nodded. "He's not been out in years. Except to the garden to tend his roses. He will go that far. Even so, all the time he's outside, he's like a frightened deer. It's pitiful to watch him."

"I can imagine. So how will we get him to the mountains?"

"It won't be easy. But I think when all is said and done he would rather be with us than be alone all weekend. Over the last three days Devin has convinced me that the possibility is there. Although I have to admit we still have reservations about discussing it with Grandfather. In the past, any mention of going outside of the park has been met with absolute refusal."

"Well, good luck. It sounds like you'll need it."

"Thanks. We will." Jack grinned, then he sobered when he caught sight of Sherri's lips. They were full, soft and inviting, and before he knew it he was standing up and touching his mouth to hers. A small gasp escaped her before she molded her lips to his and with a gentle sigh Sherri kissed him back...their first real kiss lasting longer than either of them had anticipated. When they finally broke apart neither spoke. Sherri just tucked her head against Jack's chest, feeling cherished and loved. His kiss had been warm and tender, and filled with promise. She loved him so much.

"Shall we take a walk, Sherri?"

"A walk? Where?"

"Through the park. There's something I'd like to show you."

Intrigued, Sherri agreed, "I'll get my jacket."

* * *

Twenty minutes later, the couple reached the designated spot. "Close your eyes." Jack told her, as they approached what appeared to be a new bed of flowers. Joyous, Sherri laughed out loud as Jack placed his hands over her eyes, and from behind guided her forward. "This is for you, Sherri. Do you like it?" He removed his hands and stepped forward to await her expression.

There before her was a flowerbed flanked with the bright mauve Aubrietia, and filled with Crocus. She noticed the initials J & S cut out in the grass, entwined neatly together inside a perfect heart made from pink, lemon and white Hyacinth.

"Oh!" Sherri exclaimed, "can you do that, Jack? Won't you be in trouble?"

"For what?" Jack grinned, taking her hand in his, "for announcing to the whole of New York that I'm in love with you?"

"Oh, Jack! It's beautiful." Sherri hugged him tightly. "Thank you so much, darling. It must have taken you all day to do this!"

"Three days actually," He chuckled, "and it was worth every moment just to see your face. Do you really like it?"

"Oh, yes! No one has ever done anything for me like this before."

"That's because no one before has ever loved you the way I love you."

He told her tenderly. "I have another surprise too, if you're ready?" Jack tugged at her hand.

"Another for me?"

"Yes. It might not be as pleasant as this one but…well I wondered if you'd like to meet my Grandfather?"

"Are you sure?" Sherri asked wide-eyed.

"Well since we're half way there already, may as well be now."

"You're not sure about this, are you?" she asked him anxiously.

"I've put it off long enough, Sherri." he replied seriously, "and it's not as if he bites. It's just his paranoia, and if we don't tell him what you do for a living…"

"Does he read the newspapers?"

"Yes." Jack was about to ask why when he realized. "Oh, you think he'll recognize you from the photographs in your articles?"

"He might. Perhaps it's best we don't do this, Jack," Sherri suggested, "another time, maybe…"

"There's never going to be another time, though, is there? And if we are all to go away for the weekend together…"

"Good point."

"So are you coming, or what?" Jack tugged her in the general direction of his Grandfather's home.

Sighing raggedly, Sherri nodded, deciding she might as well get it over with. It was just that after the joy she had received that day, she didn't want any of it marred by an irritable old man. Still, as Jack had said, they were halfway there already.

"All right," Sherri agreed reluctantly.

Jack smiled reassuringly. "It won't be all that bad. Really it won't. He knows about you after all. He just doesn't realize how much you mean to me. You'll see, he'll love you as much as I do when he gets to know you."

Sherri wasn't so sure. What was even more important at the moment was she feared Jack wasn't so sure either. If his Grandfather wouldn't go out, if he were suspicious of people, if he had paranoia…the visit might well prove to be rather difficult, to say the least!

Chapter Five

With his business in the city finished, Devin made his way back to his home in the mountains. He had a lot of packing to do since he had been living at the cabin for a long time, but he felt sure he was doing the right thing buying the property at the foot of his mountain home. His Grandfather would be happy there, he would feel safe, and there was room for all his family and their loved ones to live there and not get in each other's way. To top it all large grounds surrounded the estate—room enough for all the gardening his Grandfather and brother could want. In addition, there was something charismatic about the mountains Devin pondered and he wanted to live nowhere else. Which was why when he saw how much his bank balance had risen thanks to Star Spangles and a few other deeds he was involved in, he decided to buy the estate at the foot of his mountain home.

His friends Tom and Laura Sandmann had previously owned the estate and Devin had stayed there with them often. Tom was a musician and the pair had met at a Brooklyn bar where Tom was singing. Devin had been a little worse for drink and Tom had been tired. When Tom had forgotten some of the lyrics to a particular song Devin had chimed in with words of his own and the audience had loved it. From then on Tom employed Devin to deliberately supply him with alternative words to songs helping Tom's albums to sell like hot cakes. In gratitude Tom paid Devin a percentage from his sales.

Devin adored their home. It was everything his Grandfather needed, secluded, beautiful and secure. So when Devin heard that Tom and Laura were considering moving, Devin jumped at the chance to buy the estate.

The Appalachians were so beautiful and Devin wanted to live nowhere else. He constantly marveled at the peace and solitude, the wildlife, even the rich feast of fresh fruits, nuts and berries. The pure mineral water and the fresh air…mm…as Devin arrived at the foot of his mountain home, he breathed deeply of the clean air, forcing all the city toxins from his body, leaving him feeling rejuvenated and so wonderfully alive!

Oh, yes, the mountains certainly had it all, Devin thought, even as far as finding himself a partner was concerned. For it was upon these very mountain ranges, that he had met Cheryl, his dear, sweet, Cherie with her love of life and the outrageous. Devin chuckled; she had persuaded him to dance naked in the rain! He shook his head. He didn't know how she'd managed it, but one moment, he was protesting, and the next, there he was, totally nude. And though the droplets of icy rain beat down upon his body, he never felt the cold. Seeing Cheryl dancing naked beside him, made the blood pound through his veins. And as they had fallen together laughing, their bodies slick with rain, Devin had felt nothing but the heat of their passion. With their lips locked together he had lifted and carried her back to his cabin kicking the door closed on the cold wet world beyond to make love to her in a room illuminated only by the flickering flames of a log fire.

* * *

Remembering, Devin shivered, eager to get home. Cheryl had promised to walk over as soon as he let her know he was back and would spend a few days with him, before her husband's expected return from an overseas trip. Devin couldn't wait to see her.

He had to pass Cheryl and James's cabin to get to his own, and as he rounded the last crag before the cabin came into sight, he was filled with excitement. Perhaps she would be watching for him, or maybe she had already seen his approach with the aid of binoculars and had gone up ahead of him. Devin's heart raced in anticipation. It was unfortunate that the appointment with the bank in New York City had coincided with James' trip away, or they would have spent the last week entwined in one another's arms. Yet as he cornered the final bend and the cabin came into sight, Devin's heart sank. The unmistakable blue and yellow truck that James had driven down to the airport was parked squarely outside. He was back! Devin felt a tightening in his throat, as a jolt of apprehension rushed through him. Cheryl was terrified of her husband.

Cautiously, approaching their cabin, Devin couldn't decide whether to drive on by, or stop. He had never met James, but had seen his truck from time to time at the general store, when they'd both been collecting supplies. Slowing down, Devin made up his mind: he would stop, introduce himself, and try to judge if everything was all right. He couldn't just drive by, he would worry too much and he might not get another chance to see Cheryl if James was back to stay a while. Turning off the ignition, Devin alighted from his truck, making his way carefully over the loose gravel path up towards the cabin. Everywhere was quiet, unusually so, but Devin paid no heed to the silence of the birds. His mind was focused on what to say, how to act, what to do.

Raised voices sounded from within as he reached the door, and it opened to reveal a burly fellow standing to one side, his unshaven face bearing no hint of a smile. His cold gray eyes were hard and unfriendly. "Yeah, can I help you?" He demanded, before Devin had time to speak.

Devin stammered, "I, I…er…I'm sorry to bother you. I live up the mountain. I've been away for a few days, and have just this minute returned. When I saw your truck, I thought I'd stop by and introduce myself."

"Why?" The curt reply made Devin jump.

"Be…because we are neighbors." Devin felt embarrassed to be stammering.

James took a step closer, his mouth creasing into a sneer. "Well, we like to keep to ourselves. Now clear off."

Stunned to the core Devin's mouth dropped open. Cheryl had told him many things about her uncaring husband but pig-headedness wasn't one of them.

"I'm sorry…. to have troubled you." Devin stammered again, but found his feet rooted to the spot when James snarled at him, those steely gray eyes threatening.

"You got a hearing problem?" James stepped from the doorway, and advanced towards Devin. "I said, clear off. We don't need neighbors. We came out here to escape from people. Now get the hell off my property!."

Devin turned away, his throat aching. He knew he could do and say absolutely nothing. Anything would anger James further and surely be taken out on Cheryl later. To think, he had laughed at her when she had first told him what a bully her husband was. He couldn't ever imagine any man treating his wife so badly. Devin felt his blood boil. What could he do? Not what he wanted to do, that was for sure. Beat the guy senseless and take Cheryl away from him and keep her safe forever.

Reluctantly, he walked back to his truck. He felt those steely, gray eyes boring into his back, but he did not glance around until he slipped into the driver's seat. Only then, on the pretence of fastening his seat belt, did he dare look back to find James still glowering at him from the doorstep and noticed the curtains moving ever so slightly, indicating Cheryl's trembling presence behind them. Nausea rose from the pit of his belly as Devin thought about Cheryl living with a man like that. And as he drove away, Devin had never felt so wretched in all his life. He had to get Cheryl out of there and away from that maniac and soon, but how?

Chapter Six

"Grandfather?" Jack asked warily as he carefully pushed open the door to the house with one hand and held Sherri's hand with the other, "are you awake?"

The sound of the television blared out from the sitting room, and the scent of buttered toast filled the air. In one corner of the kitchen a microwave was working and a kettle was boiling on the stove.

"Grandfather?" Jack called cheerily, still keeping Sherri behind him just outside the front door.

"That you, Jack? You're just in time. Scrambled eggs and toast all right for you?" As his Grandfather spoke, the words became louder signifying the old man's approach from the sitting room to the kitchen. He hesitated when he saw his grandson hovering by the door and peered closely. "What you got there? Some flowers?"

"No. Grandfather, I have someone with me. Someone I'd like you to meet."

The color drained from his Grandfather's face and he cowered back into the recently vacated room, "Take them away, Jack." He called nervously, "Don't bring anyone in here."

"I'm sorry, Grandfather. I know how you feel about meeting new people but..."

"There are no buts, Jack. I won't have strangers in MY house! Now have them leave, please." The Grandfather's voice rose hysterically and Jack pictured him quaking in the other room, genuinely frightened by meeting someone new.

"Leave it, Jack," Sherri told him touching his arm. "Do as he says."

Turning to her Jack shook his head, "I've never been allowed to bring anyone home," he told her. Turning back to face the room he announced, "Grandfather, you've never let me bring any of my friends home, and I've always abided by your wishes, but this friend is special to me...please, Grandfather?"

"No!" The voice snapped from the other room, "take them away! Now!"

Jack sighed and tears formed on Sherri's lashes. She could see how it was affecting him, he was close to crying.

"Leave it, Jack," Sherri begged, "we'll think of something else."

Torn between wanting to introduce the two people in the world that he cared most about save his brother, and waiting for another occasion Jack hesitated, and then called to his Grandfather. "I know this is your house, Grandfather, and I know that's your garden. Now this is what I'm going to do. My friend and I are going to go out into the garden and you may watch us from the window, that way you can see my friend. I shall bring her over often and..."

"Her?"

"Yes, her. I wanted you to meet the woman that I love, Grandfather."

The old man drew in a sharp intake of breath but said nothing.

"As to your earlier question, Grandfather, no thank you for the toast and eggs, I shall be taking Sherri someplace to eat after we have left. Now I plan to show her around the garden. Is that okay with you?" There was silence. "Grandfather?"

As Jack leaned into the kitchen to ask his Grandfather's permission Sherri looked around the garden. It was a nice spot. The cottage, she knew, belonged to the Grandfather, that and a handkerchief plot of land with the bulk of the garden loaned to the family by the park commissioners. The park she could tell was just an extension of their garden as both were full of flowers, shrubs, and trees.

"Grandfather?" Sherri heard Jack enquire once more sounding exasperated. There was still no reply.

Jack sighed, "we'll be in the garden then." He closed the door gently behind him and turned to Sherri. "Sorry about that," he told her, a trifle embarrassed.

Sherri squeezed his arm. "It's okay, Jack. He'll come around you'll see."

Jack doubted it, and deep inside Sherri doubted it also. Whatever the old man had experienced in his life must have shaken him dreadfully. Goodness, if he could be like that now, whatever would he be like when he discovered what she did for a living?

* * *

After that first visit, Sherri came over whenever she could. Some days it was too cold for standing outside admiring the flowers but she did it anyway, hoping that by her steadfastness the old man would relent and invite her in out of the cold. He never did.

In fact, from that first day as he had piled eggs upon his buttered toast, he had tried not to look at the couple strolling hand in hand around his garden. He only did so eventually to check that '*she*' did not stand on any of his flowers, or that '*she*' did not pick any of his blooms. He was almost sorry when '*she*' did none of those things, as he would have liked nothing better than to have been able to have given her a piece of his mind, anything to prevent her coming back again.

When Jack came home that evening they argued, but Jack had not backed down as the Grandfather had assumed he might. "I love her,

Grandfather! So don't ask me to choose between the two of you!"

"I shouldn't have to ask you. You should know. If it weren't for me, you would have been on the streets by now. I gave you a roof over your head. Did your father want you? No. Have you seen him since, heard from him in all the years he has been gone? No. You owe me, Jack. And this is how you repay me," his Grandfather was furious.

Jack stood his ground. "I've cared for you, too. I love you, and I understand how frightening this must be for you. This is one friend, Grandfather, just one friend in all the years I've lived here. Surely you can't deny me that?"

"I almost wish I'd allowed the others. This one friend, as you put it, could be more dangerous than any of the others put together."

Jack eyed his Grandfather suspiciously. 'What did he know? Had he recognized Sherri from the newspapers? Had Devin unwittingly let something slip?' "What do you mean by that?" he enquired softly.

"This is the only friend that could take you away from me, Jack. Don't you see?"

"You're jealous!" Jack laughed. "Sherri wouldn't do that, not in the way you think. She's more than willing to meet you and I'm positive she would happily settle in here..." Jack wished he hadn't said that. He could not imagine Sherri leaving her immaculate apartment to live in a cramped cottage in the middle of the park. He went on quickly, "or maybe we could all live someplace else?" He thought about Devin's plans for the future.

"And leave my garden? To what, live in some claustrophobic apartment? Have you gone mad?"

"Doesn't have to be an apartment. There are plenty of houses with gardens. We could find one of those," Jack argued.

"Wouldn't be the same. I don't want to leave my roses."

"Then we'll transfer every last one of them."

"We'll do no such thing! And besides we won't have to because I'm not leaving and that's that!"

There was no budging Grandfather. He was adamant when his mind was made up and nothing Jack could say or Sherri could try would have him change his mind until the day Sherri slipped in the garden and cut her knee. Jack rushed into the house for the first aid box.

"Ice." His Grandfather hurried to meet him with a bag of frozen peas in his hands.

"You were watching?"

"Just lay the ice on her knee; I'll get you a dressing." His Grandfather replied hurrying toward the bathroom as fast as his rheumatism would allow. He returned moments later with some gauze soaked in cold water held over a small bowl and with a dry dressing tucked under his arm. Jack met him at the door, hovering uncertainly and understanding his look of exasperation his Grandfather opened the door wide. "Ask her to come in. Sit her at the dining table. You can doctor her leg." Then as soon as Jack had taken the dressings from him, his Grandfather hurried out of the room as Jack helped Sherri hop inside.

From the other room the Grandfather stood leaning against one wall, hand on heart, listening to what was being said in the kitchen. He felt anxious. It was the first time he had allowed a stranger to enter his house in twenty-eight years. Where he was in the sitting room he felt trapped and looked around wildly for means to escape. The window was his only option as all doors led from the kitchen. He eyed the window suspiciously, wondering if he might be able to raise his leg high enough to get through it if the need arose. Other than that, he could hide behind the sofa. Mostly he hoped Jack would not invite his 'friend' any further into the house. Even so, the pair was taking a God-awful long time patching up a simple wound. Holding his breath, the Grandfather peered around the doorframe to see into the kitchen hoping that maybe they had gone out and he hadn't heard them. He snatched his head back when he saw what they were doing! With the woman sitting and Jack on his knees leaning close he'd witnessed them kissing. Fury and indignation rose into the old man's throat. How dare they! In his house, too! He had offered his hospitality for a cut only! Still, fear glued him to the spot, and he would not, could not confront them. He would save his anger for Jack later when he returned home alone.

His heart hammering, the Grandfather drew in deep breaths. This would be no time to drop dead he reasoned, he had to calm down. He moved from the wall to sit in a chair close enough to the door to slam it in the face of anyone trying to enter. From there he was also able to hear what was going on in the kitchen beyond. There was silence for quite some time and the Grandfather pictured the couple kissing. He also wondered if Jack may have taken the woman to his room, but he had not heard any doors opening and closing, he decided they were still there in the kitchen.

He was right. With his Grandfather trapped inside the sitting room Jack had all kind of devious thoughts racing through his mind, some of which he ran by Sherri. "We could stay here till he needs to use the bathroom. Shouldn't be long. He needs it about every thirty minutes. He'd have to meet you then," Jack whispered.

"Oh, Jack that would be cruel."

"Well we could make him a cup of tea and take it in there."

"No, Jack. Look, I'm in so that's a step in the right direction isn't it? From now on I could just come on in, right?"

"Maybe. Depends whether he's in the kitchen when you arrive or not."

"Let's go now, anyway. I bet all of this is making him uncomfortable and irritable. It was kind enough of him to offer the ice and the dressing and to invite me in. That couldn't have been easy for him."

Jack nodded. "You're right. Just one more kiss before we go?" He raised an eyebrow hopefully. Sherri slapped him playfully. "Just one more then."

They kissed, drawing apart reluctantly. Jack helped Sherri to her feet. They were at the door when Sherri had an idea. Turning back, she called in the general direction of the living room, "thank you Mr. Richardson. I'll replace the peas. Bye."

Not a word came from the sitting room, but somehow Sherri thought she had been victorious. She had a feeling that they had made a gigantic step forward and when Jack squeezed her hand knowingly, she felt that he thought so too.

* * *

True to her word, Sherri replaced the peas, but she did it on a day that she knew Jack to be working in the park. It was something she'd not dared before. In all the weeks she had been coming to Jack's Grandfather's garden she had been with Jack. On this occasion she wanted to go alone. She thought Jack's Grandfather would feel less threatened if she did. In her line of work, she knew all about that. Often one to one interviews were a lot more forthcoming than when relatives were involved.

Strangely, Grandfather had been expecting her. It wasn't just Jack that could be precognitive when he chose. Old Jack Richardson, Senior had on many occasions in his life been able to 'see' something before it had happened. The only time it had let him down was the day that Horace had been murdered. Although he had been feeling out of sorts all that day he had to admit.

Thus, the door to the kitchen was open as Sherri made her way down the garden path. Leaning in ever so slightly she tapped on the glass panel in the top of the door.

"Who is it?" Grandfather asked gruffly.

"Hello, Mr. Richardson. It's me, Sherri Scott, Jack's friend. I'm returning the peas as promised." Sherri held her breath. A long silence followed and she hardly dared breathe. "Mr. Richardson?" she enquired anxiously.

"Bring them in, and put them in the freezer."

Sherri knew by his tone that it had taken every ounce of courage for him to say that. Slowly, Sherri peeped around the door, to see that the kitchen was empty and to hear him shuffle back into the sitting room.

Looking around for the freezer, Sherri finally located it by its gentle hum where it stood alongside a washing machine a few feet away from the door. Taking a deep breath Sherri entered the kitchen, slipping off each shoe and leaving them behind on the mat by the door. Then she walked to the freezer, opened it and after placing the peas inside, she returned to slip her shoes back on, while announcing, "I've done it. I'll be off now, Mr. Richardson."

She almost fell over when hovering with one foot off the ground while she pulled on her shoe she heard a gruff voice behind her ask, "Would you like a cup of tea or coffee?"

Sherri turned slowly, eyes wide, expecting anything even an axe hurtling toward her head. What she did not expect to see was an old man who resembled Jack so much, hobbling across the kitchen to fill a kettle with water before placing it to boil on the stove.

"I usually have one around about now. Would you care to join me?"

Sherri nodded, unable to speak. She thought she heard the old man chuckle but his demeanor showed fear, unease and apprehension.

Finally, she found her manners, "I'd like that, thank you. Shall I sit here?" She indicated the chair by the dining table where she had sat the day she had cut her knee. Jack's Grandfather nodded, surprising her when he moved forward to pull the chair out from beneath the table. "Yes of course. Do you take milk, sugar?"

Sherri smiled. "Milk yes, sugar no. I'm sweet enough."

The ice was broken when the old man chuckled. From that day on, neither looked back.

* * *

With his jacket collar bunched around his neck and shoulders Chas Baxter braved the elements. For the umpteenth time that day he wished he'd taken the car out that morning. Either that or he'd thought to wear an overcoat and a hat.

'Good thing I'll be home soon,' he mumbled as he eyed the apartment building where he lived alone, eagerly. "Just need to make a final stop." He grinned imagining his last task for the day, "ole Jack Richardson's annual visit. Can't miss that." Stepping from the sidewalk, Chas dodged the shoppers with their umbrellas and walked with intent into Isaac Park. The roses were gone now, their blooms wizened away by the frost, their bare brittle branches pruned low to the ground, still Chas grinned as he passed them, remembering...

It was a long time ago, water under the bridge in many respects, but people remember, and to keep the old man silent Chas had deemed this annual reminder a necessity. "Don't have to do anything, nor say anything. Just wander by his cottage and he'll be looking out, expecting me to come by. Just a look, a gesture, a grin or a wave does it every time. Ensures his silence for another year." Chas chuckled. "Still why I chose this time of year to remind him, beats me. It's always wet around about now. Must have been having a frigging mental or something that first year. Should never had said, I'll pop by this time next year, Jack...just so you never forget. I can be a stupid fucker sometimes." Chas berated as his feet crunched on the graveled paths leading across the park, "like that first time, when I mentioned my Dad. Why did I do that? Of all the bloody stupid things! If Dad knew...he'd have polished ole Jack Richardson off thirty years ago. But it was my fault...I shouldn't have opened my big mouth..." Chas groaned as he remembered what an idiot he'd been. "Why'd I have to say anything? Oh yeah, right, tell him that your Dad wouldn't be too pleased if he said anything. Of all the stupid...stupid..." Chas kicked at a stone embedded in the path, and swore when a pain shot through his toe. Annoyed, he kicked at the stone again and again until he finally dislodged it and sent it hurtling across the grass. He grinned at his success and continued walking toward the cottage. Wisps of smoke curled from its chimney, starkly white against the flat gray sky. "What shall I do this year? Wave... Say hi... I know..." Chas grinned and increased his step.

The park seemed damper and colder than any place on earth and Chas, not wanting to appear inconspicuous as he passed by the cottage, shuddered as he folded down the collar of his jacket. Rain splattered down the back of his neck and Chas picked up his pace, wanting this done and over with so he could get home.

As he expected, there was the old man peering out of the window. Their gazes met. "See, he was waiting for ya." Chas mumbled, "whatever the weather I need to keep this up. The ole feller expects this reminder." As Chas drew level with the window he stopped and saluted, grinned, and walked on.

It was all he needed to do, for inside the cottage old Jack Richardson, all alone in the house, stood as though frozen by the window his heart beating erratically. He watched the thug move out across the park and disappear from view.

"Shouldn't let him get to you." He grumbled as he moved away from the window, "should tell someone…" Grandfather shuddered and walked toward a locked kitchen cabinet, fishing the key from his pocket as he went. He extracted a sheaf of papers and taking them to the table he spread them out to read.

Time after time the headlines jumped out at him. 'Shopkeepers livid as thugs move in… Woman Found Beaten In Alley… Elderly Gent Knifed By Street Gang.' Grandfather smoothed this one with a loving hand, tears pricking at the backs of his eyes. He knew this man; they'd been best friends. And because of what they'd witnessed Horace was dead and he was receiving an annual visit from a thug to remain silent.

The newspaper articles maintained over and over that police reports came to nothing. Oh, suspicions were high, and evidence pointed repeatedly to a thug named Chas Baxter, but he had an alibi, he would always have an alibi, and nothing could be pinned to him.

Sheets upon sheets of newspaper articles spread out upon the table…and not one conviction… Why?

"You could end all of this," Grandfather spoke out loud, "you're the only one that saw all and lived to tell the tale. The reason Chas Baxter gets away with every crime in the city. The reason he's always has a watertight alibi. He isn't the one committing the crimes. It's his Dad…father and son look alike. Why does no one else know this?'

Still Grandfather knew he could never tell… he maintained his silence for the benefit of those he loved…they were the only ones important in all of this…

Sadly, Grandfather wished it could be another way, wished he were brave and unselfish…and he tried not to look at the dozens of faces of innocent people staring up at him from the cuttings as he piled them together to return to the cabinet. Mothers, and fathers, children…uncles and aunts…innocent people in the wrong place at the wrong time, or those who had tried to stand up for their rights…

Grandfather placed the cuttings back into the cabinet locked it and returned the key to his pocket. Sighing heavily, he hobbled to where next year's calendar hung behind the current year and marked off a date… the day when he knew that without a shadow of a doubt, he'd see Chas Baxter's face again.

* * *

As he approached his building, Chas was surprised to see lights blaring out of the windows of his tenth floor apartment. He smiled and quickened his step knowing who was likely to be waiting for him. There was only one other he trusted with a key.

"Dad?" Chas queried as he stepped into his apartment a few minutes later. Chas heard the sound of running water coming from the kitchen and made his way there.

His father met him on his way out. "There you are! I expected you home hours ago. Where have you been all this time?" Raymond Baxter laughed, "No, don't answer that, I can guess."

The image of his son, Raymond Baxter's life of crime had paid for cosmetic surgery to return him to the days of his youth…well, had taken twenty years off of him at any rate. It wasn't just for vanity's sake; the close resemblance to his son meant their little scam would be working a good few years yet.

"So what do I owe the pleasure of your visit?" Chas asked as he flopped wearily onto a deep burgundy sofa made from the softest leather. "Pour me a bourbon while you're over there, will you, Dad?"

"Food first! I bet you haven't eaten all day? No? Thought not. I've made you something."

Chas raised his eyebrows. "You've made me something? I can't remember the last time you did that."

"Well, don't get to liking it, cause I don't plan to be around too long.

Here, have your dinner. Nothing special, just curried beef and rice. Don't blame me if it tastes awful, I'm not known for my culinary efforts, as well you know!"

Raymond handed his son a plate of hot food, and they sat eating for a while side by side on the sofa until Chas belched, declared he'd had enough and ran for the kitchen. Raymond laughed." Thought maybe I'd added a pinch too much curry powder." He grinned as he heard Chas swallowing what sounded like a gallon of water. "Put hairs on your chest this will."

Chas peeked around the corner of the kitchen door. "Not sure I want any thanks. Be nice to be left with a throat though. God, Dad how could you eat that stuff?" he asked as he watched his father putting it away.

"Necessity. Just like your eating it is of necessity. Now get that down you."

"And I need to because…"

"We've got a job tonight."

"We?"

"Yes we."

"I don't understand, Dad, we've not worked together for nigh on thirty years. Not since…" Chas could remember the day as if it were yesterday.

"Yeah, yeah I know. When those old geezers saw everything. This is different, we ain't killing anyone tonight. And we won't exactly be side by side."

"Then why?"

"Why do I need you? Because, Sonny Jim, I need to be in two places at the same time and a lot of money is riding on this one. Believe me."

"Like you need it."

"We always need money, Boy. Can never have enough of it."

"Yeah, right. You got a house in Mexico, Paris, New Orleans, Hollywood, Australia the Bahamas. Where are you moving to next, Dad?"

"What's with the sarcasm? Don't I pay you enough? You should get out of this dump. You can afford it, or can you? What do you do with the two million dollars I send you each year?"

"That's my business."

"No. It's mine! You got debts or something?"

"No. Let's get off this subject. It has nothing to do with what's going down tonight. Which reminds me, what is going down tonight?"

"Like I say, I need to be seen in two places at the same time. Which is why, dear boy, the aroma of curry needs to be on both our breaths, so we appear one and the same. So come on, eat up."

"You need to be seen in two places at once? For a dead guy, Dad, you certainly get around." Chas grinned. "Though one whiff of your breath and they'll conclude you've been dead a hundred years."

"Funny, funny. Can't deny it though, being dead has its rewards. Do you realize that you've taken the rap for everything I've done over the last twenty odd years? Thing is you've had a concrete alibi every damn time, and no one has ever yet cottoned on as to why." Raymond Baxter laughed heartily, as his son pulled a face.

"You should try seeing the inside of an interrogation room every once in a while. They can hold you forty-eight hours while they make their enquiries you know."

"Still it must bring the greatest of satisfaction when you know they can't finger you."

"Guess so, just bloody inconvenient most of the time. I do have a life beyond crime, Dad."

Raymond raised one eyebrow in question. "You do? Is that where the two million goes every year?"

"Like I said before, it's none of your business. That's what we agreed, didn't we? You don't know anything about me, and I don't know anything about you. Save for a few contact details, of which yours grow longer by the day I might add. I'm not sure I want to stand for your double tonight though, sounds fishy to me."

"Lord, Charlie, I'm just double booked, that's all. It's not dangerous, but like I say, I stand to collect. And I mean collect!"

Chas wasn't happy but he'd never let his father down before. They were a team, two peas in a pod, and he didn't think there was anyone that knew the difference…well except maybe one did… but he received an annual reminder to keep silent.

"Won't they think it kinda suspicious. If they find out you were in two places at once? You are supposed to be dead after all."

"You're missing the point, Charlie. It's not me who has to be seen in two places at once tonight, it's you. Like you say, I am supposed to be dead after all."

"But you've always carried out the crime and I've carried the can. Why all of a sudden do I have to be the one to be seen?"

"Because there is no crime involved. We're just out there to collect."

Chas sighed heavily. Whichever way his father put it, it still sounded dangerous. A gut feeling told Chas something wasn't right.

"So we're collecting what? Money? Dad…I take it we're collecting money?" At his father's silence Chas backed off. "No. No, way, Dad. Tell me you aren't collecting narcotics?"

"The best. The purest whitest heroin you ever did see. Worth millions."

"It's a set up. You're getting stupid in your old age. Cosmetic surgery can only go so far, Dad. What you need is a brain transplant."

"Don't be insolent!"

"I'm not doing it, Dad. And that's final. You kill, I take the rap, fine. You rob threaten, rape, bust someone's skull fine, I take the rap, the rap they can't hold me to. But heroin, never! You know what will happen if we are caught with that stuff? Dad, for God's sake, reconsider!"

"There's a lot of dollars riding on this."

"And you need them because?"

"Will you stop saying that!"

Chas shrugged, "you're on your own with this one, Dad. Sorry."

Raymond sighed heavily, "I need you. The drop is synchronized. I need to collect in two places at once."

"So you keep saying. What do you mean synchronized?"

Evasive, Raymond shrugged.

"Dad...?"

"Just that. I was asked to collect in two places at the same time. When I tried to negotiate, each dealer wouldn't budge. Both set the drop for eleven o'clock tonight. One in Manhattan, the other in Brooklyn."

"At eleven, dead on the dot? No going a minute earlier or a minute later? Not that you could make the distance in a minute between Brooklyn and Manhattan."

"Absolutely on the dot or no deal. So come on, what do you say? Are you going to help me?"

Chas shook his head. "It's a trap." His mind raced. "Who knows you're alive? We've told no one, at least I haven't." Chas said suspiciously.

"Well don't look at me! A dead man can't speak can he? You know I go under a different identity these days."

"Oh yeah, and what is it now?"

'It's none of your business,' they spoke together.

Chas sighed, "Dad, listen to me. It's a trap. I'm sure of it. I don't know whether they guessed or what. Whether anyone has said anything..." Immediately Chas thought of the old fellow in the park. His father was thinking along similar lines.

"There's old Richardson. You don't think he's..."

Chas shook his head. "Nah, he's too frigging scared shitless."

"And how would you know?"

"I've been paying him an annual visit. That's why."

Raymond was impressed. "You have? Good lad. So if it's not him, then who?"

"You believe me then? About it being a trap?"

"I don't want to, but I have to admit..."

"Lord, Dad! If I hadn't made some waves about this..." Chas stood up and marched across the room and back again, dragging a hand through his shock of brown hair that belied his forty-seven years. "I can't believe you'd have gone...Dad! You could have walked us both into a bloody trap...don't tell me you had an idea of it all along..."

"In the beginning…well…yes I did. I admit it seemed suspicious. Guess I let the green eyed monster get in front of me, huh, Son?"

"Just a bit."

"So if tonight is a no go I take it we go our separate ways again? Say, have you marked your diary for those dates, I sent you?"

"Naturally."

"And you won't let me down on those?"

"Have I ever? Look Dad, that sort of thing, fine. You know it's fine, but this…God, Dad it carried a stink label on it from the very beginning…I can't believe you even contemplated…"

"Okay, okay, so sue me. I fucked up for once."

"Almost fucked up…" Chas grinned.

"Thank God for a son that saw sense, is all I can say. Well we live and learn, don't we?"

"Or in your case you die and learn. Glad you visited though." Raymond grinned and took it as his cue to leave. "Yep can't deny that. Nice spending time together I have to admit."

"You take care huh? See you in what? Two, three, five years?"

"If I'm still alive."

"Get outta here, Mister immortality…"

They embraced, a quick hug, heartfelt and emotional before Raymond stepped from the apartment without looking back.

"See ya." Chas called after him. He refrained from adding, 'Dad.'

* * *

"Eleven pm…on the dot…so where is he?"

"He said he'd be here."

"Have you heard from Larry?"

"Not yet. Want me to call him?"

"No. He'll call us if Baxter turns up. Maybe we're wrong. Maybe he is on his own. A guy can't be in two places at the same time, can he?"

"Larry thinks he can."

"Yeah, right."

"No, really. He believes that he can. Well okay not literally. But you gotta admit, how is it that Baxter has a concrete alibi for every frigging crime that goes down in this city? He's been seen. God damn it, seen! Witnesses picked him out of a line up over and over again yet other witnesses verified seeing him at every venue he said he'd been at. And those witnesses have never been the same twice, it don't make bloody sense. So Larry got to thinking, there has to be two of them, like a twin or something, one that no one knows anything about. It's the only thing it can be."

"Right."

"But looks like Larry was wrong about that."

A cell phone in his pocket vibrated and the under cover detective extracted it flipped it open and read the message. It was from DI Larry Bycroft stationed over at Brooklyn. The message simply read, 'no go'.

"So looks like we're back to square one. Baxter didn't show over there either. Can't understand it, when our contact spoke to him on the phone he was adamant he'd be here. Something must have gone wrong."

His colleague said nothing.

"Double cross? You think we were double crossed?"

"I'm saying nothing."

"Don't have to. It's written all over your face. Well I tell you this for nothing, somehow, someway we're gonna nail this guy. Someone somewhere must know how he gets away with it…there's got to be someone…and I tell you now…I'm gonna find them…you see if I don't."

His colleague remained silent. He'd heard the same sort of thing said by a dozen other detectives for years. No one could nail Baxter.

"Impossible huh?"

"Hate to say it."

Glumly, they walked toward their parked cars dark figures against an equally dark night. Neither had noticed a small device positioned on site or the black sedan parked with lights off in a corner of the parking lot. It had been there since nine, its driver inconspicuous in the back seat, waiting… watching…listening…

"Damn! Chas was right." Raymond flipped the listening device from his ear… "And so another detective bites the dust. Can't be helped…no one must guess our secret…no one…"

Content that once the detectives in question were dead that would be the end of it, Raymond Baxter made his plans. Not for one moment did he consider that the eighty plus old man in the park held the key to unlocking his secret…

If he would ever tell…

Chapter Seven

"Mr. Richardson?"

It had been three days since Sherri had returned the peas and shared a cup of coffee with Jack Richardson. He'd allowed her to stay while she sipped her coffee and had made polite conversation as new associates often did. Now Sherri was back again hoping to strengthen what little ground she had already made.

"Hello? Mr. Richardson? Are you there?"

Sherri hadn't told Jack about her visit with his Grandfather. She'd always been a great believer in doing nothing to rock the boat, so to speak, and had decided that it was far better to keep quiet about this new development.

"Helloooo?" Sherri stepped a little further into the kitchen not wishing to intrude. Her heart hammered painfully and she wondered if perhaps the Grandfather regretted inviting her in before, or even worse, had forgotten.

"That you, Sherri?"

Relief flooded through her when she heard him ask.

"Yes. Yes, Mr. Richardson. It's me, Sherri."

"Well don't just stand there letting in the cold. Come on in." His tone belied the nervousness he felt.

"Thank you," Sherri stepped into the kitchen and closed the door, "for March it's so cold out there."

He nodded and indicated the chair by the table as he walked across to the stove. "A hot cup of tea will warm you up."

"Tea?"

The Grandfather chuckled. "Or would you prefer coffee?"

Sherri's eyes sparkled. "Coffee would be wonderful."

"Then coffee it is."

"Of course you originate from the United Kingdom. They're great tea drinkers, I'm led to believe."

The Grandfather nodded as he placed the kettle onto the lighted stove, "Yes, tea just about soothes everything."

Sherri ventured another question. "Do you miss England?"

A faraway expression clouded the Grandfather's features. Sherri thought for a moment she'd asked the wrong question and waited apprehensively for his reply. It was an age before he gave it and by then the kettle was whistling merrily. He removed it from the stove and poured two cups of coffee, bringing them to the table before he answered.

"I loved England," he told her with tears in his eyes.

He handed her the coffee and sat down at the table to the left of her, averting his gaze. "I dream about it all the time."

The words, 'ever thought of returning' rushed to Sherri's mind but she refrained from asking. It was a stupid question. Of course he'd thought of returning. A man like Jack Richardson and all the burdens he carried would have thought about returning to England almost every day. Sherri reasoned.

"Whereabouts in England did you live?" She asked instead.

"At first we lived in Stratford on Avon, then we moved to the South Lincolnshire fenlands. Flat country, no hills, farming country, the land of the Pilgrim Fathers."

"The Pilgrim Fathers? So you mean Boston?"

Grandfather looked up and studied her carefully. Sherri could have kicked herself. True, she might just know all about Boston, it could be a coincidence, but she would have to be more careful in future. Everything she knew about the Pilgrim Father's and Boston was due to the fact that she was a journalist.

"We did it in college." Sherri explained without elaborating.

Grandfather appeared relieved and nodded his understanding. "Aye, yes Boston. I lived just outside of the town. Folks had a farm." Sherri wasn't certain what to say. He sounded sad and a faraway look remained in his eyes. Eventually he mumbled, "What I miss the most is the dogs. Can't have one here."

Sherri thought of the park. True, one couldn't let a dog run free there, but kept on a leash it was a great place for exercise. Then she remembered something. The Grandfather never went out. That's what he really meant.

"You could become a dog walker." When he appeared vague Sherri explained, "some people in the city that go out to work all day seldom have time for their dogs. There are a few agencies that help with that. They arrange for volunteers to walk the dogs. Some are paid a minimal fee, other people do it for nothing because they enjoy the exercise and the company of a dog they don't have to pay the upkeep of." The Grandfather seemed interested so Sherri went on, "I could arrange something like that for you if you'd like that?"

Immediately, the Grandfather became uncomfortable. His gaze swept straight to the window and settled on the park beyond. He started to shake his head before speaking "No…no…"

About to apologize and add, 'Oh I forgot you don't go out, do you?' Sherri stopped herself in time, stating instead; "It would be no bother. Perhaps we could walk the dog together."

"No, you don't understand. It's not that…" The Grandfather's voice trailed away and he gazed at her a long time before speaking. A million and one thoughts chased through his mind before he settled on a decent explanation. "I…I…I don't go out…much," he added, feeling uneasy.

"Okay, that's no problem. Tell you what then, how about if…" Sherri smiled happily, "I volunteered to be a dog walker and brought the dog around here to spend some time with you?"

"You'd do that!" The transformation to the Grandfather's face was amazing. He looked like a little boy given a puppy for his birthday.

Sherri nodded and smiled enthusiastically. "Why not? Besides I could do with the exercise. I sit far too much." She cringed, wishing she had not added that last bit. Thankfully, he was too excited to question her and his next words brought tears to her eyes.

"I'd love that. Thank you!"

"Is there any dog that you like more than any other? I believe I'll get the chance to choose which breed to walk."

"Retrievers, German Shepherds…Border Collies… We had all of those on the farm. Any one of those… Oh thank you so much, my dear."

"It will probably be a Retriever then. I don't think I could handle a Shepherd and I've not noticed too many Border Collies around these parts."

Grandfather nodded. Sherri was delighted to see that his eyes remained bright with enthusiasm and she hoped there wouldn't be any problems in signing up for dog walking.

As though he read her mind, Grandfather stated, "I suppose it will be a while before you can bring a dog here. There must be endless red tape to go through before they accept you as a walker."

"Probably. So there's no time like the present. I'll get on to it right away." She drained her coffee cup and pushed the chair back to stand, but Grandfather caught her arm. "There's no rush. Do you know how to play Scrabble?"

Sherri almost laughed out loud. Only a few weeks ago she and Jack had spent practically all of one night playing it. "Yes, I do."

"Would you join me in a game?" he asked hopefully.

Sherri nodded. "I'd love to but I'll warn you now, I'm a whiz with words."

"Age against brains then," he chuckled as he headed for his bedroom to collect the game. For the first time in as long as he could remember he began to feel comfortable with a stranger. And he admitted that she seemed nice...however only time would tell...he had to remember that all people can be nice when they wanted something...

When he emerged from his bedroom moments later he was surprised to see that Sherri was pouring more coffee. "I hope you don't mind me taking liberties? I thought the least I could do was get us set up for the game. Thirsty work, Scrabble."

Grandfather chuckled and settled the board game on the table. Sherri did the honors and set the game up. Soon both were too engrossed to notice the sound of heavy foot falls outside and were startled when Jack pushed open the door. His face was a picture, comical even, and Sherri had to laugh.

"Hello, Jack!"

"Sh...Sh...Sherri?"

"Er yes..." Sherri looked down at herself, "at least I think so. Why, who were you expecting?" Beside her she could see Grandfather's shoulders twitching as he held laughter at bay.

"I...I'm just stunned to find you here." Jack confessed stepping into the kitchen and removing his muddy boots.

"There's coffee in the pot, Jack. Sherri made some." The Grandfather waved in the general direction without taking his eyes off the board.

"Oh er...thanks." Jack walked to the counter, his mind in a spin. To find Sherri in the kitchen drinking coffee with his Grandfather and playing Scrabble! Whatever next?

"So how long..." Jack surveyed the game. They'd laid many words so he knew that would have taken at least an hour. He was surprised that his Grandfather had let someone stay that long... Hell, he was surprised his Grandfather had even allowed someone in!!

"Bout an hour," his Grandfather confirmed, "to the game, that is," he added without taking his eyes off the board, "your go, Sherri."

"So you were here before...the game?" Jack sat down at the table, his coffee cup in his hands, feeling as though he were dreaming.

Grandfather looked up. "Oh, yes. Sherri has been here most of the morning," he told his grandson, speaking as though that was nothing out of the ordinary, "she's going to get me a dog."

Quizzically, Jack raised an eyebrow. "A dog?"

"I'm going to volunteer for dog walking and bring the dog to visit your Grandfather." Sherri explained without taking her eyes from the board. She made her move and laughed, "There you are, Mr. Richardson! Look what I've put."

Grandfather looked down at the board. The word 'retriever' jumped out at him. He chuckled. "Must be fate," he said. Sherri chuckled, too.

Jack looked between his Grandfather and his girlfriend totally flummoxed.

"Even more so…" Grandfather's lips twitched as he crossed the word retriever with another. Both Sherri and Jack looked down at the board perplexed. "The twelfth?" Sherri queried. "How does that fit with retriever?"

"Well, we already have the words August and glorious, so now we've got the lot."

"The lot?" they chorused.

"Yes. Don't you two know anything? August the twelfth, the glorious twelfth, the day grouse shooting begins. The retriever would fetch the fallen birds."

His mouth agape, Jack could only stare at his Grandfather.

Sherri laughed. "So that's another thing you miss about England: Grouse shooting season?"

"I miss all of England's seasons," Grandfather confessed wistfully.

"You've never said so before." Jack was stunned.

"You've never asked."

"And Sherri did, I suppose."

"Actually, yes." Sherri and his Grandfather spoke together. They smiled at one another.

"You did?" Jack looked at his girlfriend. All of this was too much to take in at one go.

Sherri nodded, and made her final move on the Scrabble board. "I'm out!"

Looking down Grandfather groaned, "Oh no, you're not are you?" He looked upset that she had beaten him.

"Told you I was a whiz with words," Sherri laughed. "I'll come and play another time if that's okay with you? I've enjoyed this morning."

"I'd like that."

Jack listened to the exchange with disbelief. His Grandfather appeared so at ease. His eyes were sparkling, and he appeared younger than his eighty-four years, brighter, and happier than Jack had ever seen him.

Sherri stood and packed the game away, then as Jack offered to walk her back home, she shook her head, "No, it's okay, Jack. You came home for some lunch, didn't you? Stay and have it. Will I see you tonight?"

"You can count on it." Jack kissed her goodbye, and with a wave to Grandfather, Sherri left the cottage, promising to see about that dog.

When she had gone, Grandfather sighed. "Nice girl you have there, Jack."

Completely taken aback Jack didn't reply. And he was even more surprised when returning the Scrabble to his bedroom his Grandfather announced, "ask her to visit anytime she likes. I'm going to lie down. See you later, Jack."

For a long time afterward Jack remained seated at the table contemplating everything that had happened. If he'd not seen it with his own eyes, he would never have believed it.

Chapter Eight

In the city that never slept there were quiet areas akin to all cities, places where the homeless gathered. The lucky ones slept fitfully in cardboard boxes, half a mind awake to predators. Others, rested in the doorways of shops, huddled together to keep warm, taking turns to sleep while one kept watch. Many remembered another way of living others simply chose to forget. Remembering was painful, soft mattresses...food in the belly...a roof over one's head...a family. Living a life where the very necessities of every day living were taken for granted, where their whole world didn't revolve around where their next meal might come from or whether they'd have a chance to wolf it down before it was snatched away by someone else.

Hannah saw her world through tired eyes, this was the only life she'd known for a decade now and she looked older than her twenty-seven years. Her tattered clothing reeked of stale odor and dirty streets and her toes peeked out of her shoes. Her blood caked nails were dirty and broken and served her only as weapons. She had used them often.

Hannah wasn't among those that chose to forget their past she simply couldn't remember it. Although…sometimes…in the furthest recess of her mind something pricked…a memory elusive as the wind   it fluttered…occasionally…

Her turn to keep watch, Hannah surveyed her world through eyes that saw without looking…she was cold…weary…nothing mattered but watching for sudden movement…in the shadows…listening only for the sound of a footfall…

A long time ago Hannah could remember listening for other footfalls…footsteps on the squeaky stair that would signify the advance of her step father…then she could remember nothing but the squeak of the stair as he went down again. What happened in between was buried deep …tucked in the back of her mind where it could hurt her no more. Running away had not been an option…it had been a necessity…yet the life she had envisaged came with even harder edges than the one she'd left behind…and her stepfather's ways were reflected in everyone she had the misfortune to meet.

What was life that she had to endure the satisfaction of men? Hannah hungered for a life denied her…and wondered if it actually existed.

Those pretty ladies, the clothes that they wore, their carefree laughter…Hannah couldn't remember if she had ever laughed…cry, yes, she had cried…tears of self pity and pain…the wretchedness of being alone…locked in the dungeon of her mind…no one to tell and no escape…until the day another world beckoned beyond the open door…and she'd seen the way out…

Or so she had thought…

Sometimes she wondered if this was hell…perhaps they all had it wrong…perhaps one started life in hell, died and went to earth…one step closer to heaven.

She'd been born into hell…she reminisced…

* * *

A distant shuffle caught her eye…and Hannah tilted her head with the slightest of movement… never let them know you're awake…the element of surprise in numbers was a lifesaver. Allow a predator to creep up...then pounce...the sudden movement startling awake one's companions...and the predator would be down. And if by some stroke of luck that one be better off, nice clothes, good shoes, money...jewels, things to trade...things to barter for...to sell favors for...then all was well and good...

Breathing tight and shallow Hannah watched the advance of a shadow...her nails dug into her palms in anticipation...adrenalin surged in her veins...sweat broke out on her brow, beneath her breasts, in her armpits...she watched...she waited...it was almost time...

Then the shadow was no more...and Hannah's brow furrowed in confusion...where did it go?

At her side a voice as soft as butter...fresh like mountain water rippling over pebbles aroused her senses...

"Don't look at me..."

Hannah ignored the warning, turning her head at the sound of the voice...seeing nothing but the deepest of shadows...

"I've been looking for you..."

"Yeah? Well now you've found me!" Hannah whispered hoarsely. Until she knew the guy's intent she spoke lowly so as not to wake her companions.

"Aren't you curious?"

"No. You never heard what curiosity did?"

"No."

"It killed the cat."

A chuckle. "Good job I'm not a cat then."

"So what do you want?"

"You shouldn't be living like this."

"Gee wise guy." Hannah spoke dryly. "Next you'll tell me I'm destined for greater things."

"You are."

"Yeah, my name in lights, my guts ripped to shreds...I've the face the fits...heard it all before."

"Sorry. I'm not into snuff movies."

"What are you into?"

The stranger laughed. "Where do I start?"

"You tell me."

"Some other day. For now, I've brought you something."

"What?"

"A burger, coffee and a chocolate muffin."

Hannah's mouth watered.

"What do I have to do to get it?"

"Nothing, nothing at all. Except perhaps to say thank you?" The stranger asked cheerfully.

At her side Hannah heard the rustle of paper and then the scent hit her. The taste of fresh food melted on her tongue before she'd taken a bite. Hannah's hands reached out, took and stuffed the burger into her mouth. Only when she began to choke did she take the lid from the coffee and wash the food down. There was no second telling in the street world. When offered food one partook with relish and speed. Hannah never spoke again till all the burger was gone. "You said something about a muffin?"

A chuckle, "so I did. Yes. Here."

"You really did buy all this for me?"

"Yes. I've been watching you."

Alarm bells sounded in Hannah's head. She gulped down the muffin, "Watching me?" she asked between swallowing.

"Yes. If you don't mind me saying, life has been unkind to you."

Misty eyed, Hannah nodded, "and then some."

The stranger was silent for a time, Hannah felt his discomfort, knew he was trying not to offend or frighten her away...she waited knowing other people had fed her after they'd extracted whatever it was they'd come for. This one was different, and yes... "Okay, I'm curious." Hannah revealed openly.

The stranger chuckled, "Ah, now you are curious?"

"I just said that, didn't I?"

The stranger unnerved Hannah, yet she felt powerless to ignore him. He was different, though she could not see him, she knew he was different...and deep down inside she felt...that he intended her no harm...but...

"You sound sincere...but I've learned that people can put on a front..."

"Yes, they can," the stranger told her honestly, "and I'll admit I'm not all that I seem. However..."

He leaned down beside her and whispered in her ear, "I believe we can help one another."

Nervously, Hannah shifted away, "How?"

"You have some information that would be useful to me."

"Me?"

"Yes you. You're Larry Bycroft's daughter are you not?"

Hannah shuddered, "He's my stepdad. And a man in a position to know better."

"I heard what he did to you."

"I don't want to talk about it! What is this? Do you get off on perverted talk or something? Leave me alone! I ain't saying anything."

"I thought you might like to get even." He said smoothly.

"Even?"

"Yes, even. I've heard our Mr. Bycroft enjoys seeing to kids."

"And you're whiter than white, are you?"

"No. But I don't mess with kids."

"What are you going to do to him?"

"That's not for you to know. All I want to know is a few details."

"For this one burger?"

"Don't forget the coffee and the muffin."

Hannah shook her head. "You know what I mean."

"Yes. Okay, here's the deal. I can get you off the streets forever for the right details."

"For real?" Hannah didn't want to get her hopes up. Everything he was saying seemed too good to be true.

"Certainly. Can we go someplace else? We shouldn't be talking here like this."

"Here's just fine."

"Maybe I can persuade you."

Hannah heard the jingle of small change as he searched through a pocket, then beneath her nose he thrust a roll of dollar bills. Her hand reached out and she was surprised when he did not snatch the money away. From her pocket she took a cigarette lighter flicked it into life and looked at the bills closely.

"I could have saved you the trouble." The stranger told her. "I collected that little wad earlier. There's five hundred dollars there."

"Five hundred dollars!"

From somewhere behind her a voice mumbled, "someone mention money?"

Hannah was on her feet in an instant, shoving the money into her pockets, wherever it would fit. "Let's go," she told the stranger.

He took her arm. "This way. My car's parked over there."

Any hesitation Hannah would normally have had evaporated at the feel of all that money in her pockets. She went with the stranger willingly.

"Here, this one." He told her as they approached a long dark sedan. Before they were ten yards from it he clicked the keys and the vehicle indicators flashed and the doors unlocked instantly. Hannah was amazed she'd never seen anything like it before in her life!

"Remote control?" she asked impressed.

"Something like that, get in." He held the front passenger door open for her and Hannah didn't hesitate. She slid into the still warm interior, relaxing in the luxury and scent of real leather seats and waited as he walked around the vehicle to slide in beside her.

"We can stay here. It's safe enough now."

"So what do you want to know about my step father?"

"Everything you can tell me. Most importantly what are his interests? That is his other interests. Where he is most likely to be found when off duty."

"I might not be able to help you. It's ten years since I last saw him."

"I have it on good information that his habits haven't changed in years."

"Then why do you need me? Surely your other informant would have been able to tell you everything you needed to know."

The stranger nodded, and for the first time Hannah dared to look at him. It was still dark where they were and his face was in shadow, but his profile told her more than she'd known earlier. "I think I've seen you before."

"Don't look at me!"

Her heart thumping Hannah turned away. "Sorry."

"Believe me honey, it's better if you don't know who I am."

"Better for whom?"

"For you."

A shudder passed through Hannah. Sitting beside him she could almost feel the vibes that told her how dangerous he could be and with five hundred dollars in her pocket she wanted nothing more than to live and spend it. Eyes front, she dared not look at him again.

"So, back to DI Bycroft."

Hannah sighed heavily, the last thing she wanted to do was think about her stepfather. The very name brought her out in a cold sweat. As if he understood, the stranger told her, "take your time."

"He used to visit art galleries." She spoke at length. "And the library. He'd go to the library every Saturday morning. They used to close at midday. I think he'd go there to use the computers. He might have his own by now."

"Depends what material he surfed for. What sort of woman is your mother?"

Tears filled her eyes as Hannah whispered, "she didn't believe what he did to me."

"That's all I need to know. Believe me Hannah, she will do. And when she does it will be up to you to decide whether to return home."

"I'm never going back!"

The stranger nodded and asked, "So he went to galleries and the library. Anything else?"

"On Sunday's he visited his mother's grave. Regular as clock work. Never missed."

The stranger appeared interested. "Time?" He asked.

"Before ten, always. He was back before I got up at ten."

"Would that be the church yard near his home?"

"Yes."

Out of her eye corner Hannah saw him nodding. She could almost hear his mind ticking over.

"You're going to kill him, aren't you?" She whispered. The stranger said nothing. Hannah knew he was going to kill her stepfather. The thought filled her with both dread and jubilation. "Promise me something?"

"What?"

"Before you kill him…" Hannah wasn't sure what she wanted to say. She only knew that if her stepfather was going to get his comeuppance, she wanted him to know she'd been aware of it.

"Don't worry. I'll make sure he knows."

"Thank you."

"And thank you. Now, sweet lady, I have something else for you." Hannah leaned back nervously as he reached in front of her and opened the glove compartment. From inside he extracted an envelope. Hannah heard what she thought to be the jingle of coins.

"Here, these are for you." He dropped the envelope into her lap.

"For me? What is it?"

"Keys. Keys to your new home, the address is on the key ring. I own the house but you may live there rent-free for as long as you wish. You'll find the house fully stocked with everything you'll need. I took a chance on your clothes size. In a drawer you'll find details to a bank account in your name. I took the liberty of providing you with a nice little nest egg. In another drawer you'll find the address of your employer. You start work on Tuesday. I heard you could type, so it's a cushy little office job.

You'll need to tidy those nails before then." Hannah hadn't said a word it was all she could do to believe it. "Now, keep your eyes averted while I drive out of here. I'll drop you off outside your apartment building."

Hannah looked out of the window as her benefactor switched on the engine and moved away from the curb, and it seemed no time at all before he was pulling up again on the better side of town.

"You can get out now. That's the building. Use the intercom to announce who you are. The night guard is expecting you. And Hannah…"

Opening the door, Hannah hesitated. "Yes?"

"Thank you."

"Oh no, thank you!"

"You're welcome."

Her mind in a daze, Hannah stepped from the sedan and didn't look back as it pulled away from the curb. Her attention was focused on the building ahead and the feel of the keys in her hand. Her mind was in a whirl. She couldn't believe this was happening!

Taking a deep breath Hannah stepped up to the huge swing doors, gingerly pressed a button on the intercom on the wall and nervously announced her first name. To her surprise one of the doors sprang open accompanied by someone announcing, "Welcome home, Miss Carnell." Hannah almost wept with joy…whomsoever the stranger had been, he really had thought of everything…even to the point of using her old surname rather than the one her stepfather had adopted her to.

Hannah entered the bright reception, nodded a greeting to the guard and checking the apartment number on the key ring, made for the elevator.

Tonight her new life would begin. Hannah Carnell would never look back.

* * *

Being freelance meant that Sherri could choose her hours of work, and though she was always busy, she took time out to further her promise to

Jack's Grandfather that same day she'd mentioned the dog to him.

After making some enquiries she knew the location of three dog walker agencies and telephoned each for an appointment arriving at the first agency at three o'clock in the afternoon.

By five that day she had been accepted by all three as a potential walker pending references and on arriving back at her apartment had rang one out of the three that had owners of golden retrievers on their books. With the other two she cancelled her application.

Now three days later, Sherri received the telephone call that would begin to change her life.

"Miss Scott? It's Oodles of Poodles here. We are happy to tell you that your application to be a dog walker has been successful. And since you particularly wish to exercise retrievers, we have just the dog for you. Are you free anytime today?"

"I can be. What sort of time are you thinking of? It's no problem to rearrange my schedule."

"Great. Well how about two o'clock? You collect the dog from us. He's a darling. You'll have no problem with him. Providing you can give him a couple of miles, he'll be happy."

"Sounds wonderful. I'll see you at two. What's the dog's name?"

"Simba."

With thanks, Sherri hung up and anticipated the afternoon ahead and Grandfather's face when he saw the dog. Exceedingly excited, Sherri decided two o'clock wouldn't arrive soon enough.

* * *

Across town that same day, and as he ate breakfast, a cell phone vibrated in Chas Baxter's jeans pocket. Extracting it, he peered at the screen. A little envelope flashing in the top right hand corner signified that a message had been received. Scrolling through the menu Chas opened the inbox. The message simply read, "Sunday morning before ten. Find something to do."

Chas made a mental note of the details, deleted the message and replaced the cell phone to his pocket before resuming with his breakfast.

There was no expression worth mentioning on his face whatsoever.

Chapter Nine

Simba was beautiful. Sherri couldn't stop petting the dog as they walked across the park on the way to Jack's Grandfather's cottage.

With his coat the color of ripened barley folding in soft waves along the ridge of his back Sherri found her eyes drawn to the dog as he walked placidly at her side. He neither pulled on the leash nor bothered when other dogs came close, neither did he bark at strangers. He was perfect.

Sherri's excitement mounted as she anticipated taking the dog to see Jack's Grandfather and she walked quickly eager to get there.

On the way she paused at the flower bed Jack had created for her a few weeks earlier noticing that though the crocus and hyacinth had wilted Jack had planted other flowers in their place, and now pink, white and red impatiens adorned the flower bed. Stopping to look at them she did not hear footsteps come up behind her and jumped when two arms stole around her waist.

"Good afternoon, my love." Warm breath fanned the back of her neck as he kissed her there.

"Jack!" Sherri turned in his arms and gazed up at his smiling face.

"Found a dog I see. Guess I'm out of favor for today then?" He raised an eyebrow causing Sherri to laugh.

"Guess so. Seems you may have competition."

"I can handle it. So, what do you call that?" He nodded down at the dog.

"It's a dog."

"Funny, funny. I mean what's his name. I take it, it is a he?"

"Yes. His name is Simba."

"Like the lion. Cute. Is he okay?"

"He's marvelous!" Her eyes elaborated 'so are you' they told him.

"So I take it, you like the new flowers?"

"Love them. Thank you Jack."

"I'm taking a chance on frost. Should be passed now, but one never knows. If it looks like we might get some I aim to place a plastic covering over this bed. Hopefully, that will protect the Impatiens. If not…" Jack shrugged, "I'll have to replace them with something hardier till summer arrives." Sherri nodded.

"Well, should I accompany you to the cottage? Or do you want to do this all by yourself?"

"You can come. Has he said anything more about a dog?"

"Has he ever!" Jack exclaimed as they fell into step side by side and headed out over the grass toward the cottage. "Never stops talking about it. Honest my love, that day you visited, well it was like you loosened his tongue or something. He never stops talking about anything. I do believe I've discovered more about my Grandfather in the past four days than I have in thirty years. And I'm pleased to announce, he is human after all. If I'd introduced you to him six years ago, I may have discovered this sooner."

Laughing, Sherri slapped Jack's arm playfully. "So, do you think he'll like Simba, then?"

"Darling, I think he'd like anything on four legs that wagged a tail," Jack slipped his arm through hers, "thank you, Sherri. For what you've done for him. He's a changed man. Honest he is."

"I confess, I have an ulterior motive."

"I know. Getting him out and about so he'll come to Devin's place with us. Needless to say I haven't mentioned anything about that."

"Good idea. It's best not to. Do you think he will want to walk the dog eventually?"

"I don't know. Maybe...we'll see. Now come on let's go round that way to the cottage, then he won't see us arriving. Taking the dog in there will be a complete surprise."

Sherri followed Jack's lead and together the two of them and Simba arrived at the cottage door without being seen. They'd already decided the best way to surprise the old man when Jack opened the door and pushed the dog inside, holding the door ajar while they both held their breath and listened.

Inside Grandfather had been sitting at the table when he'd heard the door handle rattle, and his first instinct had been to run and hide...so he was half way to his feet when he stopped dead, disbelieving what he saw. A beautiful golden retriever was being shoved into the kitchen and then the door closed behind it.

"Sherri!" Grandfather exclaimed, knowing only too well who had brought the dog.

Sherri popped her head round the door. "Surprise!" She cried.

"Oh, it's the best..." Grandfather crossed the room surprisingly quickly and started petting the dog. Warm, adoring brown eyes gazed trustfully up at him. Man and dog fell in love.

"His name is Simba."

"Simba?" Grandfather shook his head, "Reincarnated. We had a Simba. Just like this. Welcome back, Boy." Grandfather ruffled the fur around the dog's neck. "Come...I think I can find something you'll like."

Walking to where he kept some sweet biscuits Grandfather rummaged in the jar until he found what he was looking for, "Remember these?" He held one up and the dog's eyes were bright with anticipation.

"Beg."

Simba sat down, and with his tail wagging from side to side on the hard stone floor he raised one paw and offered it to the old man. Grandfather laughed, "That'll do." He patted the retriever's head as he offered him the biscuit. Simba took it gently and munched happily sprawled out on the floor with the biscuit between his front paws. When it had gone he looked up eagerly, and Grandfather did not disappoint him as he handed him another biscuit.

"You and I will get along just fine." Grandfather ruffled the dog's ears affectionately then looking at Sherri asked, "How long can he stay?"

"Well, providing you don't let him out, he can stay a couple of hours. I still have to give him his walk, he needs two miles."

"Two miles! You don't want to walk two miles do you, Boy? I think we can exercise you well enough in here. Jack, move this table, will you, and the chairs. Sherri, if you open that cabinet under the sink you'll find a ball in there. It's one Jack and Devin used to play with. Bit old but it'll do." When each had done as asked, Grandfather walked to the far end of the kitchen and with the ball in one hand threw it to the other side of the room. The dog shot after it, its claws tapping on the stone floor as it ran. Back and forth the ball went as the dog raced after it and brought it back. It was soon covered in slobber and the dog was panting heavily.

"Water?" Grandfather walked to the sink and filled a deep dish from the tap. Simba almost knocked it out of his hands to get at it. He had soon drunk every drop. "More?" Grandfather filled the dish again, and watched the dog drink until he was full. Sherri and Jack as bystanders loved every minute of the whole thing and before half an hour was up the dog looked about ready to sleep for the rest of the day.

"I would never have thought I'd see the day when you'd have more energy than a young dog, Grandfather!" Jack exclaimed as the three sat down at the repositioned table and drank coffee. "Now I know what it means to be dog-tired. Sherri may have to carry him home."

"He did love it though, didn't he?" Grandfather's eyes were bright with humor.

"I'm not sure who enjoyed it more. The dog or you, Grandfather." Jack told him.

His Grandfather beamed. "I did enjoy myself."

"We noticed," Sherri smiled, "I'm glad."

"Thank you, Sherri." Grandfather told her happily, "I really mean that, Duck."

"Duck?" Sherri laughed. "Can't say I've been likened to one of those before."

Grandfather smiled. "It's an endearment. Where I come from, people use it all the time."

"Oh I see. Well then thank you, Mr. Richardson."

"Call me Jack…or Grandfather."

"Grandfather." Sherri acknowledged. "Save confusion."

"Wouldn't be the first time."

Muffled snoring came from the dog. He was fast asleep.

"Have you got a wheelbarrow, Jack? Maybe I'll need it to get him back."

"Yeah, I can see that…you turning up at the agency with your charge in a wheelbarrow." Jack laughed out loud.

Simba wagged his tail at the sound but his eyes remained closed.

"He'll be okay in about an hour, so while we are waiting," Jack laughed and then added the magic words, "anyone for a game of Scrabble?"

* * *

"Here lies Agnes Spencer, aged ninety-four years. Spinster, returned unopened…" Raymond Baxter guffawed at his own joke as he sat in his sedan overlooking the cemetery. It was a quarter past eight in the morning, and he was delighted to notice there were few people about. Not that it mattered if there were, for with the perfect alibi such as he had it didn't really matter who saw him do what.

Similar vehicles, same plates… Who would know? After Bycroft was dead there was nobody that would know anything…

Baxter tapped the steering wheel in time to a melody playing on the radio as he kept his eyes glued to one gravestone in particular.

"Two down one to go. Suckers!" Baxter spoke out loud remembering the deaths of DI Bycroft's two colleagues earlier that morning. He'd set a trap for them and they'd fallen straight into it. Baxter felt no remorse for killing two innocent men whose only crime was that they knew too much. Not like their colleague, who lived a double life.

"And soon everyone will know about it!" Baxter cried.

No sooner had he spoken, than did his gaze settle on a man walking with intent toward the grave of Freda ByCroft. He carried a bouquet of flowers not unlike the one Baxter had laid on the seat beside him. He readied them now, sliding a file and a gun from the glove compartment and holding the flowers and the gun together he stepped from the sedan and made his way toward the grave, tucking the file inside his breast pocket as he went. DI Larry Bycroft was just extracting the flowers from their cellophane wrapper as Baxter came up beside him.

"Never a vase, is there?" Baxter asked pretending to lay flowers on the next grave. "Bloody vandals smash anything. Someone close?"

Bycroft straightened and did not look at the speaker. Baxter wouldn't have cared if he had, but this way prolonged the event. "It's my mother. Been dead twenty-two years. Seems like yesterday. You never get over it, do you?"

"Nah. Like a lot of things though, things happen…can't be changed. Well maybe they could if other people had anything about them…Take pedophiles for instance. Don't it just make you sick when people get off doing things like that to little kids?"

DI Bycroft stiffened and turned his head just in time to see down the barrel of a revolver aiming at his forehead and he froze on the spot.

"Especially when it's kids in their care. Don't you just hate people that abuse that kind of trust?"

As Bycroft 's gaze rose to meet Baxter's, Baxter aimed the gun at the detective's genital region and pulled the trigger. "This one's for Hannah… and this one's for all those other poor kids who placed their trust in you."

Screaming in agony, the detective felt only the touch of cold steel on the back of his head before he knew no more.

Bycroft's body slumped dead at Baxter's feet. From his breast pocket Baxter pulled the file and tipped the contents over the body.

Soon people would know that DI Bycroft was not the upstanding pillar of the community that everyone thought he was…

* * *

Sherri was visiting with Grandfather when she heard. It came over the radio and she stiffened, trying to act as unconcerned as possible lest she gave herself away.

"You listening to that?" Grandfather reached for the radio his intent to turn it off, "Sherri?"

"What? Oh…er…oh…no"

"Hate news like that." Grandfather explained as he turned off the radio.

Deep in thought, Sherri said nothing.

"Sherri?" Grandfather shook her arm.

"What?"

"You okay? You look as white as a sheet?"

"I'm sorry. Grandfather, I shall have to go."

"Go? But you've only just arrived. Simba and me haven't played ball yet."

"I'll come back for him later. Keep him inside huh? There's somewhere I've got to go."

Without waiting for his reply Sherri ran to the door, slipped on her shoes and left. Grandfather gazed after her then looked back at the radio. He was sure there was a connection between the news and Sherri's sudden strange behavior, yet for the life of him he couldn't decide what.

* * *

When he saw her running past, Jack feared the worst and downing tools he raced after her. "Sherri, wait up! What's wrong?" He swung her around to face him. "Was Grandfather rude to you?"

"No, Jack. Look let me go…I have to go… Heard some bad news…"

"What bad news?"

Sherri drew in a deep breath. "DI Bycroft has been found murdered laying atop his mother's grave."

"DI Bycroft? The fellow that organizes charity runs for the kids home?"

"Yes."

"That's terrible. Who'd want to kill him?"

"That's what I'd like to know. Look, Jack I'll be back in a couple of hours. Simba is with your Grandfather. Keep an eye on him will you?"

"Which one?" His question was lost on her as Sherri started running across the grass again.

Jack shuddered, when the police started to get killed…what chance was there left for the rest of them?

* * *

By evening everyone knew. The facts spoke for themselves… there was no arguing with photographs. They showed DI Bycroft abusing kids he'd been entrusted with…and as the news broke out other kids came from all over the city to give evidence, even those he'd never touched. Compensation was a powerful thing.

His wife was devastated…and she was remembering…that was the worst of it all…her so called unruly daughter who no one had been able to handle…was lost to her…Brenda doubted she'd ever see her daughter again and her heart ached…if only she knew where to find her…

Late into the night, after the cell phones of DI Rutcliffe and DI Davis went unanswered, the worst was feared until they were later discovered, their bodies side by side behind a bar in Brooklyn. They'd been killed with a single bullet to the back of the head …the bullets came from the same gun that had killed DI Bycroft.

It was the hardest report Sherri had had to write. DI Bycroft had been her friend. She'd trusted him…and now she hated him more than words could say.

* * *

After collecting Simba and taking him back to the agency she had returned to her apartment to sit out on the balcony deep in thought.

Eyewitnesses had given a description of the graveyard killer, as he was being dubbed, a description that fitted remarkably to one she knew well…Baxter…Charlie Archibald Baxter. If that hadn't of been enough the registration of the vehicle had proved it, CAB 1. Even so, Sherri knew they'd never pin it on him.

Too bad DI Bycroft had been unable to establish the truth of his theory…Baxter a twin? Was it possible? Sherri nodded slowly. 'Yes it's possible.' She whispered, 'and that's why the three detectives were murdered. They'd been getting too close…'

Sherri shuddered…for suddenly she realized…she was the only one that knew that now…

Chapter Ten

It was the hardest thing Devin had had to do in all his life, to drive past the cabin where Cheryl lived and keep his eyes focused resolutely ahead. Out of his eye corner the distinctive glint of James's blue and yellow truck was hard to ignore and enough to keep Devin from turning to look.

Since his return to his mountain home Devin had not heard from Cheryl and he had worried himself sick over her welfare. Short of spying on the cabin to see if James went out at all there was nothing Devin could do, so he got on with packing up his things and keeping his mind actively involved on moving.

The nights were the worst when his dreams would remind him and he'd wake in a cold sweat calling her name. Sleep would be denied him then and he'd lie awake trying to formulate a plan to get Cheryl away from her husband. What appeared a good idea in the dead of night always evaporated as ridiculous in the cold light of day and he'd be left feeling inadequate and not the hero he so wanted to be.

Sometimes he wished he shared his brother's gift of precognition, that way he'd have been given insight as the best way to operate in such a delicate matter. Without that he had only to rely on gut feelings, none of which gave him any peace.

Reaching the foot of his mountain home gave Devin no satisfaction. Moving to the estate was exciting true, but he felt as though he'd left the best part of himself up on the mountain. He knew there would come a time when his relationship with Cheryl would be brought to a head but he was loath to think of it. James was not the sort to let his wife go without putting up at fight. Not because he loved her, Cheryl had confessed that her husband's love for her had waned shortly after they were wed. James liked to possess and his wife was one of his possessions nothing more nothing less. He did however enact his rights on her, and by all accounts, brutally so.

Devin's tender love making had caused Cheryl to cry that first time as they lay swathed in the golden glow of a log fire. And each time since she had clung to him with tears of gratitude and love in her eyes.

Thinking on those occasions, tears welled in Devin's eyes as he slipped from his truck to open the estate gates, taking deep steadying breaths before he returned to his vehicle to drive through to the grounds beyond.

Closing the gates behind him lent Devin a view of the mountain he had just descended and he gazed upward his heart breaking with longing and remorse to have left Cheryl behind. "Soon my love." He whispered. "Somehow someway, we shall be together. I promise, Cherie. I promise."

His heart heavy, Devin trudged back to his truck and continued the journey along the drive toward the big house.

* * *

Sherri had a dilemma. She either told someone about DI Bycroft's thoughts as regards a Baxter twin or she kept silent. It didn't need a degree in arithmetic to work out that DI Rutcliffe and DI Davies had been killed because they were colleagues of DI Bycroft. So far, it would seem, Baxter did not know of Sherri's knowledge of the matter. She also would have been killed if he'd known. So to tell anyone…that would be what?

Suicide? Right? Yet to keep it to herself then other people could die. She could argue that since no one knew for sure whether Baxter had a twin her keeping silent wouldn't be wrong, but Sherri knew better than that. Obviously Bycroft was too near the truth with his suspicions and that's why he had been killed. Although some might argue that Bycroft had been killed because of his perversions with kids, it didn't answer the question as to why Rutcliff and Davies had been killed also. So far investigations on their private lives had turned up squeaky clean. To Sherri that only left one answer, to everyone else it was a mystery.

Walking Simba these days seemed to be the only way she could unwind.

If only she could find someone, a witness, someone willing to tell, that would be wonderful, but she knew Baxter left no loose ends. There was a secret there, she just knew it, but how to dig for it that was the problem, how to dig for it and not leave a trail that led straight back to her? If only there was a simple solution.

On one of her jaunts with Simba she voiced her problem out loud, "they say that the answer very often lies beneath one's nose. They also say that at time's one can't see the wood for the trees. You known, doggie, sometimes I wish my life were as simple and uncomplicated as yours. The only worries you have regarding noses and trees is how far it is to the next one before you can cock your leg again."

Sherri ruffled the retriever's ears and he wagged his tail happily. Over the last few weeks a firm friendship had developed between the two, and Jack's Grandfather adored him.

"Well, you ready to visit the old man?" She asked the dog pushing her problem to the back of her mind. It would resurface soon enough. "The agency has asked me not to let you have any tidbits while out. Seems you've gained a few pounds. Well I'll make a deal with you okay? You and I will walk further than two miles each time to work off those biscuits. And then Grandfather can continue the pleasure of seeing your eyes light up when he offers them to you. Okay? What do you say?"

"Woof!"

Sherri smiled. "If I didn't know better I'd say you understood every word. Come on then, Grandfather will be wondering where we are."

They trotted across the immaculately mowed lawns of the park, one of Jack's jobs. Fortunately he had been commissioned to use a ride on lawn mower or by the time he'd finished he would have had to get started again, leaving no time for the flowerbeds or cultivation of seeds and cuttings in the large hothouse.

The weather had grown warmer and Sherri noticed with pleasure that the roses were beginning to shoot. Tight little buds adored the stems, though it was difficult to tell what color the blooms might be.

Passing by 'her arrangement' as she termed it, since Jack had lovingly constructed it for her, she was surprised to find that he had changed the flowers again. Now petunias of every color covered the bed and spelt out the entwined initials S and J. It was beautiful and it took her breath away. It seemed that by constantly changing the flowers with each season he was telling her that he was keeping their love alive and fresh and new. It impressed her no end.

Reaching the cottage Sherri kept her eyes on the retriever. She derived great pleasure at seeing his reaction to their arrival. He had always been a well-behaved dog, and had never pulled on the leash so she found it exceedingly pleasing to see that on their approach to the cottage he panted that bit heavier, walked a few steps ahead of her and wagged his tail and lolled his tongue that bit more than usual. But best of all were his eyes. Always warm and brown and trusting, on the approach to the cottage they blazed with delight and Sherri was sure had she released him from the leash at that stage he would have bounded the last few steps into the garden and thrown himself at the cottage door.

Grandfather had seen them coming and greeted them with the door open wide. He had changed considerably since she'd been bringing Simba to see him, he chatted more freely and didn't seem to appear so nervous when he came out as far as the gate to see them off when it was time to leave.

Sherri decided now would be as good a time as any to move on to plan B.

"Hi, Grandfather. He's eager to see you as usual. The thing is…" She went on to tell him about the biscuits and extra walking, "I know you play ball and tire him out…unfortunately the agency have equipped both me and the dog with this little gadget."

"What does that do?" Grandfather asked with interest.

"It logs each step we walk, each mile we cover and for me how many calories I burn up exercising."

"So what's wrong with playing ball in the kitchen?"

"Nothing, for Simba. The gadget will log his every step. The problem arises when they match my steps against his. A dog walker's job is to walk the dog, not sit and let the dog off the leash to run amok. I have to prove that I take as many or almost as many steps as he does. And short of having me tearing across your kitchen floor after a ball as well as Simba, he's going to log ten times more steps than I am."

"So you can't bring him in any more?" Grandfather's face fell.

"Oh no, no. That is I can. That's not the problem. The problem is that I have to clock up the same amount of steps, and a certain amount of steps. Enough to cover two miles at least."

Grandfather was thoughtful. He looked over Sherri's shoulder to the park beyond. It was quiet and with the children at school, the only people about were mothers with strollers and toddlers.

"Maybe…" He began and following his gaze Sherri held her breath. "How fast do you walk?" It was not what she expected him to say and taken aback Sherri was slow to reply. "Fast huh?" Grandfather's face fell.

"No! No not fast, we take a gentle stroll. He's a well behaved dog, he doesn't pull on the leash at all." Grandfather eyed her shrewdly, and inwardly Sherri grimaced. She'd made it too obvious hadn't she?

"I mean we have our moments. Sometimes I jog beside him as he trots along. But generally it's nice just to stroll and enjoy the park. Especially a park maintained by Jack."

Sherri saw the moment that Grandfather made his heart stopping decision…and she almost followed suit. "Could I come with you?"

It was hard not to sound too delighted. Overjoyed Sherri smiled. "Yes, that would be wonderful, Grandfather. Simba would love to have you with us."

"Just a minute then." He popped back inside the cottage, and as the minutes ticked by Sherri wondered if he'd changed his mind. Eventually he reappeared and she released the breath she hadn't been aware she was holding. He was wearing a tweed jacket and an old dusty pair of shoes that looked about thirty years out of date.

"I've left Jack a note." Grandfather told her as he walked up the garden path and opened the gate. "No doubt it'll give him a heart attack, but can't be helped. He'd have been frantic to come home and find me gone."

Sherri chuckled and slipped her arm through Grandfather's telling him "Here, Grandfather you hold the leash. You'll enjoy walking him." And so the pair set off on that momentous occasion, the first time Jack Richardson, senior had been outside of the garden of his home in twenty-eight years.

Chapter Eleven

The weeks rolled by and Sherri encouraged Grandfather that bit further every time the two of them walked the dog together. It was no pleasure trip however, for Jack's Grandfather might have stepped from his home for the first time in almost three decades but that didn't mean he dropped his guard any. It was all Sherri could do to maintain her equilibrium with his constant warnings and anxiety of what may lie around the next bend. There were times when she wanted to scream, and she could only respect Jack all the more for putting up with his Grandfather and not going completely and utterly mad.

At first Grandfather gripped her arm when they set off each day and he walked as though glued to her side. Sherri noticed his attention was diverted most of the time to what was taking place far out across the park. He would constantly stop when he saw a group of people who, in his mind were acting suspiciously. On one occasion he fairly dragged her back to the cottage when they saw some youths paying particular attention to a bush. It was only when one of the youths extracted a football from beneath it that the Grandfather sighed with relief and the color returned to his face.

Jack marveled at the fact that Sherri had been able to get his Grandfather to go out at all. The water retention in the old man's legs went down and his general attitude to life altered drastically. He grumbled less, his outlook became brighter and what was most important, he accepted Sherri into their lives as though she'd always been a part of it.

Above all Grandfather loved Simba, so it caused a huge blow the day Sherri arrived without him.

"Where's Simba?" Meeting her at the gate, Jack's Grandfather looked beyond her expecting that Sherri had let the dog run free, though she never had before.

"Grandfather, I'm sorry. The agency informed me that Simba's owner's circumstances have changed. They're able to walk him themselves now. The agency offered me another dog, but I wanted to check that with you first."

Tears formed in Grandfather's eyes, and he sobbed, "I loved that dog."

Sherri's heart went out to him. "I know you did. That's why I couldn't bring myself to walk another dog."

"Do you know where he lives?"

Sherri shook her head. "That information is confidential. If it's any consolation, I'm sure Simba will miss you as much."

"It's no consolation at all!" Grandfather marched back inside the house and slammed the door.

Undecided Sherri hovered by the gate not sure what to do. She'd known he'd be disappointed, she'd just underestimated how much it would affect him. Taking a step toward the cottage she hesitated, 'he might want to be left alone', she reasoned. Turning with the intent to leave she changed her mind, 'oh the other hand, he shouldn't be alone at a time like this.' Thus Sherri marched up to the door opened it and stepped inside. It broke her heart to hear weeping coming from the old man's bedroom and for several moments she wasn't sure what to do. It was then she spied the kettle and with the Grandfather's words of 'tea just about soothes everything' to remind her, Sherri walked to the stove to make him some.

"Tea's ready, Grandfather." Sherri called when she'd poured out two cups. She heard a clatter from the bedroom and then his face appeared around the doorframe accusation in his eyes.

"Who invited you in?" He demanded. Sherri ignored him and settled herself on one of the four chairs around the table.

"I've made it how you like it, sweet and hot." She sipped at her own grateful that she could hide her smile over its rim when he grunted disapprovingly and marched into the kitchen scraping a chair from beneath the table to sit down beside her.

"I know what you're doing. Jack and Devin do it all the time. Don't think I'm stupid, just because I'm old. Do you think a cup of sweet tea is going to stop me from missing him?" Tears gathered in his eyes again.

"No, Grandfather. You told me that tea soothes just about everything, but I don't expect it will sooth away the hurt you feel at the moment. Maybe I said the wrong thing out there, maybe I ought to have said, if it's any consolation, I shall miss him too. Simba is a gorgeous dog and we were lucky to get one so nice. I can't imagine another replacing him, and I don't intend to try."

"So that's it then?" Grandfather's tone was flat.

"That's what then?"

"Our walks."

"Not necessarily. Oh I know it won't be the same without Simba, but it doesn't mean we should stop going out."

"And what would be the purpose of that?"

"Exercise, fresh air, to name a few. If you want another, I'll confess that I enjoy your company."

A hint of a smile graced Grandfather's lips. "I did enjoy going out," he confessed.

With the cup to her mouth, Sherri held her breath.

"Though it won't be the same without the dog." He fell silent as he thoughtfully considered the idea.

"I know!" Sherri announced brightly, "We don't have to stay here. I could drive you somewhere. We could go out of town, visit other parks. Do you like galleries, or the theatre perhaps?"

Grandfather's mouth dropped open and his next remark was more than Sherri dared hope for. "You're serious? You'd take me? That would be marvelous!"

Sherri did smile then, one of pure joy and happiness. Her eyes danced with merriment, "Grandfather you're welcome…being able to take you anywhere is a pleasure…" She told him with tongue in cheek.

"I'd love to see a movie," he told her, "not one of those mucky things they show on television, but a real movie. One with a good story…a war hero story… That would be grand."

"What would be grand?" Neither had heard Jack come home. He was peering through the open window.

"Hi, Jack! Like some tea? Sherri will make you some. She makes the best cuppa, anyone would think she's British she makes them so good."

Jack laughed and moved from the window to the door, entering moments later.

"I'd like that. So what would be grand?" He looked around the kitchen, noticing the absence of the dog. He also noticed his Grandfather had been crying and putting two and two together decided it best not to ask where the dog was.

"Your Grandfather and I were discussing other outings, Jack. He'd like to go to the movies. And I happen to know just the movie to take him to see. It's showing till Friday."

"To the movies?" Jack quirked an eyebrow, the more Sherri did for his Grandfather the more impressed he became. "Devin will be surprised."

"Devin?" Grandfather queried, "why? Is he coming for a visit?"

"No, Grandfather. Not that I am aware of. It's just that since he was last here, you've done so much, changed so much. He won't believe it."

Liking the thought of that, the Grandfather chuckled. "Bout time I showed that boy I'm not over the hill yet. Talking of which, how about you taking me to visit him, Sherri?"

Sherri gasped with shock, "To the Appalachians? You're sure?"

Jack was speechless.

Grandfather shrugged, "If that's where he lives, then yes, sure I'm sure."

Sherri's heart raced and beneath the table Jack grasped one of her hands in his. This was too good to be true.

"Well, yes, certainly...I can take you..."

Grandfather nodded. "Good. But first the movies?" His eyes were bright with anticipation.

"Yes, first the movies. Tomorrow night okay with you?"

His face clouded over, "Nooo, not night time..." he shook his head, "surely they have an afternoon matinee?"

"Matinee? Oh you mean performance? I should think so. Tell you what I'll check some times and get back to you later today with them."

"Thank you. I'm really looking forward to this. Do they still bring round ices and popcorn in the interim?"

Sherri and Jack exchanged curious glances and Grandfather laughed, "I'll take that as a no shall I? What happens now then?"

"Popcorn, cola, ice creams and sweets are generally purchased on the way in, Grandfather."

"Well that's ridiculous!"

"Why is it?" Jack laughed.

"Because if you can buy the stuff on the way in, people will be rustling packets and belching from soda drinks all the way through the film. Much better to have an interim to consume food."

"Maybe you can place that in the suggestion box."

"They have one?"

Sherri nodded.

"Then I most certainly shall! No interim indeed. So when do people get up to use the toilet? No don't tell me, they get up and go whenever they want. I am beginning to see why home movies are so popular. No heads constantly popping up and down to ruin one's view."

"I'll tell you what, Grandfather, they do still have an interim at the theatre. Maybe you'd prefer to go to one of those?"

"Will I need a suit?"

"Well...yes."

"And that would mean a visit to a store." Grandfather shook his head and sadness crept back into his eyes.

Eager to find something to make him happy Sherri told him, "Grandfather, there is something you could do…only…" Her heart pounding, Sherri asked Jack, "Darling, would you mind leaving your Grandfather and I alone for a few minutes?"

The surprise was evident in Jack's eyes. He thought he knew what she was about to do and wasn't sure that now was the time.

"Just go out into the garden. And no eavesdropping!"

"Well I know when I'm not wanted." Jack rose and stomped across the floor to the door, opening and closing it behind him. "If anyone needs me I'll be in the park." Keeping his fingers crossed, he hollered from outside.

Sherri counted to twenty, "just a minute, Grandfather." She went across to close the kitchen window, "just in case." She winked at him on her return. "Grandfather, I wanted Jack out of the way for a moment because…well…please don't be angry or anything…and hear me out okay before you say anything…"

Grandfather didn't think he liked the sound of this. He nodded slowly, apprehension filling his brown eyes.

"Grandfather, a few weeks ago Devin and I started to plan a trip to Devin's place where we intend to hold a surprise for Jack. We hoped that you might consider joining us…" her voice trailed away as the Grandfather's expression changed from one of apprehension to interest and then to anger.

"I knew it! I knew it!" He flared slamming his hands down onto the table. "That's what it was about all along wasn't it? Don't deny it, girl! You came here and befriended me and got me out walking with the dog…because all the time you had an ulterior motive! And it had nothing to do with me all along did it? Well did it? Deny it if you will!"

"Grandfather!" Sherri hoped her outcry sounded indignant enough. The last thing she wanted was for him to know he was right.

Shrewdly he gazed at her. "I'm not stupid. I can see through you. I've always thought there was some reason for you doing everything you did. I began to think when you brought Simba that I might be able to trust you. But I was wrong. You abused my trust, young lady…and I will never forgive you for that! Get out of my house! And don't ever come back!"

Sherri wasn't giving in without putting up a fight. "Grandfather, okay, you win. I underestimated your intelligence. I'm sorry."

The Grandfather glared at her. "Don't... patronize...me!" he flared.

"I didn't intend to. I'm sorry! Look, please let me explain."

Grandfather pointed to the door. "There's the way out, use it!"

"No! God damn it I won't!"

"I will have no profanity in my house. Now, get out of here!"

"I'm leaving but not before you hear me out. You owe me that, at least."

With his hand hovering over the radio, his usual way of drowning out words he did not wish to hear Grandfather hesitated. "You have thirty seconds," he stated, "starting now... one... two... three... four..."

"Silence!" Sherri shouted at him, "how do you expect me to think when you are counting my time away?"

"TEN...ELEVEN...TWELVE..."

Exasperated, Sherri hurried on, "Jack's spent his whole life looking after you...he deserves time off...Dev and I thought a surprise in the Appalachians would be good for him...and we wanted you to see the look on his face when..."

"THIRTY! TIME'S UP! DOOR!"

Sherri glared at the old man as he pointed at the kitchen door, there was more she wanted to say, so much more, but already he was leaning toward the radio with his other hand and reaching for the on switch. Moments later he turned up the volume full blast and anything she attempted to add was drowned out by the classical music filling the room.

"Okay...okay..." Sherri moved toward the door, "I'm going." She slipped on her shoes and reached for the handle just as the music subsided down to nothing.

"Wait!" The Grandfather called after her.

Hope flared in her heart as Sherri slowly turned back to face him. She dared not speak.

"I'll give you another thirty seconds to tell me the truth. Your fate will depend on it. I'll know if you're lying, young lady, so don't even think about it." His face was expressionless.

Sighing heavily, Sherri crossed back to sit down beside him. It grieved her that she hadn't removed her shoes, she hoped he wouldn't mind on this one occasion. When she failed to begin he reminded her. "Time is ticking away."

"Grandfather…"

He refrained from telling her he wasn't her Grandfather, but she saw the look in his eyes.

"Mr. Richardson…"

"I'm waiting."

"It's hard knowing where to start."

"Try the beginning."

"The beginning? That would go back six years and take longer than thirty seconds. Look, okay…you know that Jack and I love each other?"

Grandfather had seen evidence of that on many occasions over the last few weeks, and could not deny it. He nodded.

"And you know that Jack would never leave you alone here?"

His gaze expressionless, Grandfather nodded again.

"Well what you don't know is that a few weeks ago, the relationship between Jack and I reached stalemate. He was reluctant to introduce you to me, and he sent Devin to tell me that our relationship was over."

"Why?"

"That's what I wanted to know. Apparently, Jack couldn't expect you to accept a woman in his life, so it was best that he didn't have one."

"That's ridiculous!"

"Is it? It seems so now. But look how it was when he first brought me here. Look how you acted toward me." Sherri reminded him.

"I had my reasons," he told her, gruffly.

"Whatever they were or are…" Sherri went on deliberately, "they were enough in the beginning for Jack to decide it was best that we split up. It was only thanks to Devin arranging a surprise for Jack at his Appalachian home that changed Jack's mind. No, I'll take that back. It was only when

I suggested to Devin that you came along too, that changed Jack's mind."

"And...?"

"And so...yes...Grand...I mean Mr. Richardson, I did set out to befriend you for my own selfish gain. What I didn't expect was how much you would come to mean to me. No, hear me out...I mean it...I've thoroughly enjoyed our walks with Simba...and seen in you an older version of the man that I love..."

"What is this surprise? What does it consist of?"

"It's an adventure. A mystery...I can show you the advertisement. It will explain things better than I ever could...I haven't got it with me right now, though."

"And you expect me to tag along?"

"Yes."

"And if I refuse?"

"Then it's all off. Jack won't leave you here by yourself." Sherri told him sadly, unable to keep the disappointment from her voice.

"And that would mean what for you and Jack?"

"Nothing." Sherri shrugged. "I'm not going to stop loving him just because he couldn't visit his brother for the weekend. I'm sorry that sounded like blackmail. What I meant was, just because he refused to go away for the weekend."

"So you'd continue to see him?"

"That would be my intention. I love Jack, Mr. Richardson."

"But you'd have no future... If Jack won't leave me, and well...I couldn't possibly imagine you coming to live here with us...even if there were room. Jack's bedroom can only contain a single bed, so too Devin's old room. And I won't give up mine. So..."

"So we continue as we are until it fizzles out." Sherri stated flatly. "Let's face it, by what you insinuate, Jack and I could never marry and live a normal husband and wife existence here in this house."

"That's about the size of it."

"So what then? What do you expect me to say now?"

"I wanted the truth."

"Then have it. If Jack won't leave you and I if couldn't live here, then we'd have to wait till you were dead before we could have a life together! And how would that make Jack feel, huh? Answer me that? And how does it make you feel? To know that but for agreeing to one thing for once in your life so many people could be happy." Sherri scraped back her chair, "I'm through with this. You wanted the truth? Well that's it. I'm outta here."

"No, wait!" Grandfather reached for and clasped her arm tightly. "I'll go."

Dumbfounded Sherri could only stand and stare. "You'll go? Where? I don't understand."

"I'll go to the Appalachians. On condition…"

Sherri's heart raced, "Name it."

"That you take me there in a car with tinted windows. That we leave early in the morning, at first light. And that you'll humor me while I look the place over before I decide whether I can spend the whole weekend there."

"I'll do better than that. I'll take you there in advance of the proposed weekend away. We'll travel there and back in one day and you can see for yourself how safe the area is."

"Safe? What do you mean by that? Has someone said something?"

Sherri acted as cool as she could. "About what?"

"Doesn't matter," he regarded her steadily before adding, "and that's the lot? You've no other little secrets you're withholding from me?"

"None at all." It was all Sherri could do to look him in the eye. Liars, she'd been led to believe couldn't do that. At that moment she realized how untrue that was.

"Then, that's settled. You'll bring me that advertisement for Jack's surprise and take me up there ahead of time. But I'll warn you now, young lady, if I think for one moment that the place is unsuitable…wild horses won't drag me back there."

Solemnly, Sherri nodded accepting his terms. It was the only thing she could do.

Chapter Twelve

Traveling in Sherri's car a little over a month later, the Grandfather had grown more and more at ease with the thought of spending a weekend in the Appalachians. For one thing it was a long way from the city and his first sight of Barrington Estate impressed him. There was a high security wall that he was pleased to note, had spikes pointing outwards at the top, making it virtually impossible to climb over without being impaled. The gates were made of strengthened steel, richly ornamented, with filigree patterns of vines overlaid with grapes in gold enamel.

"Who lives here?" Grandfather asked, as Sherri got out to push open the gates, before getting back into the car and driving through the gateway into the extensive gardens beyond.

Unsure of how much she should reveal, Sherri replied, "You'll have to ask Devin he found the place as I told you. He should be here somewhere. Perhaps he can tell us."

Stopping again to close the gates behind her, Sherri jumped as the car door opened from the outside, and Devin's cheery face appeared. "Hi," he greeted them both panting hard, "I've closed the gates Sherri, no need to get out again. I unlocked them earlier in preparation for you, and…" he waggled a set of keys at his Grandfather, "I've relocked them. And that's the way they stay when anyone is here. Firmly locked. Glad you could come, Granddad. Did you enjoy the journey?"

Eyes bright, his Grandfather nodded. "And where did you spring from?" he asked, turning in his seat to see his youngest grandson climbing into the rear.

"I've been walking around waiting for your arrival. When I saw Sherri's car approaching, I ran from where I was to get to the gates to meet you. Who'd believe it, huh, I climb up and down mountains every day, and yet I get out of breath just doing a quick sprint!" he laughed, catching his breath before adding, "well, I'm sure you have questions, Granddad. So fire away." In the reflection of the rear-view mirror Sherri saw him wink at her and she smiled.

"I was just asking Sherri who lives here. She said I should ask you."

"Mm, there's the thing. The estate is actually in the process of changing hands. At the moment until the contract is signed, it belongs to Tom, a friend of mine. Please don't think I got you here intending you should meet him. I know how you are with strangers, and I truly believed Tom would have been left by now…" Devin's words faltered, he expected an outburst any second.

"And?" his Grandfather asked gruffly.

"Well things became complicated at the other end of the chain, with the house Tom is buying. So…"

"He's still here. Is that what you are saying?" Grandfather felt the old familiar fear return at the thought of meeting a stranger.

"Yes he is. But Grandfather Tom is a great guy. And we work together."

"You work together?"

"Yes. I'll let Tom explain." Devin winked at Sherri, who could only wonder what delight Tom might impart.

"So just Tom lives here? Bit big for one isn't it?" Grandfather queried.

Devin grimaced, "actually his wife and kids are here too."

Grandfather groaned. "And how old are his children? Are they teenagers, adults or what?"

"Just children. They're about nine, I think, and they're twins, twin boys, William and Benjamin. Alias Bill and Ben."

"Bill and Ben the flower pot men," Grandfather murmured.

"Laura says that. Used to be a popular British television show for kids as I recall?"

Grandfather smiled fondly remembering, "yes."

"Well these two love gardening. So I'm sure the three of you will have a lot to talk about. And they're great kids."

"So when does Tom plan to leave? Or more importantly when do the new occupants move in? That is will the place be empty when we come for the weekend. Let me rephrase that. IF we come for the weekend, for I tell you now, my boy, if this place isn't like Fort Knox there is no way you'll have me stay here."

"I know that, Granddad."

"So is Laura from England too?"

"Her folks are. Laura has spent many holidays in the United Kingdom with her grandparents so I'm sure you will find lots to talk about. Now come on, Granddad, first impressions and all that. What do you think of the place so far?""

"It looks wonderful," his Grandfather began, "I am particularly impressed with the security, but until I have seen every thing, I can't really pass an opinion. This place needs to be like Fort Knox before I will ever consider staying here."

"Then it's a foregone conclusion, Granddad. Believe me, there is absolutely no way in to this place once those gates are locked." Devin told him, with fingers crossed.

"Is there no other way in?" His Grandfather asked, "no back gate, nothing?"

"Not unless there's a foolish pilot with a helicopter, Granddad. No, there is no other way in." Devin replied.

The Grandfather grew thoughtful, and Devin knew that look. "Look,

Granddad, don't worry. Who would want to land a chopper here? Besides it would take some navigation. I believe the previous owners had considered the possibility of that. Come look. I'll show you."

As Sherri maneuvered the car around the final bend before the house came into view, Grandfather looked up when Devin pointed above to the only part of the extensive gardens that were void of trees and shrubbery.

"What are they? Power lines?"

"No. I guess that the best way to describe them would be trip wires. See how they have been positioned? Look across there, alongside those tall trees, there are some metal poles, I've been across to them. They appear to be embedded deep in the ground. And the wires run from the tops right across the grounds. Extremely taut, and are held in place with pins to the roof of the house. Any foolish pilot navigating his propellers through those wires would stand the risk of crashing his machine and killing himself."

"Certainly not a place for flying kites then?" Sherri mused, much to Grandfather's amusement.

Driving onward, the house finally came into view, and on sight, both Sherri and Grandfather gasped. Painted in a soft lemon, with black guttering, the house was truly impressive, and a delight to look upon, and so high that the three travelers had no option but to alight from the car, before they could successfully see the rooftop.

"There's a lake. So if you fancy your hand at fishing, Grandfather, just say the word and I'll fish out some rods." Devin laughed, "I made a funny, get it, fish out some rods?" His Grandfather chuckled and Devin's mind eased. Perhaps the plan to get his Grandfather there wasn't going to be so hard after all. When he'd received Jack's letter telling him about the difference in their grandfather, Devin had hardly dared believe it.

"Those wires look pretty lethal up close, Devin. I see what you mean now." Sherri remarked.

"Ah huh, deadly aren't they? Can you imagine if they snapped?"

"I wouldn't want to think about that." Sherri replied with a shudder. "Are you certain they're safe?"

"Apparently they've been checked annually. More often if there has been any strong wind. I've been up a ladder and looked at the pins where they are fastened to the roof, so too where they are fastened to those poles. Both places seem sturdy enough. I think the only trouble one might have is if a tornado whips through here. But then who'd be outside when one of those sweeps through, huh?"

"Talking of which, is there someplace to hide if that occurred?" Sherri asked.

All the time the two had been talking the Grandfather had held his silence taking it all in. He was interested to hear the outcome of Sherri's last question.

"Yes. There's a bunker. Two actually. One in the grounds over by the meadow, and one near the stables. They've been built where there is no likelihood of fallen masonry or trees to trap the occupants."

"Can anyone get inside them?" Grandfather questioned.

Something in his tone alerted Devin and one step ahead he replied, "I suppose so, Grandfather. But if you are worried about strangers or assassins hiding down there, don't be. First they have to get over the gate or the walls. Or negotiate those wires and you've seen what a deterrent all of those are."

Sherri decided they'd reached a stage where she had to ask the obvious or be taken as stupid. "Why assassins?" she asked innocently.

Taken aback, Grandfather stared at her. He looked at Devin who shrugged and then back at Sherri. Finally he decided he could trust her with some of his story.

"There's something you don't know. I'm sure you've wondered and maybe you've been too polite to ask. Well it's this...I witnessed something terrible a long time ago...and I was threatened to keep my mouth shut. And there were certain other conditions..."

Sherri's heart was hammering so loud she thought he might hear it. "And you think that whomsoever issued the threats would follow us here from the city?"

"It's a possibility. I've tried to stick to their rules. That being not to involve the police or...or...journalists...I detest journalists..."

107

"Oh? Why's that?" Anxiously, Devin glanced from one to the other of them. Sherri was treading on dangerous ground.

"It suffices to say that because of a promise made by one of them my best friend died…that's all you need to know."

"Oh."

Happy to change the subject Devin jumped in quickly. "So what do you think of the security around the place then, Granddad. Has it surpassed your expectations?"

"Mm." Grandfather murmured thoughtfully. He wasn't entirely convinced. He believed that anyone determined enough could find a way in. Still he supposed he or Jack would have had one of their premonitions if anything had been likely to happen. Devin had never had them. In fact his two grandsons were very different in so many ways. Devin, with his roguish good looks, black hair and brown eyes lived life to the full while Jack, taller than his brother, slim athletic, light brown hair and green eyes preferred the simple things in life, asking for so little. It was one of the reasons why Grandfather found himself pondering the weekend trip away for Jack. The boy deserved it. Finally he replied, "It seems okay so far, outside that is. I can't really say till I've been inside the house."

"Then let's go. Laura said she'd be making brunch and serving it on the veranda and it's about that time now. So come on, I'll make the introductions."

Devin led them to a pair of huge oak doors and lifted a brass knocker in the shape of a bunch of grapes. Grandfather wondered what it was with the grapes, and as if he could read his Grandfather's mind Devin explained, "the place used to belong to some wine merchant. Hence the grapes." He let the knocker drop and it thwacked against the door with a heavy bang.

They waited and very soon the door creaked open revealing a smiling faced man with a mop of red hair that fell over his eyes lending him a boyish appeal. "Hi Tom, this is my Grandfather Jack Richardson and my brother's partner, Sherri Scott. Grandfather, Sherri, this is my good friend and colleague Tom Sandmann."

Tom held out a hand, "I'm so pleased to meet you, Mr. Richardson. I feel I know you already. Devin never stops talking about you." Grandfather seemed surprised as Tom explained, "you grow prize roses, I understand?"

"Yes. Yes I do!" Grandfather exclaimed happily.

"My two boys would love to hear all about that. They are very horticultural minded, and seem to have green fingers. They'll be down soon, they are showering right now, Laura, that's my wife, took them riding earlier, and they stank of the stables when they got back. Not a fine way to greet guests."

"Someone mention my name?" From behind Tom came a beautifully slender woman walking toward them. She was taller than her husband by a good six inches, revealing long deeply suntanned legs, beneath a dazzling white and yellow sundress. Devin always regarded Laura with respect and admiration. She was a woman who knew how to look after herself, her home and her family not necessarily in that order. Laura put family matters first and she loved Tom dearly.

"There you are, darling. I was just telling our guests about the twins going riding. Are they clean yet?"

"They're on their way down. I grabbed a shower ahead of them. Hello Devin. This must be your Grandfather?" Laura held out a hand to the old man who shook it warmly then she shook Sherri's hand. "Well come in, come in, Tom's always leaving people chatting on the doorstep. I'm sure you must be thirsty. What can I get you, tea, coffee, something cold?"

Tom led them into the sitting room. Grandfather had never seen a room so large in his life. From the door where Tom led them the sunny room stretched all the way down to a huge bay window that filled almost the whole length of one wall. The room was painted a magnolia or cream color with a Dado rail all around positioned about two feet from the high ceiling. From here large framed oil paintings hung, most of them depicting scenes of the Appalachians, other mountains and lakes. There was one of a cloud formation brewing into a storm, over a harbor when soft pinkish clouds met black, it was stunning and Grandfather remarked on it.

"That's one my father painted." Laura informed him.

"It's Yorkshire isn't it? Somewhere near the sea, I so love to see the bright white wings of seagulls against a black stormy sky."

"Yes, you're right. It's Whitby Bay, North Yorkshire."

"Thought so. Must admit though I've never seen boats so compatibly colored before."

Laura laughed. "That's my father for you. He decided that had he painted all the true colors it would detract from the effect of the sky. So the subtle colors you see are of his own design."

"Ah, that would explain it. Very clever."

They moved into the room and Laura showed them to a long six seat sofa. It spilled around one corner as if it had been designed to fit the room. In the opposite corner another similar sofa was placed. Between them a large oriental rug graced the room in a myriad of pastel blues, greens and gold.

"We call this the reading room." Tom explained, "hence the absence of a television. It's so cool and relaxing in here, and with the sofas as big as they are one can sprawl out and not be disturbed."

Curiously, Grandfather looked around the room. He noticed the absence of books and Tom following his gaze laughed. "I know what you are searching for. The books are next door. We found that the bookcase with its books in a myriad of colors detracted from the simplicity of this room."

Understanding, Grandfather agreed. "Well it is very impressive. I could read in a room like this and become totally engrossed."

"Then when you next visit you should do that."

They continued to chat awhile until their conversation was interrupted when the children came downstairs. A light tapping on the door indicated their arrival. "Come in children." Laura pulled the door open. "Let me introduce you to our guests."

Through the doorway edged two boys, identical twins, and Grandfather and Sherri gasped. Truly it were as though they were seeing double.

"I know." Tom laughed. "Everyone reacts the same way. Two peas in a pod these two."

"How do you tell them apart?" Grandfather asked.

"We remind them." One of the twins replied with a grin.

"We wouldn't let them make us wear sweaters with a big B or a big W on." The other boy told him.

"Hey, that reminds me, Uncle Devin. How do you know when you're in bed with an elephant?"

"Dah, heard it already." Devin laughed, "It's got a big E on its pajamas."

The guests laughed and Devin told the twins, "I've got another one for you. It's a tongue twister actually." He winked in Tom's direction.

Tom laughed "Oh that one…I told them already. That is, I tried to do."

"Is that the one about the butter?" The twins asked together.

"Sure is."

"Can you tell us? Dad kept forgetting the words."

"That doesn't surprise me." Devin laughed.

Tom explained. "That's how we met. I'm a singer and one evening while performing at a club in Brooklyn I totally forgot the lyrics when a talent agent came in. Your grandson was half cut at the time and included his own version of the song. The audience loved it and the agent thought we were a team and signed us up."

"Now I help Tom re-write songs with a few choice words, and he re-records them."

"And they sell like hot cakes." Tom added. "I've just released my third album."

"And Tom gives me a percentage. So were both happy." Devin explained.

While they had been talking the boys were standing around patiently waiting but now with a lull in conversation one jumped in, "So come on then, Uncle Devin. Tell us the tongue twister." Devin started to laugh. Their faces were so eager, and he foresaw the trouble they'd have with it.

111

"Okay then, here goes. Betty Botter bought herself a bit of butter. But the butter that Betty Botter bought was bitter. So Betty Botter bought herself a better bit of butter. But where's the bit of bitter butter that Betty Botter bought?"

Grandfather who had smiled all the way through burst into laughter. "You got it at last!" He exclaimed, "I never thought I'd see the day."

Devin turned and grinned at his Grandfather. "Well, once I realized there was a story to it, it came easy. Same with the pheasant plucker one, ahem, not to be said when intoxicated."

Grandfather blushed. "I think you should refrain from mentioning that one, my Boy!" He told him, acutely embarrassed.

Tom laughed out loud. "So this is where you heard them from?" Tom asked, "your Grandfather?"

Grinning, Devin nodded. "He taught me the Betty Botter one for years. I could never get the hang of it. It was sheer frustration."

Equally, the twins were having a difficult time with it.

"Betty Butter bought some butter."

"And it was bitter so she chucked it and got some more. Anyway it was Botter not butter.""

"No she didn't. That's why at the end no one knows what happened to the bitter bit."

"What did it matter? No one wanted it anyway."

Listening to the twins argue, the adults were grinning among themselves. "So," said Devin, "are you going to have a go at reciting it, or what?"

The twins looked at one another. "You first," said one.

"No, you go first," said the other.

"Well, when you've got the hang of it, here's another you can try." Devin told them with a grin. And winking toward his grandfather, Devin recited merrily, "my name is Eeny Meanie Macka Racka Rare Rye Dominaca, Chicka Licka Lolla Pop, Prom, Prom, Push!"

Open mouthed, the twins stood with stunned expressions on their faces while the adults laughed heartily.

112

"I think…" Laura suggested, "that Uncle Devin had best write these down, or you may spend all your lives trying to say them. Like he apparently did." She laughed and then recommended that the guests move out onto the veranda to partake of some refreshments. "What would you like? I've made some sandwiches. Or there's cake, or both?"

Devin's eyes lit up. "Both would be wonderful!" He announced eagerly. "I'm surprised you asked. You know me!"

"I wasn't actually talking to you." Laura told him. "With you it's a foregone conclusion. You eat like a horse." She smiled at Grandfather and Sherri over Devin's head. "What can I get you? There's a plate of cold cuts, with slices of warm fresh bread. Or ready made sandwiches, pastries and home made lemonade."

Sherri and Grandfather exchanged glances then both eagerly replied, "Cold cuts and fresh bread sounds wonderful."

Devin's eyes lit up and his mouth watered. "Great choice, Laura makes the bread herself and believe me, you're in for a real treat."

Devin was right. The warm crusty bread was unlike any Grandfather or Sherri had ever eaten. Laura explained it was a secret family recipe and she wasn't telling anyone.

Over lunch they chatted about the area, Tom's musical career and the reason for the family's move away from the Appalachians, basically due to the long distances Tom had to drive to his gigs.

"Don't get me wrong." Tom explained as he showed his guests around the house, "this is a fantastic place to live, but Laura and the boys seldom see me while I'm working in New York. It's so isolated here. They can go weeks without seeing another soul. That's no life for a young woman, and the children have few friends."

"So, you've never had anyone try to break in here?" Grandfather asked with interest.

Tom shook his head. "There's camera's situated around the estate that we try to monitor most of the time. A few fans have become over zealous about autographs and tried to get in, but so far, touch wood," he touched his head, "none have succeeded."

"Well I must say that's put my mind at ease. It's such a big area, I wondered how you managed to secure it all at once."

"I think you can rest assured only the very foolish would try to get in uninvited, Mr. Richardson. And then of course on top of all the security there are the dogs as well. We have three Dobermans that have the run of the place after dark."

"But they will be gone when we arrive."

"True. I shouldn't worry though. Really this place is very secure."

They completed the tour of the house, though Grandfather declined the visit to the attic, he had grown weary and longed to begin the journey home, finally getting his wish when Sherri announced it was time to leave.

"Thank you so much for allowing us into your home." Sherri told the couple. The boys were nowhere to be seen.

"You're welcome. We sincerely wish you a happy weekend here. Alas, we shall be long gone by then, and Devin will be looking after the place until the contract is signed." Again only Sherri noticed the wink that passed between Tom and Devin as Grandfather shook first Laura's offered hand and then Tom's bidding them both goodbye before getting into Sherri's car.

"What do you think then, Granddad?" Devin asked as he slid into the back passenger seat. "Will you be coming back here?"

Struck by the tranquility of the estate the security and how beautiful everything was, Grandfather was silent for some time before replying.

Majestic English Oaks provided a striking variation to the native trees of the Appalachians reminding Grandfather of his homeland. Sitting there, gazing at them he could almost believe he was back in England's Stratford upon Avon, until Devin's next question prompted him back to the present. "Well, come on then, Granddad. Don't keep me waiting any longer. What do you think? Would you like to come back and stay one weekend?"

For a few minutes his Grandfather was thoughtful before asking, "You will be here?"

"Certainly."

"Patrolling the fences?"

"And the grounds. You can count on it. I would let nothing happen to you, Granddad. No-one will know we are here, I promise you."

His Grandfather remained thoughtful. It wasn't that he didn't trust Devin. Or that he didn't accept that the place appeared sound enough to offer his protection, it was finding the courage to agree. That was the hardest of all.

Devin smiled knowingly, "I know what you are thinking. It's hard not to worry. But look at the place, Granddad. Who'd break in here? Who'd want to?" Devin smiled warmly. "Oh come on, Granddad. What could possibly go wrong?"

"Anything could go wrong, Devin and you know it. If I were discovered...."

"And why should you be? We told you. You'll come up here again in Sherri's car, the windows are tinted, no one will notice. You'll come the same way as today, except Jack will come too and you'll be coming late afternoon. It's a straightforward journey, and then once here, well you've seen the security, Granddad. Who would attempt to break in here, eh? Be realistic, Granddad, come on."

"Have you nothing to say in this?" Grandfather turned to Sherri who had remained silent throughout.

"Plenty." Sherri replied. "But it is not my position to say so. You have to make up your own mind, Grandfather. I feel as does Devin, the place is sound, the journey an easy one, and to top it all Jack will love the surprise we have arranged for him."

Grandfather continued to think. Both of them were right. And would it really be so difficult to say yes? Hadn't Jack been denied so much already? For once, he saw that every avenue had been explored, and really most of it for his own satisfaction and safety. And he had enjoyed his trip, he had to admit; in fact, he had felt himself coming back to life during every mile they had traveled on the journey up to the mountains that day. Then there was the fact that the two people looking at him in hopeful expectation had examined every eventuality, and purely from their love to see others enjoying themselves. So slowly, Grandfather found himself nodding and words followed suit, "all right…" he was not allowed to say more. Sherri twisted in her seat and hugged him tightly, her eyes bright with tears of joy.

Reaching forward Devin grasped his Grandfather's hands and thanked him sincerely, "that's great, Granddad. You won't regret this, I promise you."

Still a little unsure, Grandfather replied gruffly. "Well, I had better not."

Chapter Thirteen

He was flying…vertically…like a rocket…
his arms plastered to his sides…
his body spinning inside a whirlpool.
Mindless…unable to retain a single thought…
And the noise! Like thunder in his ears.
Then there was pain…and fear…and dread…
And he was alone in a place he'd never been before.
He thought he had died…
He wished he had died…

* * *

Working in the park's large glasshouse, Jack accidentally snapped another label in half. He'd been making mistakes all day as he had idly planted seeds and labeled the trays. All he could think about was the trip to the Appalachians and wishing he could have gone too.

Much had changed over the last few weeks, ever since Sherri had come to his house to replace the peas and to see his Grandfather. In fact, he had never seen his Grandfather look so happy, or laugh so often as he did when Sherri was around. The two of them got along really well especially after she had arranged the dog walking. What was troubling was the fact that his Grandfather still didn't know what Sherri did for a living and Jack was loath to bring it up.

When was there a right time? Jack just hoped that when it happened, it didn't put his Grandfather straight back to square one. He knew they had to tell him soon, but it was a daunting thought. Since Sherri had confessed the real reason for taking him out and about it was a wonder he had agreed to go with Sherri up to the mountains to see Devin at all, his Grandfather hated deception. He'd likely go ballistic when he found out Sherri was a journalist.

Having another premonition didn't help any. These days the ones he was having were becoming more and more violent. And as the predictions hadn't yet happened, Jack had an ominous feeling they had something to do with the weekend away in the Appalachians. Why else was he having them so frequently? True, apprehension could do that, but Jack had a feeling he was being warned. Something ghastly was going to occur, he was sure of it. However, he knew from bitter experience that his premonitions were not something he could avoid, he could lessen their impact but he couldn't change the path fate had mapped out for him, otherwise he would have talked Sherri out of going on the weekend trip.

Shuffling the labels into some sort of order ready for the next day, Jack picked up his jacket, exited and locked the glasshouse, and headed for home intending to pass by the lake on his way. He enjoyed going there. Sometimes he took bread with him to feed to the swans. At that time of day, however, he knew the birds would have their heads tucked under their wings ready to sleep for the night. He had spent quite a bit of time by the lake of late. Somehow the rippling water soothed his jangled nerves when he thought about the future.

It was peaceful and tranquil and being the chief horticulturalist Jack could cordon off any part he chose. He had done that to this spot recently so he could come here to be alone and think.

He knew Sherri intended to move their relationship a gigantic step forward at the retreat they were going to spend the weekend. For that reason Jack half-heartedly hoped his Grandfather wouldn't want to go back there. He guessed he was right to be nervous, but that didn't make him feel any better. He was thirty years old, and as his brother had said, still a virgin. He had to give it up sometime, and he did love Sherri. It was just…well… with the premonitions on the increase…he was greatly troubled. Maybe insecurity was causing his mind to play tricks on him, knowing what that weekend had in store. Jack was sure he wasn't ready…yet knew he couldn't put it off any longer. He was just being a coward or as Devin had put it, a thirty year old idiot.

Skimming a pebble across the surface of the lake Jack watched it bounce a few times before sinking then walked on toward his favorite spot. Once there, he bent down to sit with his legs beneath him. He stared at the water reflecting the setting sun from gold to flaming red, and then dulling as the sun disappeared behind tall buildings. The changing color of the water was beautiful.

Suddenly, Jack smiled as thoughts of Sherri filled his mind. She really was beautiful, long dark hair, gorgeous gray eyes, stunning figure and a wonderful nature warm and caring, in fact, every man's dream girl. Since he'd known her, Jack's loneliness had become a thing of the past. His Grandfather had never allowed him or Devin to have friends, not the sort that came back to play. If he had any, he had to meet them in the park or play at school, or go into the city to meet them. He could never bring them home. But if life had been hard for him, it had been doubly so for his Grandfather, and Jack rarely forgot that. Though over the years he and Devin were exasperated with their Grandfather's paranoia nothing they had said could change the old man's mind. So what special talent did Sherri possess that in a few months she had him walking through the park and taking a ride in her car, and to the Appalachians no less?

Obviously, his Grandfather had been smitten with Sherri just as he had been smitten with her. She was indeed a wonderful woman, warm, caring, beautiful, and with a sense of humor that made everyone laugh. She had certainly captivated his Grandfather's heart.

As the sun went down Jack rose, stretched and rubbed the dirt from the back of his trousers. He hated to be out after dark and already the sun was casting long shadows that caused him to shiver. The park was a beautiful place by day frequented with scores of people that caused him no alarm, it was just after he had locked the gates at the end of each day that his Grandfather's warnings raced back to remind him just how alone he was in acres and acres of parkland. It was too vast a place that he could check everyone had left by six in the evening. He had to assume that they'd know the time and leave or risk being locked inside. It was those that might not care about being locked inside that worried him. If Chas Baxter should dare, he'd have no one to stop him from killing Jack or his Grandfather any time he chose. It was a fear that was constantly with Jack...especially since he had fallen in love with a journalist.

As he walked toward the cottage Jack's thoughts shifted to the surprise his brother and Sherri were working on for his benefit. It was something to do with nightmares Jack shivered, nightmares? He'd had enough of them already. So what had the two concocted? It was very disconcerting, because in one breath Sherri had told him it was a nightmare he'd always remember, and in the next, she had spoken of their dreams coming true. Exceedingly contradictory and extremely suspicious, but if he knew his brother, it would be something enjoyable.

Inside the cottage some fifteen minutes later, Jack washed his hands, He wasn't sure when to expect his Grandfather home, but since they had been out all day, he thought it would be anytime soon. Jack made his way across the kitchen intending to light the stove and have a hot meal waiting for his Grandfather's return.

Collecting together the utensils he would need Jack started to prepare dinner. While it was cooking, he took a shower. He was half way through washing when he heard the sound of a door closing. Quickly he stepped from under the faucet, toweled himself vigorously before pulling on a robe, and hurried down to the kitchen. His happiness faded when he realized Sherri had been leaving, not arriving, something he had missed over the sound of the water.

"Granddad, you're home. Where's Sherri?" he asked, looking all around.

"She had to go home, Jack. She said she'd pop by and see you in the park tomorrow. I think the drive exhausted her. It's a long way you know, to go there and back in one day."

Jack noticed his Grandfather's eyes were twinkling merrily. "You enjoyed it?" Jack asked padding barefooted across to the stove to check on dinner.

"Very much. Lovely place can't wait to go back there. Is that dinner I smell cooking? I'm starved!"

Jack laughed. "Yes, Granddad. I thought you'd be hungry and you can have two helpings. I hoped Sherri would stay so you can have hers as well."

"Mm…" his Grandfather sat at the table in eager expectation, his eyes lighting up when he saw the fare his grandson had prepared, of roast chicken, vegetables, potatoes and thick onion gravy. "If I'm going to get this sort of welcome home every time I go out for the day, Jack," his Grandfather said with relish as he filled his plate, "then I'm going to go out more often!"

Chapter Fourteen

When Sherri sought out Jack in the park the following day, she filled in any gaps his Grandfather had left out. Yet though she seemed delighted at the prospect of the weekend away, Jack could tell that she had something on her mind.

"Let's go sit by the lake. You've got time I take it? No pressing engagements?"

"No. The lake would be fine. Is it still quiet there?" She smiled up into his face. Jack nodded. "I haven't taken the cordon away yet. People assume I'm maintaining the bank."

"And aren't you?"

Jack chuckled, "Perhaps I should have said, people think I'm '*still*' maintaining the bank. I actually got it finished days ago."

"Ooh, that's devious, Jack."

They laughed together and ducked beneath the yellow and red tape with the words 'park maintenance area' emblazoned across it in bold black lettering. Jack led Sherri to the shade beneath a favorite willow and they sat down on the grass together.

"With all that's been happening lately we haven't had much time to talk have we, my love?" Jack placed his arm around Sherri's shoulders and drew closer to her. "I was wondering if something was bothering you? There are times when I've noticed you seem distant. And I get the feeling it's not all to do with my family and their multitude of problems."

"Devin's right about you, Jack. You see more things than are good for you."

"Well, I won't argue with that. However, on this occasion it's not what I've seen in as much as what I've felt. Is it to do with work? I mean if it's confidential then tell me to butt out. On the other hand if it isn't maybe I can help. You know me, I can be a great sounding board."

"It's something and nothing really. It stems back to the detectives that died a few weeks ago."

"The three supposedly killed by Baxter?"

"Yes."

"And...?"

"Well..." Sherri looked over her shoulder and all around checking they couldn't be overheard then she leaned in closer and whispered, "DI Bycroft was working on a theory...he told only four people...two of them and Bycroft are now dead."

Jack's eyes opened wide with astonishment, "Are you telling me the fourth is..."

Sherri nodded.

"And it's to do with Baxter?" Jack whispered close to her ear.

"Yes."

"Oh, my God."

"Do you think I should say something?"

"To whom?"

"Anyone."

Jack shook his head, "No darling, I don't. I think you should keep absolutely silent about this."

Jack thought about his Grandfather, he too had kept silent for decades over something that had happened with Baxter, and if he could do it, so could she. Sherri had absolutely no idea that she and his Grandfather were fearful of the same thug.

"But if I stay silent and their theory has foundation a lot of people could be spared."

"Call me selfish, honey, but I think it has been well established that the foundation was concrete enough. And if you should crack it open, I could lose you." 'And my family', he added under his breath. For if Baxter linked the two of them together all their lives would be at risk.

"I don't know, Jack...I could finish this. That man has ruined so many lives and continues to do so, and gets away with it. I feel so sure that Bycroft was on to something."

"I thought he was killed due to his gross habits."

"That's the way it was meant to look, but what of Rutcliff and Davies. Their lives were squeaky clean."

"Could be a coincidence."

"And it might not have been. Oh Jack, I've been so scared. You know when your Grandfather was asking about all those security measures up at Devin's house, I found myself grateful for everything that was in place. And when your Grandfather filled me in on some of the problem that's haunted him all these years, I realized that we would both be staying there terrified of similar things."

Jack was surprised, "What did he tell you?"

"Only that he'd witnessed something a long time ago. And he had been threatened by some thug to keep quiet. I know more about it from Devin than from your Grandfather. At least I don't have to worry so much now about saying something that would give the game away."

"I know it's been difficult for you, and Sherri, don't take this the wrong way, but even Dev and I haven't told you everything." He saw her startled look and went on quickly, "sometimes I get the impression that Grandfather is withholding some of the facts as well."

"The domino effect. When one tile falls the lot comes crashing down. Next you'll be telling me Baxter is involved with your Grandfather's problem."

Jack tried not to show surprise, it would do her no good to know the truth of the matter, especially now. Best let sleeping dogs lie and all that. "Well I think you should keep quiet. You know it makes sense." He told her steadily.

"Do I?"

"Well at least don't do anything until you are absolutely sure of the facts. And don't dig where it's dangerous to do so. I bet the detectives thought they were being discreet?"

"Yes, but there were three of them, people talk. Where there's only one they keep their assumptions to themselves."

"Or they tell the one they love. Sherri, please…"

"You don't know anything about it."

"I know enough. Please Sherri, don't say anything to anyone. Chas Baxter is a dangerous man."

"I know that."

"Promise me you'll do nothing to make him suspicious."

"I can't promise that, Jack. But I will be careful."

"Oh God, Sherri you're terrifying me. I love you so much. Please I beg of you…let it go…"

"Look, I'll make a deal with you."

"I don't want to make a deal, not with this. The stakes are too high."

"Even so…I won't actively pursue this, but I will keep my ear to the ground. Is that okay?"

"Only so long as you run any decision you make by me before going anywhere with it."

"I promise."

Jack hugged her close. He decided that if that time should come he might have to tell her what Chas Baxter meant to his family, and then she would see why she should stay silent.

Unbeknown to Jack, in her heart, Sherri had already broken her promise. For she decided, if she should find out anything substantial regarding Baxter and how he got away with crime, Jack would be the last person she'd tell. Obviously his love for her was clouding his judgment, and with so many lives at stake, and despite the risk to her own life, Sherri knew where her loyalty lay.

Chapter Fifteen

Driving to the Appalachians a little under a month later, when Sherri kept checking her rear view mirror, Jack assumed she was looking at him sitting in the back. If he had guessed the truth he would have been as worried as she was.

She hadn't intended to create so many waves. She'd just made what she'd considered at the time to be discreet enquiries, asking for Chas Baxter's date and place of birth, nothing substantial. Sherri grimaced; obviously it had been substantial enough to somebody.

Larry Bycroft had been on to something, he'd assumed that Chas Baxter had a twin, and not knowing how far he had gotten with that enquiry, Sherri had taken it upon herself to check with the registrar of births deaths and marriages to see if there was any concrete evidence to support that theory. Her problem arose when the registrar asked to see her credentials, and on discovering she was no more than a freelance reporter he had reminded her about public confidentiality and had revealed nothing.

That would have been all right had she not of become paranoid that she was being watched a few days after that.

It was something and nothing really, she'd go to put the garbage out and someone would step into the shadows, she'd be driving and someone would appear to tail her, the same dark sedan on more occasions than she deemed coincidental. And the odd phone call in the middle of the night, that when answered was disconnected...leaving her with nothing but the purr of the dialing tone. All in all those things together made Sherri jumpy, and she began to wish she had left well alone.

* * *

Leaving the city far behind Jack became too engrossed in the scenery to notice Sherri's agitation each time a car pulled in front of them, or the way her gaze darted from the wing mirror to the one above the windshield when a car stayed behind them longer than she deemed necessary.

It was only when they pulled off the main highway and headed for the mountains did she relax, but Jack didn't notice that either. The long journey and late afternoon sunshine had gotten the better of him and he and his Grandfather, were both fast asleep.

The sound of gravel crunching beneath the car's tires startled them both from their slumber. Jack quickly sat up, looking with interest through the car's back windows at the shadowy trees silvered by moonlight and fading away into darkness along the overgrown track.

"Where are we?" Jack yawned.

"Hello sleepyhead. Did you enjoy your nap?" Sherri asked without taking her attention from the road.

"Yes," he whispered, his gaze meeting hers in the rear-view mirror.

"I'm glad," she told him, adding, "I hoped that with the lull of the car and all those cushions, you would be well rested before we arrived here."

"We've arrived?"

"Yes, just. The crunch of the gravel must have woken you. In a few moments we will reach the security gates."

Jack remained silent, now that the moment was almost upon him. He felt terribly nervous of being alone with Sherri. Almost as if she could read his thoughts, she slowed the car to a halt. Turning in her seat to view him asked, "You okay, Jack?"

He nodded, still unable to speak, and by his silence, Grandfather decided his grandson was worried on his behalf. "What is it, Jack? Are you having second thoughts? We can always go back you know?"

"No, Granddad. Not second thoughts. It's just…oh I don't know, just being away from home I suppose." He finished lamely remembering his recent premonition.

"Well, think of it as home away from home." Sherri winked at him as a smile quirked the corners of her mouth, and by the light of the moon, Jack could see that her eyes were dancing with delight. "Everything will be okay, you'll see."

Then to his surprise, Sherri turned off the engine and bent to pick up her purse from the foot well in front of his Grandfather, extracting from within a carefully folded piece of paper which she opened, smoothed, and handed to Jack, "This was given to me by Devin several weeks ago. It is because of this, in fact, that we are here tonight. Why don't you read it?"

Switching on the interior light, Sherri twisted around in her seat to watch Jack's expression as he read the newspaper cutting; delighted when he gasped, "Star Spangled Night Mares? Whatever is that?" His penetrating gaze searched her own. "It sounds ominous." He added, handing the cutting to his Grandfather to read.

"That's what I thought at first, but it's not what it seems. Fortunately for me, Devin had provided the remainder of the advertisement, and I was able to find out just what the word nightmare actually referred to. Alas, for you, this is to be the element of surprise. All I will say is that the word nightmare is split in two, so your clue is actually night and *mare*." Sherri told him emphasizing the last word.

"Night *mare*?" Jack reiterated. A flutter of nervous excitement ran through him.

Whatever the words implied, he was sure it was nothing bad. He knew that Sherri would not expect him to participate in anything he would not like. Nonetheless, he was intrigued. What could possibly warrant the words, *night and mare*, if not something horrific?

When Grandfather had finished reading, he handed Sherri the cutting with a knowing wink. Smiling, Sherri switched off the interior light and turned on the ignition, putting the car back into gear. The final leg of the journey began, and Sherri's eyes were bright with mischief.

She'd shown Grandfather the information about Jack's surprise weeks earlier, and he'd kept the secret very well with not even the slightest hint to his grandson. In fact, Sherri believed it was the surprise that had helped the old man to resign himself to the inevitable especially since he had seen the estate. But when she had asked if he'd like to stay in one of the fully equipped cabins in the grounds with Devin he had been adamant that he wanted to be inside the house. Therefore, she had contacted Devin to make the required arrangements, and it would appear that Devin would now be the only one sleeping outside in a cabin. Sherri didn't really mind, it was a big house and the Grandfather was a little deaf. Hopefully, he would not overhear whatever she and Jack would be doing. With that thought in mind, a shiver ran through Sherri. She was almost willing to forego the surprise in her eagerness to have Jack all to herself in that four-poster bed.

At last, the large ornamental gates rose up out of the dark before them, and Jack gasped at how high they were. "I can now see why you didn't mind coming back here, Granddad!"

"Wild horses wouldn't have dragged me back here if I hadn't thought I'd be safe." The Grandfather grinned with a sidelong glance at Sherri, who could not prevent a giggle. Unfortunately, Jack did not seem to notice his Grandfather had just dropped a very big hint as to his surprise.

"So what are we waiting for?" Jack asked as no one seemed to move, "the gates don't open by themselves do they? Should I do the honors?" He leaned toward the door handle intending to alight and go to the gates when Sherri stopped him.

"No, it's okay, Jack. We're waiting for Devin. He said he'd meet us here."

"Oh."

For a few minutes more, the purr of the engine was the only sound to be heard, as they each waited anxiously for Devin's arrival. Sherri held her breath. Devin had promised to be there, and they were on time, so where was he? Had someone known the travel arrangements and arrived ahead of them?

Jack's comment soothed her jangled nerves. "Don't worry, Sherri. Devin has never been punctual in his life, and he's not about to start now."

Nervously, Sherri laughed, "Am I so transparent?"

"Only to me." He spoke softly. Sherri turned around to look at him, and she grew weak with the love she saw in his eyes. She shivered as she felt the touch of his long fingers caressing her bare shoulder. Words stuck in her throat, her heartbeat accelerated, and she had to will herself to act as though nothing was amiss. When her gray eyes scanned every inch of his face, the desire to reach back and kiss him almost overwhelmed her.

Suddenly, a loud clanging sound brought her back to earth with a jolt and Sherri wrenched her gaze away to see what had disturbed her only to find Devin's face wreathed in smiles outside the window and full of apology as he pulled open the huge, iron gates.

"Sorry I'm late. Have you been here long? Hi Granddad, hi Jack, glad you could make it, what did you think of the ride up here?" he asked as he approached the side of the car.

Jack laughed, albeit somewhat shakily as he willed his breathing back to normal.

"Sorry did I disturb something?" Devin's face lit up, "Can't wait till you reach the house, eh?" Though he whispered, his Grandfather heard him and asked suspiciously, "Why, what's happening at the house?" He may be old but he wasn't stupid, and somehow the atmosphere seemed awkward as though he were being kept in the dark about something.

"Nothing," three people chorused, unsure of what else to say, but Grandfather wasn't buying it.

"Yes there is, and I'm not moving another inch until you tell me what's going on." He told the three adamantly. They looked from one to the other, and Jack grew fidgety with embarrassment. How could he explain things to his Grandfather? The old man would never understand. To him marriage was sacred, and intimacies between a man and a woman should only happen after they were wed. It was one of the things that kept him and Philippa apart. Jack Richardson, senior, would not dishonor his dear departed wife with a sordid love affair.

Devin's mind raced trying to think of something feasible to say that would suffice, though the longer they took to reply the more suspicious it all became.

"Well?" Grandfather prompted, "Are you going to enlighten me or what?"

"It's a surprise!" Sherri exclaimed suddenly.

"A surprise?" Grandfather wasn't born yesterday. "For whom?"

"If I told you that it wouldn't be a surprise," Sherri replied, her mind racing. What on earth could she come up with in so short a time to find a surprise that would be adequate enough for him?

Grandfather looked at each one of them in turn. They seemed to be expecting him to believe that, but it still didn't ring true somehow. But he decided to let it go for now, chalking it up as another one of those little annoyances that kept cropping up ever since this weekend trip away had been mentioned.

"We'll see," he told them, resignedly looking ahead. His three companions tried not to sigh too deeply. Sherri could gladly have kicked Devin to Kingdom Come at that moment for putting them in such a predicament. Nonetheless, she was soon driving through the gateway, lingering only while Devin fastened the gates from behind, then waited while he climbed in beside Jack. Soon Devin started chatting excitedly.

"Did Sherri show you the advert?" At Jack's nod he went on, "what do you think? Have you worked out what it could be yet?"

"Not at all, it sounds ominous though. Are you sure it's not something dangerous?" To his surprise, his Grandfather laughed.

"You know what it is don't you?" he asked stunned, "how long have you known?"

"Weeks." Grandfather enlightened him. Jack was doubly stunned. "I only wish I were younger. I wouldn't have minded having a go at it myself." Grandfather chuckled merrily.

"It's something none of us have ever done before so your guess is as good as mine as to what it'll be like. However, that time is almost upon us, because…" Devin grinned, "here we are. Well just around the next corner anyway. Sherri, what do you think, should we go straight on to the Night Mares, or go up to the house first? Anyone got any preferences? Would you like to go inside, and change, have a drink or something? Or should we start the proceedings now?"

"What do you want to do, Jack?" Sherri turned in her seat to watch his expression.

"I am anxious to know what's around that corner." he replied, in such a way that made Sherri and Devin laugh out loud, "but I am thirsty, and could do with a hot drink."

"Right then, if you will turn the car that way then, Sherri and go straight up to the house. I'll get out here and bring the nightmares round to you."

"Can you manage them all by yourself?" Sherri asked delightfully aware of Jack's questioning expression passing from one to the other of them.

"Yes. And hey thank you for booking one for me too. I never expected to join you tonight. It was a great surprise." Devin slipped from the car. "See you in about half an hour then outside the house. Don't be late. Bye."

Mystified, Jack watched his brother hurry away and smiling mischievously Sherri put the car into gear and drove the rest of the way up the long gravel drive.

Chapter Sixteen

Rounding a final corner some moments later, Sherri was only vaguely aware of the huge house in front of them, her attention otherwise taken up with the feel of Jack's fingers trailing deliciously over her bare shoulders. It was a wonder his Grandfather hadn't noticed her labored breathing. There had been times just lately when Jack had been overly attentive, and had chatted happily about their weekend away, and how much he was looking forward to it. And there had been other times when she had spoken of it, and he had become unusually quiet as though he was worried about what might happen between them there.

Now they were there though it was almost too much and with the added problem of his Grandfather staying up at the house, she hoped the whole idea wasn't about to backfire in their faces. It was all she could do to act normal in the circumstances, trying to give nothing away, while all the time, Jack's very nearness and her overpowering love for him had her body aflame. And just lately, when they had reluctantly parted, his eyes had been that bit darker with passion, and Sherri had noticed he no longer tried to hide how she affected him. She knew without a doubt that he did indeed desire her the way she desired him.

As they drew up outside the large oak doors, Sherri turned off the engine and turned in her seat to face him. By the light of the security lamps overhead, Jack's face was clearly visible, and Sherri caught her breath with the way he was looking at her.

As they gazed longingly at one another, they heard Grandfather exclaim, "Look at those stars! My, I don't believe I've ever seen so many."

"That's because it's so dark here," Jack told him dragging his gaze from Sherri's, "no lights from the city to obliterate the view."

"Yes, I suppose so." His Grandfather acknowledged gazing heavenward.

"Why don't you get out, Grandfather? Stretch your legs. You'll see more of the sky out there."

Grandfather shook his head. "You're wrong. I can see more from here. I don't think I could crane my head back far enough if I'm standing."

Suddenly, Sherri remembered something she'd seen on their previous visit to the estate. "Grandfather, this is where your surprise comes in." She noticed Jack's curious glance in the rear view mirror and grinned at him.

"There's an observatory here with a telescope so all you need is help up the steps to reach the attic. There's a huge skylight, almost the whole ceiling is glass. You can see straight up to the heavens!"

Grandfather gasped, "How delightful! Thank you. What a wonderful surprise."

"What's a wonderful surprise?" Devin had overheard as he'd opened her door.

"The observatory." Sherri made a careful show with her hands that said, 'don't let the cat out of the bag again please', and Devin fortunately deciphered her message well enough not to. "I've told your Grandfather about our surprise for him to use the telescope."

Devin beamed, what a marvelous idea, he thought. "That's right, Grandfather. You'll love it. Would you like to go up there while Sherri and I take Jack on his surprise?"

"I'd like to see Jack's face first." Grandfather replied with a chuckle.

"Yes of course. Okay, then after that, and before I join them, I will take you up to the observatory. You might have company too. There's a cat about the place. I usually find it sunning itself beneath the observatory window. It's name's Smokey. Plus, you can keep watch on us with the telescope from up there"

Grandfather laughed. "Yes I can, can't I? How wonderful. And I can keep an eye out for intruders at the same time."

Devin tried not to sigh too raggedly as he replied, "Well come on then, Granddad, I'll help you up the steps into the house and Jack can make the drinks. Make me a mug of hot chocolate will you, Jack? I left everything you'll need in the kitchen. Oh and while you're in there, remember to change your shoes. For what we have planned, Jack you'll need some with heels."

"Heels? Sure you don't want me in pantyhose and a dress as well?"

"God, Jack, that would be a nightmare!" Devin exclaimed, giving Sherri a fit of the giggles.

When Devin and Grandfather had gone into the house Sherri attempted to follow them in when Jack caught her elbow turning her back to face him, "Something wrong?" She asked gazing into his eyes.

"Not at all. In fact..." He reached forward and touched his lips to hers and a mixture of emotions too raw and overwhelming shuddered through Sherri. "I love you," he murmured against her mouth, "whatever the surprise is. Thank you."

"You're welcome, Jack."

Struggling with her seatbelt, Jack leaned over to help. "Here, let me." He unbuckled the belt with ease, and the touch of his cheek against her face sent a fresh wave of desire coursing through her veins. It was quickly followed by another as with his lips pressed close to her ear he whispered, "do you know how much I want you, Sherri?"

"Okay you two, break it up! Are you only just going in? I thought you'd be in the kitchen making that chocolate by now." Devin grinned.

Sherri managed a weak smile as she alighted from the car. "Yes, we're just going in." She muttered guiltily.

Devin raised his eyebrows. "What on earth kept you? As if I can't guess. Look I know you can't wait to ravage one another, but really there's three creatures back there, not to mention myself, that are eager to get this show on the road. So isn't it about time you had that drink you needed so badly? Besides which Grandfather is anxious to know what's keeping you."

"Three creatures?" Jack asked looking perplexed, "this I must see. What are they? Dogs?" He supposed in a place like this, there must be some guard dogs and he could think of nothing else.

"Later. Drinks first, something hot to keep us going. I noticed as I came over to the house that a mean wind is getting up. I hope it doesn't spoil our fun tonight. Though by the looks of you two you'll surely think of something else to do."

Jack blushed and Devin laughed. "Not having second thoughts are we? Sorry, just tell me to mind my own business. But hey, I don't want to alarm you, but as clear and moonlit as the sky is right now, the forecast for tonight is thunderstorms. And as the sky could cloud over at any moment, I think we should get on with this as soon as possible. Like yesterday, in fact." Devin told them laughing softly, "besides, the sooner we get on with this, the sooner you can massage one another's aching limbs, and get down to the hot stuff," he added, ducking as Jack's arm made to cuff him, "missed." Devin laughed then shouted words from their childhood, "last one ins a rotten egg!"

Laughing breathlessly from their race they found the Grandfather looking around the house. He seemed distracted, and Sherri asked if there was a problem. "No," he replied, "its just that there are so many personal things here. For example, a photograph of your grandmother, I never expected to find one here. That's all."

"Granddad?"

"Yes?"

Leading his Grandfather to the lounge Devin went on, "Sit down, Granddad. There's something I need to tell you."

Grandfather hadn't a clue as to what his grandson was about to impart, but it sounded ominous and he felt his way down into the chair behind him, sitting straight up his gaze resting on Devin and looking as though he anticipated the world to end at any moment he asked nervously, "What is it?" The foreboding feeling he had had all day was making his heart pound erratically in his chest.

"Well, it's nothing bad so you can relax." Devin told him. His words did little to relieve his Grandfather; he'd heard that before. Why, when these two were boys he'd heard that a dozen times or more over some catastrophe or another.

"Tell me?" he asked anxiously.

"Don't look so worried." Devin laughed. It was one of those occasions when a mountain had been made out of a molehill. Like when someone caught the tail end of a conversation, and you had to relate it all over again, and they wondered what was so important about it that you'd felt the need to. He hated it when that happened, just as he hated what was happening now. Because, though it was no one's business that he had bought the house, it would affect all of his family in the long run.

"The house is mine, Grandfather." Devin told him quickly, "I've bought it."

For a long while his Grandfather said nothing, but it was obvious he disbelieved every word his grandson had said and that was confirmed when he announced sarcastically, "Oh look, there's a pig flying by."

Jack started to laugh, but as his Grandfather looked deadly serious, his laughter faded.

"It's true." Devin told him, "The house is mine. Which is why you are seeing so many family treasures around the room. I moved in four days ago."

"It can't be!" His Grandfather exclaimed. "Where would you get the money to buy a place like this? How dare you spin me such a wicked yarn!"

"It is true, Grandfather." Jack intervened.

"Yes it is." Devin reiterated, "and before you ask, no I didn't get into debt, well no more than most people. The bank agreed I could meet the repayments on the loan and I put a huge chunk down first. I'm getting a steady income from what Tom allows me and from Star Spangles. You should be happy for me owning a place like this, Granddad. I thought you'd be pleased."

Now his Grandfather believed, but there was still that ominous feeling hanging over him, and with eyes mere slits he challenged. "You expect me to live here don't you? That's what all this is about? I knew there was more to this than met the eye. I knew there was an ulterior motive for coming here! You want me to leave my roses to live in the back of beyond where nothing ever happens. Well I'm not!"

Devin's first thought was to argue and point out all the benefits, but he knew how stubborn his Grandfather could be, so he tactfully replied, "Actually no." This stunned his Grandfather, along with Jack and Sherri, but both kept quiet, hoping Devin knew what he was doing.

"You didn't?" his Grandfather was clearly stunned. "You mean you bought this place to live here all by yourself?" Then he paled as he thought of something fresh. "Oh no, Jack. You're not going to live here with him are you? Then this is what it's all about. You're coming here, you and this lady friend, and you plan to leave me all alone in the city? How could you!"

"Jack's not living here, Grandfather." Devin hated to lie and it took everything in him to meet his Grandfather's penetrating gaze at that moment. "I bought it for myself and the woman that I love."

His Grandfather's mouth dropped open and it took several minutes before what Devin had said to register, and then he asked, "The woman that you love?" He looked at Sherri, what was going on here?

Following his gaze Devin laughed, "No, not Sherri, Grandfather, similar name but somebody different. Someone you have yet to meet. Her name is Cherry. Well Cheryl, to be precise. I'm going to ask her to marry me and live here in this big house and we will fill it with children." The moment he said it, Devin wished he hadn't.

"Children! Children! How can you even think of bringing children into a world such as this?"

Devin had had enough. Clearly, his Grandfather was in an argumentative mood so he told him, "Look, Grandfather, you're here for the weekend in my house. So try and enjoy yourself, okay? Now we are going to have some hot chocolate and then Jack, Sherri and I are going outside for a couple of hours. But before we go, we'll help you up to the observatory."

"Don't want to go!" The Grandfather folded his arms and sat stiffly acting as if only a bulldozer might shift him.

"Please yourself, I've not got time for this. Look, the television is over there, and here's the remote control. There's books in the cabinet, a radio over there." He indicated to a shelf where a CB radio stood, and then making a distinction told his Grandfather, "and there's the other kind of radio. The one you're more used to."

"So what's that contraption?" The Grandfather asked pointing to the radio unit on the shelf.

"Citizen's band, Grandfather. It's like a telephone but runs by aerial. There are a few numbers written down on the pad alongside for emergencies in case you need anything. However, if you need us while we are out, I am carrying this pager. Just dial number one and you will reach me straight away. Okay? See, I've tried to think of everything."

Grandfather said nothing. He was peeved about having nothing to grumble about. Devin moved by him, and on his way out told Jack and Sherri, "let's go make that drink."

"Will he be all right?" Sherri asked anxiously as they reached the kitchen.

Jack nodded. He had seen his Grandfather behave like that many times.

"He'll come around." Devin assured her, "He likes to make waves where he can."

"It's the paranoia." Jack felt the need to explain, "I am led to believe it's a form of panic attack. He can't help it. It takes him longer than most people to get his head around new ideas. Apparently, he has always been a bit like that. Like me, he's precognitive, you see? And after what he literally saw, well that just escalated the problem. Now he sees everything as a threat to his existence."

"I see." Sherri replied sadly. She had come to have affection for the old man. It was sad he couldn't accept things at face value, and that he always had to be pessimistic over everything. Many times of late, she caught herself wondering if there was anything she could do to help him, but doubted the possibility. The thugs that had ruined his life and taken away his best friend were probably in jail or dead now, it was sad he wouldn't believe that. Additionally, what seemed to bother him was how wicked the world was. He acted as if he had taken all its ills upon his own shoulders.

"Maybe he's depressed," Sherri suggested thoughtfully, "he took it real hard when I could no longer bring Simba round." Jack and Devin stopped what they were doing which was boiling milk, collecting mugs, finding spoons for the sugar and chocolate, and looked at her. Devin had put a packet of cookies someplace earlier and he'd open them if he could just remember where he'd left them.

Seeing the expression on their faces, Sherri explained, "I mean if he had something to occupy his mind he might not let things get on top of him so much. What is he interested in other than television and roses?"

"Well, I thought that was a marvelous idea you had when you mentioned the observatory. But he's being stubborn now. It's doubtful that he'll go up there tonight. Sometimes he cuts off his own nose to spite his face. After all, it's no skin off of our noses if he does or doesn't want to do any given thing."

"That's cruel." Sherri told Devin.

"You wait till you've lived with him awhile then you'll see what is and isn't cruel. Jack needs a medal for putting up with him so long and staying sane. I know I couldn't do it. I was out of there just as soon as I was able."

"Well if he still wants to go up there, I'll take him," Sherri told the brothers showing she could be just as stubborn if she put her mind to it.

Devin replied, "it's not that either of us doesn't want to take him, he just won't go. You'll see, he's making a statement now, or thinks he is. I bet when we go in there he'll be in the same position looking like a wet weekend and the television will still be off."

Jack laughed, "yeah, but you can bet your bottom dollar that while we are in here he'll be all over that room looking into everything. Only when he hears our return he'll hurry back to that chair where we left him."

"Really?" Sherri was stunned, "how devious." Jack and Devin laughed loudly.

"I do believe she's getting the picture." Devin told his brother.

* * *

Unfortunately, their Grandfather wasn't. Grandfather had moved to the television set to switch it on, but the screen was fuzzy and the sound distorted. The Grandfather was in a right mood by the time he switched it off and returned to his seat as he heard the three returning. And like Devin and Jack had expected, there he was when they came through the door looking like a wet blanket, only more than they had assumed. He didn't seem to have calmed down one iota. "You took your time!" He snapped, "am I to sit here waiting for you all evening?"

Jack and Devin ignored him, which did not help matters, and Sherri handed him a mug of hot chocolate.

"There you go, Grandfather." She told him kindly. Gruffly, he muttered his thanks and took the steaming mug, placing it down on a table at his side almost immediately.

"I wanted tea!"

"Sorry, Granddad, we've not unpacked it yet." Jack told him, "and Devin didn't have any."

"Try the chocolate, Grandfather. It's delicious. I'll make you some tea later." Sherri told him kindly.

Begrudgingly, Grandfather sipped the chocolate, "Too hot!" He barked.

"I'll bring some cold milk." Sherri offered since no one else seemed to bother.

When she brought it and topped up his mug, she waited while the Grandfather tasted it to test its temperature surprised when he grunted, "too bitter!"

Behind her, Devin chuckled. Sherri shot him a disgruntled look and went back to the kitchen, returning with some sugar. "How much, Grandfather?" She asked as she spooned sugar from the jar and hovered it over his mug. He indicated a little with one hand and she poured it in and stirred. He took a sip.

"Not enough!" He told her. She added more and stirred it briskly. This time when he tasted it he complained, "Too sweet." Exasperated Sherri stood back, uncertain how to help save throwing the lot away and starting again from scratch.

And then he said, "It's too chocolaty, too."

That did it! Sherri snatched up the mug and waltzed off to the kitchen and when she returned she was empty handed.

"Where's my hot chocolate?" Grandfather grumbled.

Jack and Devin creased into laughter at her reply.

"Down the sink, Grandfather." She told him before picking up her own mug of hot chocolate to begin drinking.

The old man glared at her, "But I'm thirsty." He told her with annoyance.

Her mouth to her cup, Sherri eyed him over the rim and pointed in the direction she had just come in and out of several times for his benefit. Then when she had swallowed she told him, "There's the kitchen, Grandfather. Why don't you go and make yourself the perfect cup?"

Devin laughed whispering, "She's a fast learner." Jack chuckled. Grandfather just fumed, and then he turned his attention to something else that riled him.

"Can't watch that thing!" He pointed to the television set.

"Why ever not?" Devin asked.

"Don't work."

"Yes it does. Anyway how do you know? I thought you said you'd sat there waiting for our return?"

"I have."

"Mm."

"What's that supposed to mean? Do you think I'm lying?"

"Nothing would surprise me, Granddad." Devin told him as he made his way to the set and switched it on. Sure enough the picture was fuzzy. "Strange how you knew that," Devin mumbled.

"I'm psychic." Grandfather snapped. Everyone laughed loudly.

Grandfather seethed, but knew when he was beaten. He remained silent as Devin fiddled with some knobs and the aerial until he got a picture on all the channels. "There you go, Granddad, you can watch it now." He told him leaving it on a music channel as he straightened.

"You can turn that load of ya ya off for a start."

"You're the one with the remote control, or is there something wrong with your fingers now?" Devin asked sweetly.

Again, Grandfather grew silent. He could be quick off the mark too, when he wanted, but right now…Devin knew he was just being too pigheaded to think fast enough. Grandfather wished he could think of a suitable retort to wipe that smug look off his grandson's face.

"Well if you're ready?" Devin asked of Jack and Sherri as he downed the remains of his hot chocolate, and ignored his Grandfather totally.

Hesitant, Sherri looked from one brother to the other. Surely, they weren't going to leave Grandfather behind in that mood? Mind you, she couldn't blame them, but then she wouldn't be able to enjoy herself if she was thinking about him all the time. Thankfully, the Grandfather's mind was racing along similar lines.

"Aren't you going to take me up to the observatory first?" he asked no one in particular though each felt the question was directed toward them.

Devin drew in a deep breath, and standing behind his Grandfather, lifted his arms in a motion that suggested he would give anything right then to be able to clobber the old man over the back of the head. Sherri pursed her lips tightly trying not to laugh; Jack turned away and giggled softly.

"Come then, Grandfather. Jack and I will take you. Is there anything you need? Sherri can follow with it."

Of all the things Devin thought his Grandfather might want with him he was surprised by his reply.

"Only one thing. Bring that photograph up will you, my dear?" Sherri almost did a double take. My dear? Where had that come from? "The one of my wife. I'd like her to be with me while I look at the stars."

Chapter Seventeen

Finally!

The three breathed sighs of relief when they alighted from the house an hour overdue for Jack's surprise. "I didn't think he would ever get the hang of it!" Jack exclaimed. "This lens, that lens…blah, blah, blah…"

Sherri giggled, "You deserve a medal, Jack. I never knew he could be like that."

"Sometimes he can be a real pain. Thank God for you, huh? Or I'd have gone mad by now. Thankfully I was only alone with him for seven months between Devin leaving to see the world and you coming into my life, Sherri, otherwise I don't think I would have lasted this long. You can understand why people put old folks into nursing homes can't you?"

"You can, indeed." She sympathized. "I'm glad my grandparents never got like that."

"He's worse because of what he endured." Jack told Sherri gathering her close to his side. It had seemed eons ago since he'd last had his arms around her.

"Well enough of the pessimism" Devin announced, "Let's get on with what we came here to do, and enjoy ourselves huh? I take it I can leave you two alone for a few minutes without having to return and untangle you, can't I? I just have to check on a few things."

Acutely aware of Devin's parting shot, Sherri and Jack walked about idly in his absence, hardly daring to look at one another. Both were thinking about the night ahead and Sherri's emotions almost got the better of her each time she glanced in Jack's direction.

"Stop it, Scotty." She scolded under her breath, "you are supposed to be composing yourself, girl, not running amok with your fantasies." Even so, for a few delicious moments Sherri found it impossible to think of little else.

A few yards away, Jack was also having a hard time with his feelings. He knew there was his surprise to come, but somehow things had become complicated and he'd lost his enthusiasm. His Grandfather could often make him feel that way and it wasn't difficult to worry over what might happen when they returned with the old man in that mood. It could well be that his Grandfather would ruin everything with his childish tantrums. Not only that, but Jack wasn't comfortable being out after dark.

Oh well, Jack sighed heavily 'whatever will be will be.' He had no time to feel sorry for himself for at that moment Devin returned and what came up behind him left Jack totally staggered!

"Horses!" He exclaimed. "What are you doing with those?"

Sherri appeared at Jack's side she had almost missed Devin's arrival while engrossed in her feelings. "This," she told him happily clutching Jack's arm, "is your surprise, darling!"

Devin grinned at the look on his brother's face.

"I don't get it." Jack stated flatly. "I thought you said it had something to do with nightmares?"

"And so I did my love, night as in night, and mares as in horses."

Enlightenment dawned slowly and Jack's face lit up. "I'd like to say I'm relieved, but I don't think I am. Do you mean I am expected to ride one of them?"

"It'll be a piece of cake, Jack." Devin replied his voice bubbling with laughter. "Come on, take a closer look. I'm not an expert rider either, but these horses are used to novices like you and I."

Jack hesitated uncertainly.

"Look, don't worry, Jack. This will be no ordinary ride. See, the mares are equipped with a battery charged harness, and at the flick of a switch…" Devin touched the saddle to demonstrate, "ta da, see the harness lights the way ahead. Clever isn't it? The lights are star shaped too, hence star spangles, but that's not all…."

Jack gave his brother an irritated look. "You really like to drag it out, don't you?" With his arms folded in front of him he asked, "tell me then, what's not all?"

Devin hurried around to the rear of one of the horses, "Here's the clever bit, Jack. Each mare's rump is covered with a fine coating of luminous glitter, again star shaped, and when the moonlight shines upon it, the mare's rump is dappled in star spangles. It's great isn't it? See…get it? Star… Spangled… Night… Mares."

"It's going to be wonderful, Jack." Sherri told him hugging his arm tightly. Her eyes sparkled with happiness. "Devin has ensured that the clearing is clean from debris and pot holes. So we could gallop if we want to do, but other than that, with all this woodland, just riding together beneath the moonlight, well we thought it would be an experience to cherish forever."

Jack nodded, it did sound delightful, and it wasn't as if he were nervous of anything, it all just seemed so unbelievable. "You did all this just for me?" he asked incredulous.

"Never." Devin exclaimed. "Why are you so important? We did it for all of us. I've been meaning to try this for ages."

"Give it up, Devin" Sherri exclaimed, punching Devin playfully, before turning her face up to Jack's. "Don't you believe it, Jack, the whole thing was planned with you in mind, and unbelievably, Devin is the brainchild of this little gimmick too. He may never have admitted it, but when a joke of his went down like a lead balloon, someone listening was given a great idea, and so Star Spangles was born."

"That sound's like my brother. I've heard his jokes before." Jack replied dryly.

Sherri chuckled and reached up to stroke the forehead of one of the mares, "Hello," she told the horse. "You're nice." The mare rewarded Sherri by blowing softly into her hair.

"Well, are we going riding or not?" Devin asked handing out hard hats in the appropriate sizes.

"You just make sure you stay close." Jack told him, "Strange place, strange sounds, there's no way I want to be out here at this time of night by myself."

"I promise, Jack. We'll ride either side of you. Now come on, there's no telling if the storm will come near us, but you never know. The forecast said it might fizzle out before it reaches this area. Let's hope so huh? I wouldn't like to ascertain how horses react to thunder and lightening."

"Not well, I can vouch for that." Sherri replied speaking from experience. "Jack, will you need a leg up?

Jack shook his head, "Just show me how it's done, and I'll copy."

Handing the reins to Sherri and Jack in turn, Devin explained, "It's simple, watch me. You face the mare's rump, gather up the reins, place your left hand on the horses' withers, your left foot into the stirrup, put your right hand onto the back of the saddle, and hoist yourself up. There, that's all there is to it."

"Then put your right foot into the other stirrup." Sherri added, "Go on, Jack, you next. And then I can adjust the length of your stirrups."

"It looks easy." Jack mused, unconvinced.

"It is." Devin and Sherri chorused. "So come on, Bro. Quit stalling."

Jack did everything that Devin had told him, yet when it came to hoisting himself up, everything seemed awkward, and he just could not get the hang of it. Feeling somewhat foolish, Jack settled back to the ground exasperated with the whole thing, so Devin dismounted, and prepared to slide his hands up Jack's legs.

"What are you doing!" Jack exclaimed.

"No funny business, that's for sure. Just giving you a bunk up." Devin laughed out loud, "now hold on to the mare's withers, and I'll soon have you mounted."

Devin heaved his brother upward until finally with one almighty shove, Jack was astride the horse.

Staying on would prove to be another thing entirely.

Chapter Eighteen

Cheryl Sullivan looked around the cabin anxiously, hoping she had left nothing out of place. James was not to know that she had left him. Not until she was far away. If he should return and discover that she had gone before she had got off the mountainside, then there would be no hope for her. It had to look as if she had just gone out to collect some wild strawberries.

The fire was banked, the mixing bowl set up with flour and margarine blended together, the rolling pin at the ready, and her apron nestled upon the work surface as if awaiting her return. Everything made to look as if she had just popped out for fresh fruit, nothing out of the ordinary, nothing to make him suspect she was anywhere but on the mountainside.

Things had gone from bad to worse ever since James had returned from his trip abroad. Cheryl couldn't put her finger on it, but it was as if he knew that she had been seeing someone else. That was impossible of course, because up here in the mountains, there was no one that would have seen the two of them together. Yet, something was not right, and Cheryl had become afraid of her own shadow when James was around.

And then something he had said had been the final straw.

Just four days ago, she had watched as Devin's truck had disappeared down the mountain only the second time she had seen him since his return from New York City, a month earlier, the day when he had called by to introduce himself to James as their neighbor. Since that time, she had made one hasty CB call to him, other than that neither she nor Devin, had been able to find a way to see one another, although under the circumstances she had realized it was probably better that they hadn't tried.

James' suspicions had made her jumpy, her conversation stilted. His eyes followed her everywhere, his questions bordered on mistrust. And then there came the outright threat to her life. Cheryl would never have believed he would say such a thing, for all his nastiness, she would never have believed he was capable of murder, if she had not heard it with her own ears.

He'd been sneering at her as usual, but this time something was different. His eyes when he stared at her were unusually hard and chilling sending shudders of apprehension through her.

"There's someone else."

Cheryl looked up sharply trying hard to hide a slight tremor as she replied, "Someone else..." suddenly her mind raced, 'someone else? For him?' and her heart pounded with hope....'he'd found someone else! He was leaving her? Oh yes, yes, please let it be so!'

Suddenly he was on his feet, his rough fingers pulling her upwards so that her face was inches from his own, "You..." He rasped through gritted teeth, "You bitch!" He threw her away from him laughing sadistically as her head hit the sideboard and started to bleed.

"You deserved that you bitch! Who is he?" he fumed through gritted teeth, coming across to where she lay, and yanking her onto her feet again. Cheryl's head swam from the pain of the blow and from confusion.

"He?" She queried. "Who?"

Another blow sent her reeling, "You take me for stupid, woman? I see it in your eyes, I see it in your face, I know you've got someone else." he seethed, glowering over her, tempted to kick her hard, but Cheryl rolled away, staggering with the aid of a cupboard to stand upright.

"I…I thought…you meant yourself?" she stammered, the hot tears rushing down her cheeks.

"ME!" her husband shouted. "Me! You thought I was the unfaithful one! How dare you!" Another blow sent her reeling, crashing to the floor, her head, her shoulder, her ribs throbbing with pain.

"There's no-one else." Cheryl murmured weakly, but even to her own ears, the words sounded false.

"LIAR!" James strode across the floor, yanking Cheryl by her hair to stand in front of him, "Let me tell you this!" he spat, "you'll get nothing from me, no divorce, no settlement, nothing. You hear me? I'll see you dead first. It wouldn't be the first time I've killed a wife!" Cheryl had struggled, but he held her tighter. "And you can tell your lover, whoever he is, that I'll make him pay, you hear me? No one takes anything that's mine and gets away with it. You hear me! He'll pay. And don't you think I won't find out who he is, I will! And no mere beating will be good enough for him, no!" He sneered, "oh no, you were my life, he stole that from me. And what does the good book say, a life for a life, huh? You hearing me, Cherry!"

Wide eyed, Cheryl nodded.

"A life for a life Cherry, nothing less. You tell that son of a bitch I'll find him, and when I do… he'll die…slowly." He laughed sadistically, then, shoved Cheryl to the floor, before leaving the cabin, and slamming the door behind him.

Cheryl pulled herself up from where he had let her fall, and stood at the window watching him get into his truck and drive away. Her whole body was numb—a coldness creeping into every limb as the shaking started. Her teeth chattered, her head throbbed, and Cheryl longed for Devin's loving arms at that moment, more than she had ever longed for anything in her life. However, she could not go to him, James would not have gone far; he'd have anticipated her first move would be to go to her lover, and he'd be watching, and waiting. No, whatever she did, she couldn't involve Devin. Not this time. It would be far too dangerous.

* * *

Now remembering that terrible episode, Cheryl couldn't believe that it had happened just four short days ago, it seemed more like four years. The time spent with her husband was an ever-present strain, as his eyes had followed her every move, and she had never believed her husband to be capable of murder. But, she reflected, he'd told her he could, something about his last wife? Cheryl knew Janet Sullivan had died, just always believed James' version that she had been killed in an automobile accident.

Cheryl knew if her husband could kill one wife and beat another senseless, then what would he do to the man that she had turned to when she had first begun to learn what he was capable of?

Gathering her few possessions together beneath the covering of the fruit basket Cheryl left the cabin behind, hoping to get off the mountain before James returned.

Her intention was to find Devin. She could think of nothing else, and simply could not spend another night under the same roof with the monster she had married.

Chapter Nineteen

With a cup of foaming coffee and a packet of biscuits George Mansfield studied weather charts with interest. There was a storm approaching.

Idly flicking crumbs away from his desk, George heard a beeper a few yards behind him. He'd turned the volume down earlier when he'd needed to concentrate, but now he read the monitor with concern. The chart showed a graph that indicated the likelihood of tornadoes.

Scrolling to bring up fresh data, George turned up page after page pressing the printout key and gathering copies required for faxing to various departments within the building. This was standard procedure it didn't mean that this storm was going to be any worse than others that had preceded it.

George gave this one no special consideration even though it appeared to cover a wider area on the grid than normal. After thirty years in the business George knew how unpredictable storms could be, often they fizzled out and came to nothing.

With the specific charts highlighted George eyed his coffee on another desk, and leaned forward to pick up the mug. As he did so, he didn't notice that his elbow accidentally caught the computer's delete button. The system altered rapidly, bringing up old data that revealed the shape of the storm when it was brewing hours earlier.

Gulping down his coffee, George glanced over the rim of the mug and frowned, 'what on earth?' He checked the system, not understanding how the storm could alter just like that. One moment it had covered two counties and the next a few kilometers.

George nodded, perhaps that was it, anything was possible, even storms that died out in the blink of an eye.

Relieved, George began munching on biscuits again. Reaching for his coffee, he looked at the dregs with distaste. The biscuits were too dry without dunking. Perhaps he should make more coffee.

Eyeing the apparatus doubtfully, George made his decision. Everything appeared normal again, and the storm had died down, thank goodness. He hesitated for several seconds until a loud stomach rumble made up his mind. He'd only be gone long enough to wolf down a meal. Even if the storm did start up again, he'd still be back before he needed to send warnings. George left the room, biscuits forgotten, his mind firmly fixed on rump steak and all the trimmings. Urged by his rumbling stomach, George's feet could not carry him to the canteen fast enough.

* * *

Outside the weather center, an ill wind was brewing, buffeting debris around the car park and whipping at trees, causing havoc wherever it could.

On the tail of the wind came the "Almighty" as it would later be known, a tornado unprecedented by any other.

Racing behind the storm, the Almighty struck the weather center's radar with full force, sending it spiraling upwards and down again. It crashed somewhere in the center of the car park, in a mangled wreck. The driving rain that followed lashed in torrents. It was illuminated by fiery streaks of lightening that split the sky, before the Almighty cried out, its steely breath smashing everything in its path.

Oblivious to the turmoil outside, George finished his long awaited meal, and made his way back to the station. He was tired after his long shift and the recent meal, and his eyes were heavy. Reaching his room, he blinked rapidly, disbelieving all he saw. All the monitors flickered swiftly, and the beeper was sounding wildly. George hurried across to the system, pressing appropriate buttons to connect with the radar and received nothing. Frowning, George made his way to the window. Everything inside the room indicated mayhem, yet the weather center radar had not picked up anything to show for that.

Suddenly the lights went out, the computer screens flickered and died and immediately all came back on again accompanied by a humming sound that signaled the generator had kicked in.

Pulling the drawstring to the blinds, George peered through the tinted glass. He was shocked to see a great streak of fire pass yards from his face, blinding him momentarily. He heard an ear-splitting crash, followed by a mighty roar as the storm rocketed through the weather center. Struck dumb and motionless, George froze. Armageddon was his first and foremost thought. It had come.

No, God had promised to arrive as a thief in the night. This was not Armageddon. Had it been, it would have come without warning. There would not have been an irrational storm perpetually changing its course. Armageddon it was not, not yet anyway, and George was somewhat relieved. At least it still gave him time to put things right with God and for that he was grateful, as he had sadly neglected spiritual matters of late.

Vowing all that would change; George quickly set about making amends for the time lost in reporting the oncoming storm.

Oncoming? George chided. His head was going to roll for this one. Thirty years in the business, and he'd let the biggest storm get away without notice. Oh well, perhaps early retirement might be a blessing in disguise. He could at least warn the next town that the storm was fast approaching.

Frantically, George tapped at some keyboards searching for data. Cameras and radars positioned along the highway showed trails of destruction for miles. Someone would be contacting him shortly and screaming in his ear. George started sending faxes to the appropriate destinations. He would do all he could to rectify the matter, knowing full well the futility of that.

Already, the storm was well ahead of him and out of control, with innocent unprepared people in its path. As George closed his eyes and groaned with great sorrow the telephones began to shrill.

* * *

Helena Brooks locked her office door and pulled the collar of her coat tighter about her neck as she made her way towards her car. Star Spangles was closed for the night. The mares were tucked up safe and warm in their stables and those out for hire would be out until the morning. Helena liked the job, she really did, it was fun, but at times after seeing that everything was as it should be for effective day-to-day running she wanted never to hear the word, 'horse', ever again.

Her car and home beckoned, her family would be waiting for their supper, and Helena checked her watch, wondering if they would appreciate pizza at this hour. "Who are you kidding?" she laughed to herself, "that lot would appreciate pizza for breakfast." Just at that moment, a car rounded the corner, its headlights momentarily blinding her. She heard the car door slam and footsteps. Helena fingered her purse, lifting the catch, ready to search out the alarm she carried in case of attack, when she heard a voice she recognized. "It's okay, love. It's me, Glen." Her husband's voice filled her with relief. Helena relaxed and then a sudden thought made her cry, "Glen, why are you here! Is something wrong?"

"Something and nothing really. The kids are fine. It's just this damn storm. I was worried about some of the horses that are out tonight. Many of those people won't have access to the news while out riding and they might be in serious trouble. I thought it might be best to check out some of those locations and see about taking a ride over there, to check everything is Hunky-Dory. We don't want anyone breaking their necks, do we?"

Helena agreed at once, her concern plainly evident in her eyes. As they reached the office she unlocked the door, and turned on the lights.

"Switch the computer back on, will you, Glen? I'll fetch the files. We have to locate and contact everyone. The horses must be stabled while this lot is going on. We can compensate with a free night some other time if the need arises."

"Sure." Glen flicked on the computer, waited while it whirled into action, and took the files from his wife as she handed each in turn. The location of each horse was available on the computer hard drive. Glen checked the route planner for the quickest way to get there.

This, Glen did with each hire in turn, wondering if the storm had reached that part of the country at all, and then telephoning the customers accordingly. Most, he was relieved to note, had long ridden and were enjoying supper with their families; with the mares tucked up safely for the night in sturdy brick stables, which was another condition of hiring.

There was one or two, however, where he received no answer, and asked his wife to keep calling while he made his way over there. "If by any chance they answer the phone, just call me on the cell will you, honey? I'll detour and go on to the next place. Don't want to be out driving all night in those conditions."

"You should contact the boss, Glen, it's not our business to risk our necks. I've already done a full day here, we'll not get thought of any better for it, you know? Wouldn't mind if we did, and we've our own family to think of."

"The kid's are fine, I've left them next door, and they're probably having a ball right now even as we speak. Craig has his relatives over, you know, the ones that have just returned from Tokyo? There'll be all those photos to sort through, and you know how much our kids love to play with Craig's kids."

"So long as they keep out of the tree house then."

"Don't worry, I left strict instructions against that." Glen pulled on his jacket that he had draped over a chair as he had entered the building earlier and checked the pocket for his car keys and phone, extracting the latter to ensure the battery wasn't low. "Everything will be okay, honey. You'll see. Just make sure you keep trying those numbers and let me know if anything materializes. I'll see you soon, huh?"

Helena nodded, somewhat uneasy, as she'd heard that before, "No heroics remember? You're worth more to me than a dozen horses, no, a million horses, you come back safe, you hear me?"

Glen walked across to his wife and hugged her hard, "Know something, Mrs. Brooks?"

"What?"

"I love you."

"Now quit that, it won't alter the way I feel, no softening me up, get away with you. You just do as I say, you hear? No doing your knight in shining armor bit, okay?"

"If you insist." Glen rubbed his stubbly chin over his wife's cheek, kissing her ear, triumphant when she shivered with longing.

"You hurry home, I've got plans for you." she whispered huskily.

Glen laughed softly, "you've got plans for me! Huh, just you wait until I get you home! We have a house void of kids tonight remember? And the world's your oyster baby."

Helena laughed, smacking her husband's rear playfully. "Oh you. Just make sure you remember that and hurry back, huh?"

Glen noticed with pleasure that his wife's eyes were bright with mischief, holding a promise that was hard to ignore. "I'll hurry home, I promise. And I do love you. Without any of the conditions."

"And I love you. Now be off with you or the only storm that will be left raging tonight will be in me."

Glen's eyes crinkled at the corners, "Promises, promises. I'll hold you to that." Kissing his wife long and hard, Glen reluctantly withdrew from her arms, "I'll be as quick as I can." Then opening the door and stepping through, his final, "see ya," was almost lost to her as the howling wind tugged it away.

Chapter Twenty

Beneath a starry, moonlit sky, Sherri didn't think she had ever known a more wondrous sight. Sitting astride a beautiful horse, with Devin riding one side of Jack and she the other, the three chatted happily about all manner of topics. The moon filtered rays of refined silver down onto the horses, bringing forth the promised effect of glittering stars upon the rumps and flanks of the trusting animals.

Jack had quickly mastered the art of riding, providing they walked at a steady pace, and while Devin and Sherri stayed close by, he relaxed, enjoying the experience tremendously. Jack was no stranger to sounds and scents of the great outdoors, but this, riding of a horse, the motion, the feel of the faithful animal beneath him, was something he would never forget. The harness, with its beam of star-studded light, moved gently with the motion of each horse, casting tiny rays that filtered through the woodland and along the track flanked by rhododendrons in full bloom.

"This is great, isn't it?" Devin exclaimed more than once, pleased by the delighted faces of Sherri and especially of Jack. Devin had never felt so pleased with himself. It was clear that this 'surprise' was bringing his brother and Sherri closer together.

Conscious of their eye contact, the long, tantalizing looks passing from one to the other, the gentle touch of hands, the invisible current blazed between them, signifying a night of forthcoming passion. Devin was almost envious, and for the umpteenth time that day he wished that Cheryl were there with him.

He hadn't seen her for several weeks and when he had last driven past her cabin on the way to move some of his belongings into his new house he had noted that James's truck had still been parked outside. She had managed one brief call to him when James was out, and he mentioned his weekend trip to the estate at the bottom of the mountain. Devin wished she could join him there.

He was unaware he was daydreaming, until Jack nudged him hard laughing, "earth to Devin. Where are you?"

"I...er, oh, sorry, Jack. Were you saying something?"

"Yes, I was saying that this is wonderful. I had no idea what you had planned for me, but nothing could have prepared me for this. I shall remember it all my life."

""We could always do this again, sometime." Sherri offered.

"Really? That would be great!" Jack exclaimed.

"The best bit is yet to come. There's a clearing just a few yards ahead. Would you like to venture going a bit faster, Jack?" Devin asked, adding, "It's real easy, you just adjust your position to the gait of the horse. Believe me, you will love this. To feel the wind in your hair, the speed of the horse, it's simply great. You'll see, you'll love it. Trust me."

Jack found that he did. Horse riding was a new experience to him and instructed by Sherri, he urged his mare onward by pressing his knees inward and his body forward, so the mare soon picked up the pace. Within seconds, he found his body swiftly maneuvered into the gait of rise and fall. Then before he had had time to adjust to that, he was forced back into the saddle as the mare's strides took him into a canter. For a fleeting moment, the thought of having little control worried him, until he heard Devin call out beside him, "It's great, isn't it?" And he had to agree that it was.

Coming up alongside him, Sherri rode her mare with the skill of experience.

"You've done this before?" Jack called to her with laughter in his voice.

"Yes." Sherri called back, "many times. Are you ready to gallop?"

"You mean they can go faster than this?" Jack sounded surprised.

"Faster even than that. Beyond a gallop, a horse can bolt…" Sherri began.

"And believe me, Jack that's fast. Just squeeze your knees a little harder and we'll gallop." Devin was shouting, urging his own horse on to demonstrate and Jack was stunned as Devin's mare surged ahead her long tail fanning out behind her, the glittering array of starlight turning silvery by moonlight.

What magic! The motion, the moonlight, Jack felt liberated and he urged his mare onward in an attempt to catch up with his brother, well aware of Sherri clicking her tongue to urge her mare into a full scale gallop at his side her gay laughter tinkling behind her.

The ride was breathtaking. Jack had never experienced anything like it in his life. This moment, this glorious, wondrous moment of riding through the night with Devin and Sherri at his side, the beautiful creature beneath him, its quivering flesh eager to please, it was awesome and Jack drank in every moment of it with intense pleasure.

It took only moments to cross the clearing, yet even before they had quite reached the other side Devin had become vaguely aware of a darkening in the appearance of the night around them. The rump of the horses no longer sparkled as large clouds eclipsed the moon.

Slowing his mare to a trot, Devin waited while Sherri and Jack drew level with him their faces wreathed in smiles altering slowly as they acknowledged his silence.

"What is it, Devin?" Sherri asked breathlessly, following his gaze to where ominous clouds were gathering.

"I think that storm's brewing. We ought to take the horses back to the stables before it hits us." Devin replied gravely saddened that their enjoyment was to be cut short so soon.

"There'll be another time, don't worry. I promise. We'll do this again. Won't we, Jack?" Sherri hoped he would agree.

"Oh yes." Jack replied with pleasure, "I never thought I would enjoy myself so much. That was truly wonderful."

"Come on then," Sherri turned her horse back toward the clearing, "at least it's not over yet. We still have to negotiate the return journey and I for one, cannot wait." With that, she was gone calling over her shoulder, "race you." As her horse surged forth into a gallop within the space of a heartbeat.

"What are we waiting for?" Devin challenged. "You heard the lady. Now 'git." He yelled, urging his mare onward, happy to hear Jack's laughter bubble behind anticipating another exhilarating gallop.

* * *

Glen slowed his van at an intersection, checking his map for the right direction to take, as a fiery glow streaked across the sky, followed by crashing thunder. "Whoa," Glen whistled. "That was some baby. I sure hope them gee gees are stabled by now. If anyone is out on them they are sure gonna get one hell of a ride."

Tracing a line along the map with his finger, Glen noted the area of his last call. Helena had rung with the good news that two out of the four he'd gone out to see, had been contacted, and Glen was happy to detour. The previous call had been closer to home but this one, well, it was sure out in the sticks somewhere towards the Appalachians, in fact, Glen whistled, that was a fair old journey and obviously intended for someone who wanted real privacy.

Checking his rear view mirror, Glen was pleased to see that traffic was sparse and he switched off the engine, 'no use wasting fuel' he spoke aloud while unfolding a sheet of paper that would inform him of the recipient of the mares that evening. The name jumped out at him, Devin Richardson; sure, he'd heard that name before, the boss was always joking about good old Devin making him millions. 'Huh millions, in your dreams man.' Glen laughed, but he had to admit that the idea was taking off at a remarkable rate. This week alone, they had proposed and passed the motion of buying in another dozen mares. There was a waiting list for Night Mares as long as his arm, and Glen found that he had to be impressed that this Devin had sparked off a great idea and thought it might be nice to meet the man and shake his hand if nothing else.

Using the map's chart, Glen could make out his route clearly. He checked the fuel level and whistled again, happy to find that for once, the tank appeared full, but then the gauge had been known to stick. Glen tried to remember when he had last filled it and couldn't. Usually he and Helena worked shifts together and used the one car, her car, whereas the van was used for outings over rough terrain taking the kids out somewhere wild. Glen grimaced, perhaps the van would make it, but he wasn't certain that it would get him back, not after all those gear changes through the rocky region, and he wasn't sure of the location of the nearest gas station. There was nothing else for it, he would simply have to risk it, he'd call Helena, tell her he'd be home as soon as he could, and just keep his fingers crossed that there would be enough fuel to get him there and back.

The radio crackled as he turned it on but any news that was announced made light of the storm's strength, almost as if they didn't know of its existence. Glen could not understand why the Weather Center had not warned everyone about its savage advance. And the storm showed no signs of abating, just continued to move nearer and nearer to the mountains at an amazing rate of knots.

Glen shuddered, still undecided about continuing onwards. Any possibility of warning the riders was, after all, shattered now, for the storm had raged ahead of him displaying an awesome display of celestial lights. Glen could only hope that the horses were stabled and the riders tucked safely in bed for he didn't like to think of anyone still outside trying to ride petrified horses. The risk was too great, and there would be certain casualties.

As Glen drove faster, he found he could only continue to hope that the reason why no one had yet answered his repetitive call was that they were fast asleep or otherwise entertained, and not that they were lying in a ditch somewhere with a broken neck.

Chapter Twenty-one

Traveling down the mountainside, even with very little luggage, Cheryl found the way harder than she had imagined and her body ached terribly from James's beating. She was worried about the ominous approach of dark clouds and the rumble of distant thunder. During thunderstorms, Cheryl preferred to be tucked up safely for the night beneath the bedclothes.

Of all the nights to run away from home, she had to choose this one. Still, soon she would find Devin and all her worries would be over. James would never find her, Devin would take care of her, they would build a new life together, and in time she would forget the horrors of her life with James.

Picking her way over the rocky terrain Cheryl made her way ever downward. She had seen the estate many times. If the gates were locked it wouldn't matter for she knew of another way in. She would get cut to ribbons doing it, but what the hell, getting cut to ribbons would be nothing compared to what James had in store for her for an alternative. Cheryl footsteps faltered. What was she doing? Suppose James did find her? It didn't bear thinking about. Then she remembered Devin, his tenderness and the way he loved her, and Cheryl forced all thoughts of her monstrous husband from her mind.

* * *

For the umpteenth time, Glen stopped the car and checked the map. With no streetlamps, it was hard to see it with the dim interior light, especially as the night grew ever darker with thunderclouds covering the moonlight. Running his finger over the map, tracing the road he had traveled, Glen sighed with relief. He'd made it. Now he could relax. He felt exhausted.

Folding the map, Glen leaned back and closed his eyes. They were gritty and sore, and they ached. 'Just a second or two' he promised himself, 'then I'll go check on those horses.'

Moments later he was fast asleep.

* * *

Returning from a trip into town, James hurried back to the cabin. Cheryl hated thunderstorms and he loved to gloat at her fear.

Pulling up outside the cabin he had built some years previously, James noted the gentle puffs of smoke coming through the chimney, and knew the signs. Cherry would be preparing a meal, possibly baking.

Baking, baking, she was always damn baking! Cheryl was the perfect wifey. James sneered. Really, he couldn't fault her in that way. Meals always on time, hot and filling, the bed made, the cabin always neat and tidy, homely…homely! Huh, typical! "Trust me to find the 'perfect' wife." He spat. "WELL YOU JUST DON'T EXCITE ME ANYMORE!" He yelled out towards the cabin, not in the least surprised when Cheryl never came to the window. Did she ever? Did she care about anything he did these days?

Fed up, James slid from the truck. No matter what he did, whether he kissed her, abused her, insulted her, his wife reacted the same, just getting on with life, the same old way. She was so weak! Never reacting any differently, no matter what he did to her. Well he'd show her, this time, she had gone too far, and beatings clearly were not enough.

In his eyes, Cheryl had committed the unpardonable crime. Having an affair was something he had never even considered. After all that was a man's prerogative, wasn't it?

Incensed now, James strode towards the cabin, his mind filled with ugly, consuming thoughts. It had been a long time since he'd 'had' Cherry, he realized, and that was her fault too. Even with her petite figure, long dark hair and baby blue eyes she just didn't turn him on anymore.

Kicking open the cabin door, James strode inside shouting as he entered, "Cherry! Stop whatever you're doing and git yourself onto this bed. It's time I had what I'm entitled to, woman."

Unzipping his trousers, James turned full circle, searching the seemingly empty cabin for any sign of life. Cheryl was nowhere to be seen, but he noticed the stove had been stacked, and there was dough ready for rolling on the work surface, also some strawberries in a bowl, but no Cheryl.

"Guess you've gone a picking cherries, Cherry." James spoke to the room, as he held his swollen manhood in one hand, "No matter," James fondled himself lazily, "the longer you take, the madder I'll get, and then the harder it'll come." Aggressively, he grinned, his deranged mind showing definite signs of insanity. "So you take all the time you need, my love," he whispered hoarsely. His manhood throbbed in eager expectation growing larger as his anger increased, pleasing him no end. "Yes, Cherry," he added with glee as his eyes glazed over, "you just take all the time you need."

* * *

Believing her troubles were over the storm mocked Cheryl as it passed overhead with arrows of fire.

"Lightening!" Cheryl shrieked diving for cover beneath a small tree realizing her mistake instantly when a streak of lightening singed the grass next to her.

"Trees! Cheryl Sullivan, you know you shouldn't be under trees in a thunder storm." She laughed with quiet hysteria. "James probably sent the lightening strike to get me...WELL YOU MISSED!" she shouted foolishly but feeling better for it. "Oh stop being so melodramatic," she chided herself, "you're not home dry yet."

There had been no sign of James at all, for which Cheryl had been thankful, but that didn't mean he hadn't realized she had gone. He could be searching for her on the mountain, even as she thought it.

Picking her way carefully down the final slope Cheryl breathed a sigh of relief. Somewhere inside the large estate was Devin. Cheryl felt a warmth ripple through her at the thought of him. So near and yet so far, and he had no idea she was coming to him.

He would be surprised, but she hoped he wouldn't mind her turning up like this. He'd told her he was staying with a few members of his family, and Cheryl thought it would be nice to meet them, yet regardless what they thought of her gate crashing their get together, she had no other choice. She'd had to get away from James. Devin would understand that, wouldn't he?

Cheryl really hoped so, as for the first time since she had set off, she began to have doubts about descending on these people unannounced.

Chapter Twenty-two

Disorientated and confused, Sherri struggled to stand, not knowing why she was lying on the cold wet grass anyway. Her head throbbed, and she could remember little. Drawing her brows together, she tried to establish where she was. Isaac Park? Had she been going somewhere and been attacked? Oh dear God no, not Baxter!

Squinting to see through the dark, Sherri could make out the shapes of huge trees, telling her she was not in Isaac Park, and the sound of the wind whistling through the branches carried with it another sound, a moaning. Someone was moaning. Who? Frowning, Sherri passed a hand across her brow, feeling the matted hair beneath, sticky from the outpouring of blood from a gash on the side of her head. She groaned and tried to remember what had happened.

"Sherri? Is that you? Are you all right?"

"Who's that?"

"Devin. Is Jack with you?"

"Jack?"

"Yes, Jack. Did he fall too?"

"Fall?" Sherri's heart raced. Fall? Where from?

"From his horse."

"His horse?" Sherri drew her brows together and winced with pain. "What horse?" she murmured, confused.

"You must have banged your head or something. Don't you remember anything?"

"Very little. Where are we? Where's Jack?"

"Can you stand?"

"What kind of answer is that?"

"It isn't. Can you stand?"

"Just." She replied getting to her feet and holding onto something that felt like a tree trunk for support. "I'm up. Where are you?"

"Over here. Can you see me?"

"Yes. At least I think so. It's just so dark. Devin, whatever happened to us?"

"I'm not rightly sure. We were riding horses, and there was this ear-splitting noise, and the next thing I know I'm laid here. I think I may have broken my ankle."

"Horses? We were riding horses? Why? Where are you? Maybe your ankle is sprained?"

"I wouldn't get that lucky. No, it is some divine retribution to halt my globe trotting, you'll see. All those broken promises I made to Granddad, about returning from each trip to give Jack a break. I'm being punished, and have to stay put, whether I like it or not." Devin sighed raggedly unable to stop his voice trailing away on a tinge of laughter. For a moment Sherri almost believed him, until she heard the note of humor, and smiled, she could always count on Devin to make light of a tricky situation even though on this occasion he sounded in great pain. Shuffling over to where she believed him to be, Sherri soon located him, or rather he located her, as he placed a hand upon her leg, halting her from stepping on him.

"Can you help me up? We have to look for Jack. He could be anywhere. This is a big estate Sherri, though he should be around here somewhere. If we, experienced riders, could fall off, he would surely have been unable to stay mounted."

Sherri started to remember. She could see the three of them galloping through the clearing, trying to get back to the house and stables before the storm hit, when a streak of fire etched the sky, and hurtled a thunderous cry above them. Her horse had reared, Devin's horse had bolted straight into her mare's back, teetering him crazily for dizzying moments, before throwing him to the ground, and Sherri had just seen Jack's wild-eyed mare bolt forward, before she too had slipped from the saddle.

"He could be anywhere, Devin."

"We must get some flashlights from the house, Sherri. I believe it's this way. We'll keep our eyes and ears open huh? Maybe we'll come across him."

"Maybe."

"Try to stay optimistic, Sherri." Devin urged as he leaned on her for support. "Horses usually stay together. If we look out for them then maybe Jack will be nearby."

Sherri knew he was only saying that to make her feel better but it didn't help. They had put a novice rider on a horse in the middle of the night. Anything may have happened to him and if it had, she would never forgive herself.

* * *

"She's taking her time." James stopped his relentless pacing, and his anger ceased for just a moment, as he began to wonder what could be keeping his wife.

He went to the door, idly pushing his engorged flesh back inside his trousers, and fastening the zipper as best he could with one hand, while he picked up his jacket from where he had dropped it with the other.

Stepping outside, he scanned the area. The sky had grown darker since he had arrived home, and he hadn't realized. Turning back to the cabin, he frowned. He hadn't noticed Cherry had lit the lamps either. She only did that when she expected to be back late, so that the light from the lamps acted as a beacon to help her find her way home.

174

There was something unusual though…

If Cherry was in the middle of baking and had gone to pick fruit, why had she left the lamps burning? She couldn't pick fruit in the dark, could she? She'd never done so before. And if she had anticipated enough to light the lamps then she was also expecting to travel a fair distance, either up or down the mountainside. It was possible she had gone down, but he hadn't passed her on his way home, so perhaps she had gone up instead? But why, what could possibly be upwards? Fruit, yes, if she had really gone out for fruit, but the lighted lamps made mockery to that idea.

James thought hard. It was a long time since he had gone further than his own cabin. Who lived up that way now? He really hadn't a clue.

Just then he remembered something. A few weeks back a chap had come by to introduce himself as their new neighbor. He'd gone that way! Was that who Cherry had gone to visit? In fact…James's temper increased, 'was that who the bitch was seeing?"

Running now, James, yanked open the door of his truck, tossed in his jacket and slid inside, starting the engine. "Well, if that's where you both are then I'll soon surprise you." He seethed, pulling open the glove compartment, pleased to note his revolver tucked safely inside, "Now I can kill two birds with one stone…" he laughed sadistically, "and I don't mean maybe!"

Chapter Twenty-three

Reaching the house, Devin paused with his hand on the doorknob and gazed upward.

"What is it?" Sherri asked from behind him, "why have you stopped?"

Devin grinned wryly. "Just look at that." he nodded indicating the sky, "absolutely clear now, not a cloud in sight. And those stars! Why the sky is full of them."

Sherri shuddered. "It might be the eye of the storm. If so, we need to find Jack before it gets rough again."

She'd promised to make all of Jack's dreams come true, while instead, had, in effect given him a living nightmare. She fought back a sob and Devin placed his arm around her shoulders. "Don't worry, Sherri we'll find him. Come now, let's freshen up, and get back out there. I don't want to alarm you further, but Star Spangles will be coming to collect the mares in a few hours."

Sherri groaned. "Oh no, that went right out of my mind. Where are the flashlights? I'll get them. You wait here, and listen out for the horses."

"No, I'll come with you. I need to look at my ankle." He told her, wincing with pain as he eased his injured foot up each step.

For the first time Sherri noticed his discomfort, which up until then he had cleverly disguised from her, and told him, "You shouldn't take off your boot, Devin. Whatever it is you have done, and however much it hurts, the boot will be supporting it. You take it off, and the swelling with come up tenfold. Then you will never get your boot back on until it heals, and that may take weeks. Best let a doctor take a look at it first."

"Such a pessimist." Devin tried to laugh, but found it hurt too much.

"You ought to stay here, Devin. I'll go look for Jack."

"But you don't know the place, you'll get lost."

"Don't worry, I'll be alright. Perhaps one of us should stay here anyway, your Grandfather will be worried. I'll try not to be gone too long, and if I need your help, I'll come back at once."

"You promise?"

"Yes."

"All right then, Sherri, and I'll not remove this boot until you are back, just in case you need me to come outside again. But first run inside and get a flashlight. They're in the cabinet under the sink."

Helping him into the house Sherri left Devin in the hall as she ran to the kitchen, returning moments later with a flashlight.

"You'll take care, promise me?" Devin asked anxiously, as she approached.

"I will. Try not to worry."

"That's easier said than done."

"I know. But while the storm has finished and it's quiet out there, Jack will hear me when I call."

"If he's conscious."

"Devin!"

"I know, pessimistic again, huh? Sorry. Off you go then."

They hugged one another tightly, "See you soon, Dev. Go rest that foot okay?"

Devin nodded slowly. It was a long time after she had left that he remained by the open door looking up at the starry sky. He felt desolate and miserable…the weekend surprise for his brother that he had planned with such precision…had now become a real, living, nightmare.

* * *

It took no time at all to reach the other cabin. James pulled up just out of sight, but was dismayed to find that there was no vehicle parked outside. Perhaps he had been wrong after all. 'No harm in looking though', he told himself, and alighting from his truck he shrugged into his jacket before making his way quietly over to the cabin. First off, he listened at the door, and hearing nothing, he peeped through the windows. Nothing. There didn't appear to be anyone home. Just in case, James knocked hard at the door. And when there was no answer, he tried the handle. It turned, and the door opened. James was not surprised. Way up there, where thieves were few and far between, no one locked their cabin. It was an unwritten law of the mountains to leave cabins unlocked in case any lost or injured traveler needed help or a bed for the night. Although that same law, insisted that doors were always kept closed, because of bears. In view of this, James had no qualms about entering. It was a sparsely furnished cabin, well kept, and tidy but James could see that whoever lived there, hardly had two coins to rub together. This dismayed James. He had considered Cheryl to like her home comforts, and he couldn't imagine why she should choose someone who had next to nothing. No, he told himself, he must have got this wrong. This guy couldn't be the one Cherry had been seeing. He wished that he had asked for a description from the fellow at the store who had seen the pair of them together. With a final perusal of the cabin, James, had seen enough, and made to leave when he noticed a notepad alongside a CB set. Maybe that would tell him something.

James flicked through the pages. Only one thing jumped out at him, his own code for the radio back at his cabin and beneath it the name, 'Cherie'. James frowned, 'could it be? His wife was called Cheryl, and he called her Cherry so Cherie could be a derivative of that too couldn't it?

Cherie, Cherry, Cheryl, yes, it made sense. Picking up the notepad, James saw something flutter from beneath the pages and drop to the floor, and he bent to pick it up. Lifting it to the moonlight streaming through the window, he noticed that it was a newspaper cutting, and there was a message written in ink at the top of it. "Barrington Estate, May thirteenth." So! They were together, and this piece of paper had just told him where. Barrington Estate, and he knew where that was! Dropping the notepad, James marched from the cabin, slamming the door shut behind him and headed for his truck. "No one, but no one, makes a fool out of me." he stormed as the engine roared into life and sweeping the vehicle around in a large arc, James was soon speeding down the mountainside, his destination plain.

Chapter Twenty-four

The sound of a vehicle passing by at speed startled Glen awake. He was surprised to find he was in the van. Disorientated, he stared out the windshield, trying to recollect his surroundings. He was in a place he had never seen before. Was he dreaming?

Ahead, the bright red glare of brake lights startled him. It was then he remembered it had woken him.

Unconcerned, he watched the lights disappear. Whatever their problem, it had nothing to do with him.

The dashboard clock showed him it was the middle of the night. Glen tried to remember what he was doing in the van at that time. Whatever the reason, he wished he was still asleep. He yawned, and his gaze settled upon a map spread out on the passenger seat, his cell phone on top…it was then that he remembered.

"Oh, Lord!" Glen struggled to sit up, checking the clock again. How long had he slept? An hour? He couldn't have! He'd meant only to rest his eyes a few minutes. And that car…had it been driven by someone in trouble, rushing another to hospital?

Glen pulled the seatbelt around, buckled it and made to start the engine. He checked the rear view mirror out of habit, not expecting to see anything way out there, and froze! Something moved behind the van, something ghostly…

* * *

Wandering down the wall side for the best part of an hour Cheryl had finally found the place she searched, only to discover that someone had bricked it up. Now what?

There was no other way in, and she was wet, cold and exhausted. She had to find somewhere safe to rest. Under a bush was her only option. Sliding beneath feet first, Cheryl paused when she heard a vehicle approaching. Automatically she lay flat and watched it pass by. The distinctive fluorescent stripe of her husband's van terrified her. She'd been right to assume he'd come after her, wrong to believe he'd not know where to look.

Heart thumping, Cheryl pulled herself out from beneath the bush. She was too close to the estate. If James could not gain entry, he might drive back and wait nearby, or park his van beside her. That would be terrible.

Cheryl looked down the road. It appeared empty. Even so, she stayed near the edge where she could dive for cover in the long grass if the need arose.

Head bent she walked, listening intently over the whistle of the wind for sounds of traffic, and too late walked right into a parked vehicle she hadn't noticed was there.

From where she stood it looked empty. Cautiously she moved by it, peering through the windows, checking the back seat to see if anyone rested there. Nothing. As she came to the driver's door, she froze! A man was looking at her through the window, his face obscured by a dim light within.

As the door opened, Cheryl screamed.

* * *

"Hey, hey. It's all right, look; don't be afraid. I'm not going to hurt you. Are you lost?"

"Who are you?" They asked together. Glen laughed. "I'm Glen Brooks."

"Cheryl."

"Hello Cheryl. This is going to sound corny, but what are you doing out alone on a night like this?"

"You wouldn't believe me if I told you."

"Pardon?"

"Oh, nothing. I'm looking for a way into the estate actually. My boyfriend is there."

"Your boyfriend?" Glen sounded surprised. He hadn't meant to do. What he knew of Devin Richardson was minimal. The thing was he'd always assumed him to be married.

"Yes. I need to contact him," Cheryl replied, wondering why she was telling a perfect stranger all these things.

"What's his name?"

"His name? Why should you want to know?"

"I might know him. I was on my way to the estate too."

"You were! That's marvelous. Do you have a key to the gate?"

"No, but I have a cell phone, and a contact number. Tell me your friend's name, and I'll call and see if he's there." Cheryl closed her eyes as relief washed over her. "Here, why don't you get into the van out of this wind?"

"No!" Cheryl stepped away, frightened, "You just make the call okay?"

"Sure. Give me his name then." The woman clearly mistrusted his motives, but then, could he blame her? Out there alone, meeting a strange man, both of them miles from home. He could be anyone.

"His name is Devin."

Glen nodded, he'd expected as much. "That would be Devin Richardson then?"

"You know him?"

"Yes. Look, do get into the van. It's so windy out here, and you are wet. You'll catch your death. I won't harm you, I promise. I'm not that sort of man. Here, take a look at this photo." Glen extracted the picture from above his sunshield. "This is the wife and my kids. See, I'm just your run of the mill average fellow, and I'm offering you assistance. Nothing else."

Looking at the photo Cheryl first noticed a pretty middle aged woman with curly mousy brown hair and a smiling face that showed she was happy with her life. In front two small boys were laughing at their Dad giving a little girl a piggyback. With his receding gray hair and smiling eyes, Cheryl could clearly see the photo was of Glen and his family.

"Thank you," she sighed with relief handing him back the photograph, "thank you so much."

Glen waited outside the van while Cheryl slipped into the passenger seat, noticing her watching him warily as he slipped back into the car beside her.

"It's okay, relax. I'll make that call."

Cheryl watched as he dialed the number, it seemed an age before anyone answered.

* * *

Peering anxiously out of the window, Devin had never felt so sick or so helpless. He supposed he should check on his Grandfather, but knew he would never manage the stairs. When the telephone rang, Devin jumped out of his skin, it was the last sound that he expected, and he hobbled over to it, wincing with every step. He was glad that he got to it before it stopped ringing. "Hello?" He enquired, snatching up the receiver.

"Devin Richardson?"

Devin froze. There weren't many people that knew he was there. His first thought was that Cheryl's husband had found out about him. Stiltedly, he replied, "Yes... speaking."

"Hello, Devin. You won't know me. My name is Glen Brooks. I work for Star Spangles. I'm sitting outside the estate. I came to warn you about the approaching storm, but it was obviously faster than I was. We tried ringing, but there was no reply. Anyway, is everything all right? Did the storm affect you at all?"

Devin sighed with relief, still what could he say? He didn't want anyone coming over here for his Grandfather's sake. The old man had been cranky enough for one evening as it was.

The pause worried Glen. "Something's wrong, isn't it?" He asked.

"Nothing I can't handle. You don't have to worry." Devin hoped he sounded convincing.

"What happened?" Glen asked.

"The horses bolted. We all took a fall, but everything is fine now. The mares will be waiting for collection as planned." Devin hoped the half-truth would suffice.

Glen sighed with relief. "That is good news, I'll go back then. The horse-box should be with you in a few hours, though if your ride was ruined, you could have the mares for tonight as well."

"We're only here for the one night," Devin told him, "thanks anyway."

"It's okay. You know the drill. Just call when you want a couple of horses again, okay? Better still, can you get over to the office soon. I know the boss has been trying to reach you. Something about expansion?"

"We've spoken already. Keith brought the mares out to me personally."

"Oh…" Glen hesitated, hoping Devin might elaborate. He and Helena had wondered what the boss's new plans had been for days.

"If that's everything then, many thanks for checking on us. I appreciate it. Goodbye." Devin was just about to replace the receiver when Glen exclaimed, "hold on! I have someone with me who would like to speak with you."

Devin's brow furrowed with confusion. "Someone for me? Who?"

Glen passed the phone to Cheryl. "Hello, Devin?" She enquired nervously.

"Cheryl?"

"Yes. Devin, can you let me in? I really need to see you."

Devin froze. Cheryl here? Wanting to come in? No, she couldn't. She couldn't. But how could he say that? What would she think? And why had she come? How had she come? She couldn't drive, had she walked all that way? Had James followed her? His mind raced with questions.

"Devin?" Cheryl queried at his silence.

"Whereabouts are you?" Devin asked, thinking, 'Maybe I can take her to the cabin in the grounds. Perhaps Grandfather won't see her then,' he hoped.

"Somewhere along the perimeter fence. Glen Brooks will give me a lift up to the gates before he goes back. Can you meet me there?"

"No, too far. I've hurt my ankle. Twisted it I think. Can't walk too well. Look drive up to the fence by the junction, and shine the headlights through. That'll be closer, and I'll head towards you and hand you the keys to the gate." He knew from that point his Grandfather would not see them. The trees would obscure his view.

"That's great, Devin. Thank you so much. I can't tell you how much I need to see you."

"You don't need to, Cherie. I've missed you so much."

"I love you, Devin. Take care huh?"

"I love you, too. See you soon. Bye now."

Devin replaced the receiver, his mind full of anxiety. He hoped his Grandfather wouldn't see anything with the telescope. And where was Jack?

Earlier he didn't think things could get any worse—now he wasn't so sure. What on earth would happen if James showed up too? Devin didn't want to think about that.

Chapter Twenty-five

If he were dead, why did he ache so much? That was Jack's first rational thought as he drifted back to consciousness.

He had to be in heaven.

Each time he lifted one eyelid startling light made him shut it again. He was blinded and his head thumped painfully. Gingerly he maneuvered himself into a position where he hurt less, though getting there was excruciating. He braved opening his eyes again, squinting to see what was the cause of such brightness.

Behind the light, Jack made out the shape of a vehicle, and realized the light was coming from that. So if he wasn't in heaven where was he?

Even so...what had happened that made him believe he may have been?

Had he been in an accident? Traffic was not allowed through Isaac Park, and Jack knew from the scents around him that he was outside, and lying on grass. So where was he?

Closing his eyes again he thought hard and with difficulty. Try as he might, he couldn't remember. It was so frustrating!

Maybe he was in the midst of a nightmare. If so he could wake himself out of it, unless it was something else. A premonition. He'd had them all his life, but he never quite got used to them. He had to stay with them till they were done, or he only saw half of what they were telling him.

To that end, Jack relaxed, allowing the images to flow through his mind. It was obviously a warning that he was going to have an accident. With eyes open he watched intently, learning how to avoid the calamity of being injured when the accident started to occur.

The premonition involved someone else with an unusual gait as though they had injured a foot.

Jack watched, eyes squinting towards the bright lights as the silhouette of a man came closer and suddenly, Jack recognized him.

It was Devin!

Jack tried calling out, but nothing happened, his throat pained him, no sound would come. Why? Of course it was a premonition!

No it wasn't!

Swiftly, everything came crashing in on him. This was no premonition! It was real, it had happened! God, how he wished he had been shown this one in advance! Before him rolled the whole event, the night away, the horses, Sherri... The storm! Oh no, the storm! Sherri, where was she? Oh God! He would die if anything had happened to her!

"Devin! Have you found Jack?" The sudden sound of Sherri's voice filled Jack with joy. He looked for her, but could see nothing beyond those lights. What were they from anyway?

"Eh?" Devin sounded puzzled.

"Hello you in there? I was looking for Jack. Remember? Did he come back?" Sherri smiled indulgently wondering if like her, Devin had lost his hard hat and hit his head after the mares had bolted.

"Jack?" Devin seemed puzzled and distracted she noticed. He kept glancing toward the railings. And what was that car doing there?

"Yes, Jack. You know? Your brother?"

Sherri's heart began to thud erratically. Was Jack injured so badly that Devin had called the paramedics? Or...no...Sherri shook her head slowly, wincing at a pain in her neck, she mustn't think like that…

"Sorry, I don't know where he is, Sherri." Devin told her and his voice sounded vague, and strained.

"What is it, what's wrong?" Sherri was bewildered now. Suddenly she noticed someone had alighted from the car and was coming toward the railings, and from their silhouette, it looked like a woman. Who on earth was it?

Sherri watched as Devin reached through the railings to grasp the hands of the woman and heard the woman speaking his name.

"Who's that, Devin?" Sherri called following Devin to the railings.

She was surprised to see the other woman snatch her hands back and start to sob uncontrollably.

"Devin, what's happening? Tell me?" Sherri cried, "Who is this woman?" No sooner had she said it then did the other woman cry similarly, "who is this woman, Devin? Who is she?"

Cheryl could not believe what was happening. Devin was with another woman! No! He wouldn't, he wouldn't! Grief stricken, Cheryl sobbed. Were all men the same? She'd trusted Devin, thought he was different, but this woman…Cheryl's breath caught in her throat. The woman was beautiful…Cheryl gasped. How could she hope to compete with someone like that?

"It's not what you think, Cheryl," Devin had summed up the situation precisely, "this is a friend."

"Huh, you expect me to believe that? I trusted you Devin, I trusted you…" She sobbed harder and ran back toward the car burying her face against Glen's shoulder as he got out to see why she was so distressed.

"No!" Devin shouted, "You've got it wrong. Cheryl! This is Sherri Scott. Sherri is here with my brother. Believe me, Cheryl. I love you!"

Sherri smiled, Devin in love? Well that was a surprise. But this woman, why had she turned up here, and now of all times? And who was the guy with the car? Reaching Devin's side, Sherri touched his arm, "Care to fill me in?" she enquired softly.

"This is Cheryl." Devin answered.

"That, I'd gathered. Hello, Cheryl. I'm Sherilyn."

"Cheryl is coming inside."

"In here? Into the estate?" Sherri shot Devin a startled look that asked 'what about your Grandfather?' Surprised when he ignored her silent protest.

"Cheryl needs help, Sherri. I've got to let her in. Something is wrong. She wouldn't have come here otherwise."

Sherri took Devin's arm, turning him to face her. "What's the problem?" She asked.

"I don't know yet. But Cheryl's husband is abusive; I think she has run away from him or something, and came here to find me."

"Her husband?" Sherri queried.

"Yeah. Don't look so shocked. He doesn't deserve her. She is warm and caring. He is a bully and a monster. I love her, Sherri." He added, helplessly.

Sensing a story Sherri told him, "If she needs protection I might be able to find a way to get her husband off her back. I have connections. Would she speak to me?"

"Maybe. Not tonight. Right now, I want to take her to the cabin, let her talk, be with her. I'm worried about Jack though."

"I'm sure he's okay. Try not to worry." Sherri tried to smile. "Let me know when you find him, and if you need help. Cheryl and I will be at the cabin."

"How's your Grandfather? Did you check on him before you left?"

Indicating his ankle Devin answered, "Couldn't. Besides, no time. You left and then the phone rang. It was a guy from Star Spangles, and he had Cheryl with him. Sorry, I know no more than you do at this stage."

"Okay. Well, when I get back to the house I'll check on your Grandfather. If he saw any of this through the telescope, he's going to be frantic by now. Do you need any help with the gates before I go?"

Devin nodded, "I'd really appreciate that."

From where he lay, unseen in the long grass, Jack could only watch helplessly while Sherri opened the gates, waiting while one of the two people from the car entered. He couldn't understand who she was, or why his brother was allowing her in. More importantly he wondered how a stranger about the place would affect his Grandfather's stability

As the car turned, just a halo of light was left. From that, Jack could see his brother with two women at his side. The troubling thing was, they were now further away from where he lay, heading in the direction of the house until they separated, two toward the cabin, and one for the house.

Suddenly a shout rang out, and all three stopped dead. Jack moved quickly to see, and pain lanced through his spine! 'Oh no,' Jack groaned, 'what on earth have I done?'

Just how serious were his injuries?

Chapter Twenty-six

Driving recklessly, James swung the car around. 'If Cherry had gone this way' he reasoned, 'I would have spotted her by now'. Bringing the car to a sudden, screeching halt, James thrummed the steering wheel with his fingertips, peering out through the windshield, looking for any movement that couldn't be the wind. It was difficult. The storm, though long gone, had left turmoil in its wake, trees creaked in the slightest breath of wind, and there was something eerie about the night. Something sinister, James couldn't quite put his finger on it, but turning off the engine, and winding down his window, he listened intently. Yes, that was it, everything was so still, so quiet, as if it awaited something, the calm before the storm?

Not a creature stirred. That's what it was! Of course, even after so much rain, his headlights would have picked out a myriad of moths dancing on the beam, but this time there was nothing, not a moth in sight.

James opened the door, and got out of the car. Even the air felt ominous, if that was the right word for it and James frowned. He'd experienced something like this before, but where? When?

Racking his mind, he tried to remember, when suddenly a rush of air swept by causing him concern. James reached for the handle of his car, fear rippling through him, as the car moved out of reach and his body was sucked and whipped back and forth crashing between metal and something ferocious that had no substance.

With all his might, James fought to reach the handle, wrenching the door open just wide enough to slither inside. He sat panting for breath for several seconds, aware that the treacherous wind buffeted his car sideways off the road.

Suddenly James knew, he should always have known, should never have forgotten, but it had been buried long ago, the experience, the horrible, nauseating experience of his family losing everything that they'd owned to the spiraling twister that picked up and carried everything away in its wake.

Turning on the ignition, James put the car into first, second, third, forth, fifth gear and accelerated forward, trying to outrun the approaching twister, hoping he could find some shelter where he would be safe.

His first and foremost thought was the estate, there had to be somewhere there, somewhere he could hide. The building was sturdy, hundreds of years old, so maybe it would have a large basement where he could stay.

A memory flitted through his mind and he was as a child again. Hearing his mother scream, the cry of his sister, his father trying to protect his family, shielding them with his body, even though the bunker was reasonably sound. And then the horror, as the departing twister revealed the calamity that was once their farm. There was nothing. Even the debris of the collapsed buildings had gone, leaving only wind-tousled grass for miles upon miles and not a building or a fence in sight. He'd only have been a toddler, so he had suppressed the memory, now the experience might save his life.

Reaching the perimeter fence, James stopped the car. He knew the gates were locked, and the vertical railings would be difficult to climb. Here, some of the railings were criss-crossed with horizontal bars, James didn't really know why. All he knew, as he started to climb, was that if he had to make a choice between the barbed spikes at the top of the fence and the oncoming twister, then simply, there was no contest.

Placing each hand between the spikes, James carefully maneuvered his body to straddle them, mindfully climbing over, and bit by bit, sliding himself head first down the bars on the other side. Heart in his mouth, he found himself suspended as sweat broke out on his brow, and between the spikes his boots became wedged, so that he could go neither up nor down. To yank hard, and pull off the boots, he would force his body down faster than anticipated, maybe cracking his skull on the hard ground beneath, but once again, the thought of the chasing wind, which was already beginning to suck and pull at his clothing, was enough to make him take the risk.

Wiggling his feet this way and that, James loosened his boots, then with a mighty pull on his arms he slid further down the bars for mere seconds, his legs somersaulting over his back and James screamed as his spine was bent backward. He let go of the bars at the same moment, allowing his body to fall sideways but in so doing, his head came down with a resounding crack against the hard gravel path that ran the length of the perimeter fence.

Holding his throbbing head in his hands, James scrambled to his feet. There was no time for delaying, the twister was hot on his heels, and James ran dazed and disorientated towards the big house.

* * *

His intention had been to try to get home but the buffeting wind that suddenly raced in from nowhere terrified Glen. The steering wheel was being ripped from his hands. Switching off the engine, Glen alighted from the car and called to the three people inside the estate, louder and louder until they heard him and came back to see what he wanted.

"Could I stay here?" he yelled, unsure. Their mannerism spoke of friendliness but Glen was given the impression that just the arrival of someone they did know had annoyed them enough.

Sherri looked at Devin, and Glen noticed the hesitation to agree. "I don't want to sit out here in my car, nor attempt the road," he shouted over the roar of the wind, "I'll not be any bother. It's a big house, I'm sure I could find some lonely wing some place where I'll be out of your way."

Reluctantly, Devin agreed. What else was he to do? Everything was going horribly wrong, and they hadn't even found Jack or the horses yet. "Yes. Come in. You're right. It is a big house. There will be plenty of room. Do you want to bring your car inside? You could drive us up to the house, it'll save the leg if nothing else," he had to shout to be heard over the roar of the wind.

Glen smiled, "Of course, hold on." He struggled to return to the vehicle, swung it back around then opened the door for Devin and Cheryl, expecting Sherri to follow, surprised when she cried, "did you hear that?"

"What?" Three voices chorused together.

"Over there, someone cried out. It must be Jack!" Sherri started running.

Undecided, Glen looked at his companions. "Want me to go with her?"

"It might be James!" Cheryl cried anxiously burying her face into Devin's chest. "He must have followed me!"

"No," Devin told Glen tapping him on the shoulder, "take us up to the house, and then you can come back if you want to."

"I do want to. If someone is injured they'll need the car to bring them to safety." Glen revved the engine, drove forward and seconds later his tires were sending gravel flying outside the house and he was helping his passengers out. "What's your friend's name?" He shouted above the sound of the wind and the roar of the engine with a nod of his head in the direction Sherri had gone.

"Sherri." Devin called back, as Cheryl helped him up the steps to the house.

Moments later, Glen reversed the car, turned and sped back the way he'd come just as the sting of the Almighty thundered into the estate.

* * *

James stilled himself to listen. Someone was coming. Though his head throbbed, and the wind howled behind him, clearly he could hear that the sound of staggered footsteps upon the gravel drive leading from the house exceeded the pounding in his head. Peering from behind a tree, James watched the approach of the person. It wasn't easy to see, and with the wind bending the shrubbery this way and that, James could not get a clear view, but from out of the sound of the howling wind, came a shout, a female voice! She must have heard him scream and had mistaken him for someone else.

James gasped, it didn't sound like Cherry but then the wind whipped away her voice the moment it was borne and besides, what other woman would be there? James felt the hope and the fury rise up inside him like a tidal wave, she was calling to someone, someone called Jack. Blind rage filled James, and too late, James remembered his gun, left behind in his car in his hurry to flee from the wind, yet there she was, right before him, and he wouldn't get another chance this good. Heat fused James's body, an erotic sensation that he associated with only two things, sex and murder. Both fuelled his body to a height that he could not resist, and, he sneered, now he could have both, one after the other and as the footsteps came closer James clenched his fists and held his breath, waiting.

Chapter Twenty-seven

The howling wind was terrifying and Sherri knew that she was in a perilous situation, but she was sure that Jack was close, and this lessened the fear a little.

Stopping to listen intently, Sherri held onto a tree for support as the outer blast of the oncoming twister buffeted her body this way and that. She heard a noise, one that sounded like someone else was in the grounds and looking back saw Glen was following on foot but the sound hadn't been made by him even though he was calling to her, "Sherri wait up. You forgot your flashlight."

Sherri slowed looking around her wildly, convinced that someone else approached from the other direction.

Mistaking the name Glen shouted from Sherri to Cherry James heard the anxious warning and was overjoyed. It was her! It was really her, but he'd have to be quick, he'd have to be fast, no time now for rape, he'd have to strangle her quickly before the other had a chance to reach them. James was jubilant, at least she was closer to him than her lover, and in this howling wind he wouldn't hear her struggle. By the time the guy reached her it would be too late and he, James would be waiting…when her lover caught up…he too would die.

Everything seemed to come together at once, James, Sherri… the tornado. For as Sherri fought away the whipping leaves from her face and shielded her eyes from the sting of the hail she felt something pulling her hair, forcing her backward and as a hand clamped over her mouth a menacing voice sounded in her ear, "Got you! You bitch!"

"Oh no! Oh God, it's Baxter!" Sherri's mind screamed and she struggled with all her might.

From his vantage point in the tall grass Jack watched the scene unfold just yards in front of him and willed himself to reach out and seize an extremely lethal shard of shattered wood intending to lunge it at Sherri's attacker when suddenly the ferocious wind snatched it from his hand and catapulted it straight into the attacker's back. Stunned Jack watched it sink through flesh and shatter bone as if controlled by some higher source.

As Sherri struggled James suddenly felt an erotic sensation of another kind, one that seared his back, sending his legs into jellied spasms as the heat from his blood pounded through the open wound exposing his spine.

"What the…" James spluttered, trying to turn around to see. Suddenly, the whole night was filled with a terrible sound, the deathly, churning, ear-splitting savagery of a ferocious wind. For mere seconds, James's whole life ran before him, like some deliciously slow tapestry passing before his eyes. A whole lifetime of events mapped out in front of him, and James fought hard against the pull of death. No! He would not let it kill him, whatever it was. His hands reached around and felt the shard of wood sticking out of his back but he was strong, he could survive. James fought back unwilling to die when suddenly he felt his whole body transcend time pulled up and away, sucked beyond the pain of one horrific nightmare, into another more deadly than that.

With grazed and bloodied hands, Jack crawled toward Sherri, standing speechless and shaking beside a tree a few yards away. She noticed him seconds before he too was whipped away from the earth, leaving Sherri far behind screaming his name.

The phenomenon was mind blowing. Jack had never felt anything like it in his life. The sound of it was thunderous, and his body spun around and around as though he was in a giant whirlpool. His clothes twisted tightly around him as the twister took him up and up and palpitated his entire body, attempting to wring the very life from him.

* * *

At the time, Sherri could not have explained it had she of wanted to do. Back at the house however, and after a stiff drink she was able to tell a concerned Devin and Cheryl just what had happened.

Shakily holding the glass of amber liquid in her hands, Sherri searched their faces, wide eyed, willing them to understand. "It was awful," she ventured at last, "there was this man, he called me a bitch…he tried to kill me…but then, then…"

"What happened, Sherri? Go on." Devin prompted gently.

"It sucked him away. Oh God, Devin, it was awful!"

"It was a twister, Sherri. You did know that didn't you?"

Sherri nodded. "Yes. I realize that now, but at the time, no, it came on so sudden. It was very windy, but then suddenly…I've never felt anything like it! Oh my God, Devin, what if he's…I couldn't bear it if I lost Jack."

"Jack?" Both Devin and Cheryl said together.

Eyes wide, Sherri stared at them. "Yes, Jack. The twister snatched him away. Haven't you heard a word I've said?" She wailed accusingly.

"Yes, but…you were talking about some stranger, some guy that tried to kill you. Where does Jack fit into all of this?"

"He was there too!" Sherri cried.

"Then you found him!" Devin exclaimed.

Cheryl was looking from one to the other, not understanding what was going on.

"Yes! This man had his hands around my throat. Was trying to strangle me, and then Jack appeared and everything went horribly wrong. Oh God, Devin it was awful!" Sherri buried her face into her hands and sobbed.

"So who was the other guy? Oh my God, it wasn't Glen was it?" Devin asked then immediately disregarded that thought, "no, he wouldn't. I mean I realize we have only just met him, but why would he want to kill you? Besides, he escorted you back to the house, so forget I said that. Sherri, is there any chance that you can describe the guy that attacked you?"

"He came out of nowhere." Sherri replied thoughtfully, "he was big, tough, heavy voice. He was strong too, no way I could get out of his grasp."

As she spoke, Cheryl was remembering what that felt like.

"Did Glen see anything?"

"Doubt it. He was around the corner. I didn't even know he was coming after me until he shouted for me to wait up."

Devin was thoughtful. "Did Glen call you by name?"

One step ahead of him, Cheryl gasped, "oh my God! Devin, no!"

"What?" Sherri looked from one to other of them, "what's wrong?"

Gravely, Devin told her, "I was wondering if Cheryl's husband had gotten inside the estate. If so, when Glen shouted your name, it's possible with all the noise the wind was making, it might have sounded like Cherry instead of Sherri and you do look alike. Would be an easy mistake."

Wide eyed, Cheryl whispered hoarsely, "That's it. It's got to be. It was clearly a case of mistaken identity and with all the commotion, James truly believed that Sherri was me out there!"

Devin nodded, "Yes," he told her, "it does seem that way. Do you know what happened to the fellow, Sherri?"

"I told you! The wind took him!"

"No, you said it took Jack."

"It took them both. The attacker first, Jack after. It should have taken me too, but somehow it just breezed past, threw me to the ground, but nothing more. Thank God!"

"Yes, thank God you're all right. Let's hope Jack is too. As to James, if it is him, he deserves to be dead!" Devin stated aggressively.

"I wouldn't get that lucky." Cheryl whispered, with tears falling down her cheeks. "Oh Devin, will I never be free of him?"

Devin turned to her enfolding her in his arms, "Don't worry, my love. Even if he has survived the twister, Sherri is a journalist and she told me earlier she might be able to find someone who can help you. Look, don't worry, whatever happens, I promise you, Cherie, James will never hurt you again. But until we know where he is, you keep close to me, okay? Glen can look after himself. He'll find where the lounge is, the bathroom, bedroom etcetera. He's had a nasty shock but he'll be okay."

Cheryl held Devin tightly, looked on by Sherri, wishing she could be in Jack's arms that way. The thought brought forth a fresh flood of tears. "I have to find him Devin. Jack, I mean, and you can't walk far with that ankle, but I don't want to be out there with that crazy guy either. Can you suggest anything?"

"Yes, I think you should stay here. No one is safe outside in that wind."

"No, Devin you didn't hear me. I *have* to find him."

"Sherri believe me I know that, but it's not something anyone can do right now. Can't you hear it? The wind hasn't calmed any. Maybe there's more than one twister. Good job this old house is sturdy or we too would have been swept away by now. Look, I think we should try to get help as soon as possible, I will call someone, let them know the house is occupied. In the meantime, if you want to do something constructive, you can check on Grandfather."

"Grandfather!" Sherri gasped. "Oh my God, with everything that's happened he's been the last person on my mind. I'll go at once and call down if I need anything."

Swiftly mounting the stairs two at a time Sherri stilled to listen when a sound caught her attention and she turned to look back down the stairs, stunned when she saw the object of her visit from upstairs now tugging open the front door and stepping outside.

"No! Grandfather!" Sherri turned and raced back down the steps yanking open the door only to find the old man was nowhere to be seen. "Devin!" She screamed slamming the door shut and rushing back into the lounge, "He's gone...outside..."

"Who's gone outside?" Devin cried hobbling to her side, his eyes filling with anxiety.

"Grandfather." Sherri cried, "I just saw him leave. I was half way upstairs when I heard a noise and I saw him pulling open the door to go outside. By the time I got back downstairs to look for him he'd vanished! Oh, Devin! The wind must have taken him also!"

"No!" Devin hopped toward one of the shuttered windows, peering through the slats to see outside. "I can't see through!" he cried, hurrying out into the hall. Sherri helped him yank open the front door and both surveyed as much of the area as possible before being forced to slam the door shut again on the crazy buffeting wind.

"I'll find him!" Sherri made the decision, "you'll see. Don't worry. I'll find them both." Before Devin could grab her she'd pulled open the door and stepped outside, slamming it closed behind her.

By the time Devin had pulled it open again and peered outside Sherri had gone, caught up in a blast of wind that had taken her off her feet the moment she had stepped outside.

Chapter Twenty-eight

The Almighty gathered momentum, speeding out across the estate, encompassing half the area in its wake, and collected everything within itself, uprooting trees, old brickwork, ornaments and gravel upon the drive, its hungry unrelenting appetite knowing no bounds, swallowing everything in its path.

Sherri was thrown and tossed about by the ferocious wind unable to grasp hold of anything as she hurtled by. All manner of debris was thrown at her and she was petrified for Grandfather. Why had he left the house? It didn't make sense. A house full of strangers might have terrified him but surely, he had known about the storm? If she found it difficult to stand, how would he fare, a frail old man?

Forced around a corner Sherri frantically reached out for the ivy growing upon the house walls and held on tight. Leaves ripped in her hands, the entwined branches coming away in her grasp like bits of dried paper. That was no good, as fast as she took a handful it broke away. Sherri fought to stand but the wind knocked her from her feet then lifted and carried her in its wake until it smashed her against the house wall.

Miraculously she was thrown into a crevice just large enough for her to scramble into as the wind whizzed past her.

She could see now, well as much as that was possible through the debris thundering past. Across the way, maybe a hundred yards or so she could see a building and guessed it to be the cabin. It was sturdy and surrounded by shrubs and there was a light standing in its window. If Grandfather, had been swept that way, perhaps he had made it to the cabin and was taking refuge there.

Inch by inch and using shrubs to help her Sherri edged her way around the outer extremities of the tornado. The wind tore at her face and tugged away the hand she held to her brow to protect her eyes. It was sheer horror just trying to make her way around the buffeting wind.

The hundred yards seemed like a hundred miles, but finally Sherri made it to the cabin, feeling her way around its sides until she found the door, then trying the handle and shoving, as the wind literally forced her inside.

'Its not Grandfather then.' Was Sherri's first thought as she fell inside the cabin. Had it of been he would surely have fastened all the locks, unless he'd been too injured to do so. However, a quick perusal of the cabin told her that the Grandfather was not there. In fact no one was. She was alone in the cabin. The lamp had obviously been placed there in preparation for Devin's overnight stay.

Though she had everything to occupy her and keep her at the cabin until the storm abated Sherri didn't dare. If the twister swept by, the cabin could be taken up into the heavens like a pile of matchsticks and would offer her no protection at all. No, wherever Jack and the Grandfather were they weren't dumb enough to come to the cabin as she had been.

However, the first thing that Sherri heard as she attempted to tug open the wooden door was the whizzing sound of a ricochet, and then another and another. "Gunshot?" Sherri queried. Yet it didn't sound like gunshot, more like something held taught and released, a high-pitched pinging sound that whistled above the thunderous cry of the raging wind.

Slamming the door shut, Sherri leaned against it. What was that sound?

She'd never heard anything like it. She covered her ears, as through the thick walls of the cabin it sounded crystal clear and dangerously close. She thought she heard a muffled scream, gone in an instant, snatched away by the ferocious wind, and when nothing more came she hoped she'd imagined it. Still the sounds of the ricochet had her diving for cover beneath a table. There she remained until the strange noises ebbed away, daring only to crawl out when she could hear them no more.

Finally, leaving her place on the floor, Sherri scrambled to the window, and gasped as the sight beyond leapt at her like a viper!

With the sky heralding the dawn streaks of brilliant hues of pink and gold could be seen through an almost open void. Where once had stood the old oak trees, now the twisters had ripped apart the ground, and huge gaping holes were the only mark left of the trees that had once stood there, their snapped and fleshy roots exposed to the oncoming daylight. If such an evil wind could rip apart such robust trees, what chance did Jack and Grandfather have?

Tugging open the door Sherri summoned her courage to step outside. With one twister past and another bearing down on her, she began to run fearing for her life with every step.

Her breath rasped in her throat as she dared to look back to see the long column of dust bending like a blade of grass and hurting toward the cabin. In seconds one half of the cabin was ripped apart, and Sherri instinctively ducked as huge logs were thrown through the air like matchsticks.

They fell around her as she ran, some landing in front halting her progress. She careered around them praying for her life. When one missed her head by centimeters Sherri screamed, but she never stopped running.

From his vantage point by the drawing room window, Devin watched her go with his heart in his mouth. The twister was hot on her heels and he couldn't bear to look. He had to look!

There was something fantastic about the whole affair…the twister bearing down on her like some crazy thing throwing logs to halt her progress. Horrified, Devin could do nothing but watch.

As Sherri turned, the twister followed likewise… gaining…then suddenly like an answer to a prayer…the tornado was lifted above the ground and sucked back up to the sky.

From out of her eye corner Sherri saw it happen, and stopped amazed at the sight. Just like someone had picked it up from above, the column of dust debris fell as the funnel receded back to the storm clouds above. The reprieve was short lived, with the death of the one another was born, twirling from the sky to touchdown…it careered across the estate toward her and Sherri ran, harder than before…faster…faster…

Just because she could see the swirling dust didn't mean that's all there was of it. Sherri knew that wind like air, was invisible and she was all too aware that the tornado was right behind her, propelling her forward, though the debris was some way behind. Getting out of its path was difficult, and there was nowhere to hide. With her sides aching…her mouth parched, Sherri had a sudden thought of those cartoons where an animal is running straight ahead beneath a falling telegraph pole and she'd scream, 'go sideways! Go sideways!'

That thought saved her life. Realizing that the twister wasn't literally after her… just happened to be going her way Sherri careered off to the right sweeping in a wide circle, coming up behind it. She laughed at her stupidity, how ridiculous she must have looked from the house running in the path of the tornado, having it chase her. How easy it would have been to have changed direction earlier and avoided the deathly demon as it hurtled behind.

Looking around just to be certain Sherri noted with satisfaction that there were no more tornados and then she remembered what she had to do. Find Jack that was the most important thing then find Grandfather, and then the horses. Whatever had become of that other man she didn't know, she just hoped she didn't find him first.

With Sherri and the tornado out of sight, Devin rested his forehead against the cool glass of the window, and casting his eyes heavenwards, he prayed, as he had never prayed before. 'Please let Grandfather and Jack be alive'.

Then he noted with raw irony, the heavens star studded and twinkling in the remnants of a night sky and he told himself raggedly, "Well Devin, you did it. You certainly did it. For if nothing else, this certainly has been a star spangled nightmare." And he didn't know whether to laugh or cry.

Chapter Twenty-nine

Jack, lying back against the downy earth, enjoyed his view of the sky. It was an intense shade of blue, with fluffy white clouds, and Jack derived immense pleasure from the sight of it. Overhead, from time to time, a bird would soar, its outstretched wings gliding in effortless flight.

For how long he had been unconscious he did not know. Neither did he know how far the raging wind had taken him. The spiraling, crazy wind had been suffocating, terrifying, before ejecting him earthbound with such force that he was sure that he would die.

Reliving the entire episode in his mind, he realized that nothing would ever compare to such an experience, and that he had lived to tell the tale at all, was indeed a miracle. But he had not entirely survived it unscathed. This time he was certain his back had been broken. When he had fallen from the horse, he had at least felt pain. Now there was nothing.

Tears filled Jack's eyes. The weekend surprise had been ruined. And nothing would ever be the same again. He'd spend the rest of his days in a wheelchair. Housebound just as his Grandfather had been all these years. Jack knew it would drive him insane. He wished the tornado had killed him.

The sound of a twig snapping startled him, and he turned his eyes in its direction in time to find Sherri dropping to her knees at his side. She cradled him close, sobbing tears of relief and joy at finding him alive. "I'm here. It's all right. Everything is all right. Hush now."

Tears slid down Jack's cheeks as he foresaw moments like these slipping away forever. When Sherri discovered he was paralyzed, she would want nothing more to do with him. What good was half a man to a woman as beautiful as Sherri?

"Oh Baby, I've been so worried. I thought I'd lost you. Are you all right, Jack?" Sherri asked at last, pulling back a little to scan his face anxiously.

Jack couldn't reply.

"There was a storm." Sherri told him, "with tornados, three I think, one worse than the others."

Jack tried to speak. Nothing would come. He remembered earlier when he'd tried, he hadn't been able to speak then. He drew his brows together and tried again. Nothing.

"What's wrong, Jack? Something in your throat?"

Jack could only stare up at her helplessly. In his eyes, she read his fear, and bewilderment.

"Can't you speak, Jack?"

The sadness in his eyes followed by fresh tears gave her his answer.

"You must be in shock, Jack. Don't worry, I've heard of things like this." Sherri told him tenderly. "It's to be expected really. You've suffered so much in so short a time. We all have." She finished then seeing the question in his eyes she told him, "every one is fine. Don't worry. We all escaped unscathed." Sherri sensed now was not the time to tell him that his Grandfather was missing. "Look, you stay here. Don't try to move. I'll call an ambulance."

His eyes begged her not to, Sherri ignored them. She had to face facts that all was not right with Jack. He was deathly pale, might have internal injuries and she didn't like the way he was laying, all twisted and not seeming to notice. She refused to think on how serious his injuries might be.

"I promise, I'll be right back." She told him bending to kiss him. Jack watched her go. The moment she was out of sight, he had never felt so forlorn in all his life.

* * *

With the house full of people and the cabin too dangerous to take shelter in, the Grandfather had found his way to the stables and settled for the rest of the night on a pile of hay he had pulled from one of the two bales put there for the horses. He slept fitfully, believing that any moment someone would be holding a gun to his head, that the man who had threatened him these past twenty eight years had followed him to the estate and was about to kill him.

Worse still, and with this Grandfather really was incensed, Jack's girlfriend whom he had come to trust and care for had been lying to him. Coming down the stairs to investigate the commotion, he'd overhead Devin telling some strange woman that Sherri was a journalist! Grandfather had panicked and sought a place of hiding under the stairs until he could find a better place. Then when Sherri had mounted the stairs to check on him, he had fled for the door, yanking it open and surprised that he could but reasoning that adrenaline could move mountains when needed. Once outside though, his feet had been whipped away from under him and he'd been thrown along the drive by a pounding and relentless wind surging against his back.

He knew he couldn't stay in the stables, but was unsure what to do. If only he knew where Jack was. For he had witnessed the event with the aid of the telescope, a streak of lightening had sent the horses bolting and throwing their riders from their backs. He knew that Devin and Sherri were safe, not that he cared for the latter now, but what of Jack, where was he? Had he been injured...or worse...Grandfather shuddered...no he would know if Jack had been killed he was sure of it.

Well one thing was certain—While he had breath in his body he could at least look for his grandson, and then assuming all was well, he'd give him a piece of his mind for bringing such a woman into their lives! A journalist? Jack might just have well brought home the death squad!

Chapter Thirty

Weddings and children…Mountains and forests…
A joyful future
Devin and some woman… Jack and Sherri…
And Philippa…

Why Philippa? Grandfather's brow furrowed with confusion. He held on to the stable wall for support as the premonition ended. They always came over him suddenly without warning. This one had left him bewildered.

"That was a strange premonition… Can't understand why Philippa was in it…looked like she was wearing a wedding gown…" Grandfather pondered, "must be the first time one of my visions has left me in the dark. Oh well, no use worrying about it right now, I have to find somewhere else to hide."

Gingerly taking a few hesitant steps outside, Grandfather noticed all was clear and he set off, his intention to find one of the bunkers his grandson had spoken of weeks before.

However, as Grandfather was leaving the safety of the stables Sherri saw him, "Grandfather!" she yelled running toward him, "there you are!"

For a split second, he stood his ground and then with unbelievable agility he started running away from her shouting, "Leave me alone! I don't want to talk to you. Don't you people ever give up?"

Sherri stopped dead. 'He knows?' she asked herself, 'but how?' She ran after him begging him to stop, "Grandfather, please wait up, I'm not a threat to you, please believe me."

To her relief, he slowed down but the face that he turned to her was furious. "You're all alike!" He spat, "all of you. You creep into our lives earn our trust and then wham! You turn on us; well I won't tell you anything you hear? So you can tell your editor that coming here and getting to know me was a complete waste of time. Does Jack know what you do for a living? Yes, he must do, Devin knows. How would one know and not the other? Did Jack think I would talk to you and change my mind, tell the world what I know? Did he, did he! Well I won't, I won't ever tell, you hear me I won't ever tell!" He turned to run again and Sherri on the brink of running after him stopped dead. "Alright, Grandfather, just go back to the house. Devin is worried about you."

"What about you?"

"What do you mean?"

"There's no way I'm going back to the house if you're going to be there."

"Don't worry, Grandfather. I won't." She thought it best that she didn't tell him about Jack needing an ambulance and they hadn't established where James had gone to, so Grandfather might be in danger wandering about alone.

Grandfather stared at her a long, long time, and only when Sherri made the decision to start walking did she see the Grandfather do likewise, hesitantly back toward the house.

'He really is afraid of me. I wonder what happened to make him feel that way? Doubt I'll ever know now." Sherri headed toward the garage where her cell phone had been left in her car. Her heart felt like lead. All

212

her dreams for the perfect weekend had been shattered, and she realized with raw irony that the star spangled nightmare that had held such promise, held for her only one thing now, the nightmare of going back to square one, for surely after this the Grandfather would do everything in his power to keep Jack away from her.

* * *

Driving along the graveled drive to await the ambulance some minutes later, Sherri was shocked all over again at the devastation caused by the wind. Debris lay everywhere, and the cabin was standing precariously with one wall torn completely away, the roof suspended over nothing.

She slowed the car to look, then accelerated to put the view behind her. The storm had gone now and after she saw Jack into the ambulance she would leave the estate. It was unlikely she would ever come back again so what did it matter what sights she saw? Even so, as she rounded a corner out of sight from the house she recognized the clearing where only hours earlier she and Jack and Devin had galloped the horses. She could not prevent herself from stopping the car and getting out to walk around part of the trail, remembering how wonderful riding the horses had been.

As she walked, she looked about her, total devastation had befallen the area, and it was so sad to see all the gaping roots of the old oak trees that littered the grounds as if a chainsaw massacre of another kind had befallen them.

Walking back to her car, Sherri caught something with her shoe and tossed it onto some grass ahead of her. It was blue and white and stood out in the grass and bending to see what it was Sherri discovered Devin's pager at her feet. Turning it over in her hand, Sherri observed the few buttons and remembered the CB unit up at the house. She looked back that way and wondered if it might be possible to send a text message just to explain about Jack.

Devin had to know what had happened to his brother, the thing was, would the Grandfather answer the unit instead? She hoped not. She had no wish to distress him further. If she had Devin's new telephone number she would have used her cell phone to make contact. She looked the pager over. Some, she knew, just notified the owner that they needed to get to a phone and quick; others had a small screen for text messaging. Overjoyed, Sherri noticed this was so. Checking first that it was working, she entered her message "Jack injured. Have called ambulance. Awaiting its arrival at gates." She then waited in hopeful expectation of a reply. Soon the beeper sounded and vibrated in her hand and she read the incoming message.

"How bad is he?"

"Not good."

"Will he make it?"

Sherri had no answers. Her hands shook as she keyed in the message, "I hope so."

There was nothing after that. Sherri stared at the screen expecting something until she heard the bang of a heavy door. Shortly thereafter, Devin came across the lawn leaning on Cheryl for support.

"Grandfather told us what happened." He called the moment he got close enough. He grimaced, "You should hear him. I'm happy to get out of there! Jack will sure be glad he missed it at any rate." This made Sherri smile as Devin had hoped.

"I need to go back to Jack." Sherri told him. "Can you wait for the ambulance? You can sit in my car. Just send them out across the meadow."

"The meadow?"

"Ah huh. The tornado chucked him down right up against the boundary wall, another fraction and he'd been on top of those spikes. I'm really worried about him, Devin. He doesn't look right at all."

"He's lucky to be alive." Devin whispered. Sherri said nothing. She didn't want to go there, besides...from what she had seen...no...she couldn't let herself think that way...Jack would be all right...he was strong...once he was in hospital...he'd be fine, she reasoned. It was unthinkable he might die from his injuries. He'd survived, hadn't he? Still

Sherri faced the niggling truth of the few people that had experienced a twister and lived to tell the tale. Tears coursed down her cheeks. Angrily she brushed them away.

"Give him my love, Sherri," Devin told her attempting to pull her close. The news had terrified him.

"I will." Sherri replied giving Devin a quick hug before running back toward the meadow where she'd left Jack.

Watching her hurry across the lawn, Devin had a terrible feeling that he might never see his brother again.

Chapter Thirty-one

Due to a stranger's presence inside the house, the Grandfather had climbed the stairs with difficulty and had retired back to the observatory where he felt safest. The cat that Devin had spoken of had crept in during his absence and was washing itself under the window. Grandfather wandered over and looked out. From there he could see everything that was going on. With so much damage around the estate he had a clear view with the aid of the telescope and saw Devin and 'that other woman' walk to meet Sherri at the gate, speak awhile, then part. Grandfather set the sights on Sherri, wondering why she was coming back into the grounds and leaving the other two in her car.

He sighed heavily, and grumbled aloud, 'should have stayed at home. Should never have let them talk me into this. Bet the whole thing was planned. Have me stranded here and bring in people I've never met before…well…it won't happen…I'll stay up here. That's what I'll do!" He looked around the sparsely furnished room. There was an armchair and a swivel chair, a small table and a blanket box. Sherri had given him a thermos of tea the night before, he still had some left and there was a box of assorted biscuits and some fudge in a jar. Not a lot, but enough to keep him there for the day at least. He could always sneak down to the kitchen to re-stock when no one was around.

Satisfied, he hobbled to the door, sure he had seen a key inside the lock earlier. Yes, there was one. He extracted it from one side and turned it in the other, smiling smugly. "There, that'll keep them out." he chuckled, "think they can change my life do they? Well they'll see!"

He settled himself into the armchair. It was a little hard, he could have done with some cushions, but there were none. Scanning the room with eyes of distaste, his gaze settled upon the blanket box and he wondered what was inside.

The room was growing lighter all the time as the sun rose, but it was not enough to see clearly, and Grandfather dragged the lamp closer so he could see into the box. Lifting the lid, he found it full of blankets no less, but not just any old blankets. His first sight of them sent memories flooding his mind, and Grandfather stumbled backwards panting hard.

It had been years since he'd seen them, wasn't even aware Devin had them. Had assumed those blankets put together patchwork style by his dear wife, had been taken to charity shops with all her things about a year after she had passed away. Obviously his son's wife had stored them someplace out of sight then when she too had died Devin had looked after them.

Gingerly he reached inside, pulling the top blanket out, and returning to the chair he laid it across his lap gently stroking its softness. Memories were swift, thundering through him at random. Grandfather closed his eyes, and let them drift over him, taking him back...back...

* * *

It all begun with roses, the Horticultural show, the winner's celebration...walking home late at night...the murder...

Strange how one moment in time can change life forever...strange how one single item could set off a chain of events that will rule the lives of many.

If he'd never grown roses…If Horace hadn't gone running to the press…if Chas Baxter hadn't of issued his threat…

So many lives could have been spared the insecurities of simply living…

Suddenly the scene from yesteryear rolled before him as vivid as though it were happening all over again…

* * *

"Boo!"

Absorbed in tending his beloved roses, Grandfather Jack staggered back and glared at the youths that had crept up on him.

"Who are you? What do you want?"

Leaning over the fence one youth whispered savagely, "who am I? Chas Baxter's the name. I'm surprised you didn't know that, Jack!"

The name meant nothing to Jack and sensing trouble he hissed, "Leave me alone! Just go, get away from me. Just leave me alone!"

"And why would we want to do that?" With a sneer, Chas broke away from his companions and strode up and down, up and down idly pulling the heads from the roses and crushing them in his hands.

Tears rushed to Jack's eyes, and he forced them resolutely away. He would not let these creatures see how much they were hurting him. He would not. He would not!

"Such pretty flowers…she loves me, she loves me not, she loves me, she loves me not…" The youth ran out of flowers. His friends giggled as he cried, "she loves me NOT!" Reaching across the fence, the youth grabbed hold of Jack's checked shirt and yanked him forward until their faces almost touched.

"She loves me not old man! Why don't you have more flowers?" He asked savagely.

Over Jack's shoulder he saw more roses in a profusion of colors growing around the garden and Chas dropped Jack so quickly, that the elderly man almost lost his balance. Jubilant, the jean-clad youth leaped over the fence, his intention plain.

"NO!" Jack cried knowing the youth's intent. "Please!"

"Sorry, old man. Have to." The youth began tugging at the rose heads chanting. "She loves me…she loves me not…she loves me…she loves me not…Ah ha! SHE LOVES ME! And just because she does…" The youth took the rose and tucked it haphazardly into the breast pocket of Jack's shirt, "there you are old man, not only does she love me, but it's a red rose, a symbol of love, huh? Aren't you the lucky one?"

Cheeks wet from tears, Jack's gasped for breath.

"It's okay old man, you don't have to thank me. It's all part of the service." Chas Baxter walked back to the fence, but rather than leap over it as he had on the way in, he opened the gate, walked through and shut it demurely behind him as if it were the most precious thing in the world. Then suddenly he turned and glared at Jack who was standing with his head bowed beside his decimated roses, and shouted, "but of course! I'm forgetting you don't know what the service is, do you?"

Groaning with sorrow, Jack closed his eyes tightly refusing to look at the youth.

"You wouldn't be ignoring me now would you, old feller?" Chas jeered.

"I do believe he is." It was the first time one of the other youths had spoken, but with those few words, fear rippled through Jack.

Now the third one spoke, "Give him a smack, Chas." Laughter followed but no one moved and Jack found that fact relieved him only slightly.

"Let's see now, have you any more pretty flowers?" Jack looked up then, his eyes darting to the side of the house, wishing he had not done that the moment the gaze of the three youths followed, and instead of one leaping the fence as before, they all came over now, their intention plain.

"No. No! PLEASE!" Jack cried, staggering one or two steps and then falling to his knees, "what do you want with me!" "Please leave me alone! I'm no threat to you!"

Amazingly, Chas halted his companions. They turned back to the old man and laughed when they saw him there on the ground, his knees sunken into the damp earth of a rose bed, crushed flower heads and petals strewn around him.

"Well that's real nice to hear, ain't it guys? Because you know, Jack, it's a pity old Horace hadn't felt the same way."

Jack gazed up at the youths, his eyes asking questions his lips dared not.

"That's right Grandpa, old Horace knew too much, saw too much. And my Dad see, he wasn't too impressed with that…so…well, there was nothing else we could do…You do understand that don't you, Jack?"

Jack's mouth opened and closed, his lips forming a thin straight line as he forced back the tears and tremors that threatened to crumple him at their disgusting feet.

When the other two youths stepped off his property Jack hoped they were leaving, when the one named Chas yanked him to his feet and spat angrily, "Just you remember, plants can grow again, friends cannot. See how easy it is to crush a flower beneath one's feet? Just you remember, Grandpa we're watching you. Old Horace, well he ain't here now, he's pushing up daisies, or should I say roses. Well, whatever, just you remember we're watching you, and if you don't ever want to join your old buddy, you'll keep this buttoned okay!" The youth touched Jack's mouth with one long finger brushing the scent of roses across his lips.

"I'd rather die than be harassed by you!" Jack cried courageously, at the precise moment when a child's cry was heard from inside the house, quickly pursued by another sounding younger, hungrier.

"How about them, then? Grandchildren are they? Wouldn't want them following old Horace to an early grave would we?" Chas taunted maliciously.

Jack cowered beneath the glare. "No...no..." he whimpered hoarsely.

"Then just you stay quiet and everything will be..." Chas laughed, kicked a rose head with his toe and added, "dare I say, blooming good?" The three youths laughed in unison as Chas hurled the elderly man to the ground again as if touching him made him sick.

"Just remember Grandpa, what you saw remains in here!" The youth tapped Jack's forehead, "you tell no one, no friends, no reporters, and especially not the law, because you know why, old man? We'll be watching you. Wherever you go, whatever you do, know this...we'll ALWAYS be watching you!"

* * *

Twenty-eight years later...it still seemed like yesterday...and it had all begun with roses...

* * *

The ambulance sirens, blaring as they approached the estate, cut out when Devin unlocked the gates and pointed to where the paramedics needed to be. With his sprained ankle he couldn't drive, and Cheryl had never learned. They could only sit in the car watching the ambulance thunder across the grounds and out of sight.

"What now?" Cheryl asked, "are we to wait until they come back with your brother?"

Devin nodded. "I think that would be best."

"Do you think James is alive?" Cheryl asked aloud the thought that had been bugging her all morning.

"We need to make sure either way, Cherie. When the ambulance has gone perhaps Glen will help us look."

"You should go with your brother to the hospital. Besides, that ankle may be broken."

Devin shook his head. "Don't think so. Besides I'm not leaving you here alone until we find out what happened to your husband."

Cheryl fell silent. Deep down inside she hoped her husband was dead. Then she felt guilty about thinking such things. One should never wish another dead—it was the three monkeys thing, see no evil, hear no evil, speak no evil, the problem being she had both seen and heard it from James for years, so why couldn't she speak like him too?

As they sat there in silence, each with their own thoughts, a bright flashing light reflected in the rear view mirror and both watched it edge closer. Devin expected it to stop, and had his hand on the door catch to open when it went sailing past and the sirens begun blaring again. Out of the back window they caught sight of Sherri's anxious face, and while it was good to know his brother wasn't alone, Devin was exceedingly concerned as to the state of his health. Ambulances only used their sirens in an emergency.

"You know we're forgetting something, don't you?" Cheryl stated when the ambulance was out of sight. Devin turned to her, his eyes asking questions.

"We should call the police. James tried to kill Sherri and if he's alive and uninjured he may try to kill us too. Look, let's go back to the house. Glen will be leaving soon, and so far he's the only able bodied one among us. Well, except me of course, but I can't drive, so that leaves me at a certain disadvantage when it comes to getting out of this place."

"I don't intend to get out of here, Cheryl." Devin told her, "it belongs to me now."

Cheryl gasped. "You've bought it?"

"Yes."

"It's a big place for one, isn't it? Or are your family moving in?"

"They might do. Even so, it's still a big place for three, even four if Sherri joins us. Be nice for five though, maybe even six, seven or eight." Devin's eyes were brimming with mischief.

"What are you getting at, Mr. Richardson?" Cheryl asked perplexed.

"Mr. Richardson? Mm, let me see now. I guess, what I'm getting at is hoping you'll agree to being Mrs. Richardson and move in here with me. We can fill it with children. What do you say, my Cherie."

"Oh Devin!" Cheryl wrapped her arms around his neck and hugged him tightly, "I'd love to!"

Strange, how out of a tragedy could come such joy. And Devin had never felt happier…it was only his brother's health that bothered him now. Oh and his Grandfather…Devin groaned, and Cheryl pulled back. "What's wrong, my love?" She asked him with concern.

"In a word…Grandfather. He will take some getting used to, Cheryl. And he won't make it easy for you. I'd really like my family to leave New York and come here to live. It's a big place so surely all these people can find something to occupy their time? I have a feeling Sherri might write books. She could write one about this weekend and call it Star Spangled Night Mare." Devin said ruefully, "while Jack will likely grow exotic plants. Is there anything you have ever wanted to do and haven't had the opportunity for, my love?"

"The only thing I have ever wanted was to be someone's mom."

Devin squeezed her hand. "Then that's easily done. How many should we have? Three, four…six…eight!"

Cheryl laughed, "Two would be nice…maybe three…even one. Oh, Devin to have a family is all I've ever wanted. But what will you do though?"

Devin cocked his head and winked. Cheryl slapped his arm, "I don't mean that! I mean for a living, dork!"

Devin laughed telling her, "Well, I did think of becoming a guide for the caves and subterranean levels hereabouts. I know the Tourist Board is always looking for good scouts that know the ropes, like I do. I could do that, or I'll think of something else. We'll be all right for money though, so long as Tom and Star Spangles…" he paused slapping a hand to his mouth, "the horses! Cheryl, where are the horses? Quick, help me out of here, will you? We have to go look for them. They could be anywhere and the horse box will be arriving to collect them soon!"

All kinds of scenarios flashed through Devin's mind. Horses injured, broken legs, necks, taken by the twister, killed, suffering…he had to find them. If none of those things had happened, they would still be tacked up, reins may have been caught in branches, stirrups caught in bushes. The poor things would be petrified. He chided himself for not thinking of them sooner…then chided some more when he realized that he had done…when Glen had first driven in.

As if reading his mind Cheryl asked him, "surely the horses are Glen's responsibility? He'd be out looking for them wouldn't he?"

"Not if he was lead to believe they were stabled, no. Cheryl, this is my responsibility, I have to find them…but you are right about one thing, Glen could be helping." They had walked up to the house as they chatted and Devin suggested, "You go in and find him I'll wait out here. If you see my Grandfather don't say anything about Jack, okay?" Devin told her leaning against the house wall for support.

Mounting the steps two at a time Cheryl called back cheerfully, "Okay. I'll be right back."

"Wait! On second thoughts, I should really tell Grandfather about Jack."

It was a daunting thought, everything had gone wrong and his Grandfather would gloat that he'd been right about that all along.

Chapter Thirty-two

"We were always together, Gloria and me," Grandfather told the cat as he fondled its ears, "we did everything together, emigrated from Britain together, raised our son, saw him married, looked forward to grandchildren. You ever had children?" He asked the cat. It ignored him, blissfully content on his lap, purring loudly. Grandfather smiled and continued his narrative. "We had two special friends Horace and Philippa. They helped Gloria settle into life in America. Met them at a flower show and invited them back for coffee. Got on like a house on fire, we did. Were soon seeing one another almost every day.

Horace grew roses too and he and I spent hours cultivating them. And we loved walking. All four of us took long walks together which was as well because Horace had packed on the pounds since his redundancy from the Electronics Industry and the exercise kept him fit. Kept us all fit." For a few moments Grandfather fell silent reminiscing on those days of sightseeing with his wife and their friends.

"They got by. Philippa cleaned offices after hours. Horace didn't like her being the breadwinner...but..." Grandfather shrugged, "needs must.

Horace tried to find work...but...well, no one wants an old guy when there are all these new ones cramming for employment. The world is a strange place, puss. People think they save money employing kids and teaching them the ropes. Sooner do that than employ an older guy who knows what he's doing and doesn't need any training. Society is round the twist. Still...Horace soon adapted...grew his roses...enjoyed early retirement. Would have continued too...if only..." Grandfather fell silent and dabbed at his eyes. Even after all these years what happened to Horace never failed to move him.

"One evening after she'd finished work Philippa stayed at our house with Gloria. They loved to bake and wanted to try out a new recipe. That night they didn't come out for a walk with Horace and I...just as well really...

We saw something puss. Something I never want to see again. A man gunned down in cold blood." His eyes haunted, Grandfather shuddered. "Our wives wanted to call someone. A doctor...the police... we didn't know what to do...but I felt that we shouldn't involve the police. We were seen, you see. Those thugs saw us and I recognized one of them. We were terrified for our lives. We had to keep quiet. Maybe they'd leave us alone if we did. Besides...we'd run...and they didn't know where we lived...

Horace though, he felt differently, his father had been in the police force, see? Horace's morals were different to mine. He remembered how often his father had wished to get just one lead, just one break in an otherwise unfathomable case that would lead to conviction...and another criminal off the streets.

I begged Horace to reconsider. I told him things were different than they had been during his father's day. I tried to convince him that in the course of time the murderers would be found out, the case closed...the crime punishable in a court of law...so for us it was better to stay quiet...say nothing... We had our families to think of, for goodness sake...

I really thought I'd gotten through to Horace although with our varying views our friendship faltered. We often argued. Philippa and Gloria were caught in the middle, each defending her own husband...our friendship suffered...to the point that they didn't visit us anymore...and worse...when Gloria met either one of them while out shopping they avoided her. It upset her terribly.

One day...it all became too much..." Grandfather sobbed, tears openly streaming down his cheeks as he remembered. Through a voice thick with emotion he went on, "I found her... slumped in an armchair...she had been dead for hours...she didn't even live long enough to see the birth of our first grandchild." His throat ached with grief...and as it sensed his pain the cat snuggled against him. Grandfather hugged it to him, burying his wet face in the cat's fur until composed enough to speak again he went on; "nothing was ever the same after that...time moved on...baby Jack was born...two years later...Devin...

Horace remained as hostile as ever...but Philippa started talking to me again...I was both pleased and angry over that. I think she felt guilty about what she had done to Gloria...but it was too late...I forgave her in time...Philippa I mean...and we are close now...but...we'll they say time is a healer...but it's not...not a day goes by that I don't think about Gloria...I loved her you see...still do...always will..." A sob caught in Grandfather's throat. Still he went on, as if telling the cat his life story was important.

"Philippa told me that the murder was getting to Horace...he could no longer sit by and say nothing...I tried reasoning with him...he wouldn't hear a word I said...and he was furious with Philippa for telling me. I think he felt betrayed by that. In the end it was as though he'd decided even if the worse should happen, then at least his father would have been proud of him for trying to do what was right.

I was tending my roses when I heard. Philippa came running through the park with tears streaming down her face... sobbing uncontrollably...the police had been...the body of a man carrying identification of Horace Yzaguirre had been found in a pool of blood just off 34th Street. A man walking his dog had found it. Philippa was asked to identify the body...she'd just returned...it was Horace. Killed by the blade of a single knife to the throat. He'd not even had time to give evidence.

That was the bit that got to me...Horace hadn't even given evidence... How in God's name had the thugs known of Horace's intent to tell? Were they watching? Had they been watching these past two and a half years? Had they been expecting that one or both of us would go to the police? That's all I could think of...until the day thugs threatened me...they did, you know? They came right up to me in the garden one day...you don't want to know what they did." Jack sobbed remembering how the thugs had destroyed his beautiful roses. "And then...then...they threatened to harm the boys... our lives were never the same after that." Grandfather swallowed with difficulty...and sucked in his cheeks repeatedly in an attempt to force back a cry of anguish. He was silent for a time, continuing to stroke the cat drawing on its warm body for comfort. It seemed happy to be with him, and in that moment he was glad to have it there. Glad that he had told someone...let it go...at last...even if that someone was only a cat.

"Chas Baxter was his name. The thug, the one that threatened me, but it wasn't him that killed that man that day, that one was like him but older, they're related you know? And I keep news cuttings see? I've got a scrapbook. If I wanted to be like Horace I could go to the police and reveal everything, the unsolved crimes...the homicides...I know who's to blame...but...why should I? As long as I keep my mouth shut my family won't suffer...that's why I can't tell them see? That's why I could never tell anyone...but you...you're the first...and you won't tell anyone will you?" As if in response the cat sat up and stretched and rubbed its head beneath Grandfather's chin. He smiled.

"Oh they know bits, mainly through Philippa but they don't know about the relationship. No one does. The Baxter's think they're clever, but I know how it's done. If I wanted to I could spill the beans...but I never will not for anything. You know, when it came down to it, no matter what Horace felt about his father, about what was right and what was wrong, in the end it all boiled down to money. Horace didn't go straight to the police with what we had seen…no…he made arrangements to speak to a reporter. Huh." Grandfather laughed derisively, "probably envisaged the morning papers to reveal Baxter's arrest…instead…the exclusive that hit the press was that Horace's mutilated body had been discovered in an alley off 34th." Grandfather drew in a long ragged breath, "never trusted reporters since. Know why? Because I found out that the one meeting Horace had promised him thousands of dollars if his story was as good as Horace hinted. But when it came down to it…Horace had been deceived…that reporter was in no position to make such an offer…and he'd held such a big carrot before the donkey that Horace could not resist. My old friend died for that, puss. He died for a lie…and the greed that went with it. And now…I find there's a reporter in this house! Nothings changed. They're all the same! By her deception I've been sucked in just as Horace was. She abused my trust! I will never forgive her for that! Nor Jack." At the mention of his grandson Grandfather drew his brows together, "Jack. Where is Jack? It's been hours since I've seen him."

Frowning, the Grandfather picked up the cat, stood, put the cat onto his vacated seat and draping his wife's cozy blanket around his shoulders he went to sit behind the telescope. His intent was to use it to search the grounds for his eldest grandson.

Starting from the cabin, Grandfather swept the telescope slowly over the lawn to what had once been the woodland. Now the trees resembled a stack of fallen dominoes. Would take months to clear and plant new trees then years before it became woodland again. The odd bush remained standing some lying flat against the ground, their branches snapped, leaves ripped away…the Grandfather passed these by without a second glance.

He'd gone by two, maybe three bushes when he stopped. Froze… backtracked… something registered… possibly just the shape of a bush…he didn't know…he had to know!

Slowly moving the telescope back again, at first he encountered nothing, but as his heart continued to hammer in his chest, the

Grandfather returned to each spot, focusing the lens that bit sharper, that bit closer...there...something was there...suddenly he reeled back in shock...falling off the stool...laying on the hard wooden floor his terrified eyes staring straight up at the ceiling.

No!

Grandfather panted for breath and scrambled back to his seat. His hands trembled as he laid them upon the telescope. With one eye to the lens he looked again. Slowly, slowly he moved the telescope until he recognized the bush, gingerly he swept the sights over...it was an ear he noticed first. A little bloodied lobe peeking beneath a mop of dark hair...probably pierced by a thorn. A trickle of blood had been smudged from the ear to the...cheek...to the throat...

Grandfather paused, his body shaking as he panted for breath. Nausea...light-headedness...drifted over him in waves.

Swallowing hard, he moved the telescope, closing his eyes tightly before opening them again to see, mustering all his courage to do so. Chas Baxter's face peered out from the bush...his eyes fixed and staring toward the house...up toward the observatory...

Falling backwards off the stool, Grandfather screamed.

Chapter Thirty-three

In the nick of time the ambulance reached the hospital and under anesthetic Jack's injuries were dealt with. It was too soon to know if the four vertebrae he'd broken would prevent his legs from working, as one break was a hairs breadth from his spinal cord. It could not be established if it were swelling or something worse that caused his paralysis.

His speech was another matter. There was nothing physically wrong, more psychological. Doctors told Sherri that in their opinion the trauma Jack had suffered had contributed. Either that or perpetual screaming had strained the muscles in his voice box. All they could do was wait and see what his recovery would be. They gave her no indication how long it might take.

Secure in the knowledge that he was in safe hands, Sherri made her way back to the estate. She was well aware that with Devin's injured ankle, no matter what the Grandfather thought of her, he was stranded at the estate until someone could drive him back to New York. That he was unlikely to allow her to do that, well, Sherri decided she would cross that bridge when she came to it.

The estate was eerily quiet when a taxi dropped her off later that day. She decided to walk from the gates down the winding gravel drive up toward the house. The first thing she noticed was a horsebox, with Glen's car parked alongside it. There was no sign of life anywhere.

"Hello?" She called softly peering into the gloom of the hall as she pushed open the door to the house. "Anyone here?"

Silence.

Sherri entered, closing the door behind her with a soft click. She padded across the wooden floor of the entrance and peeped into the drawing room where everyone had been assembled earlier. It was empty.

"Devin?" Sherri called, walking from the drawing room to the lounge, "Cheryl?" she asked timidly unused to saying the woman's name, "you here?" Silence met her as she edged into the kitchen. The stove had gone out, and the kitchen was cold.

Just as she was deciding everyone must be out in the grounds, a strange sound came from far above her. She recognized the location immediately. The observatory!

Taking the stairs of the long winding staircase two at a time, Sherri made it to the top breathless. She ran down the hall to its end and started mounting the stairs leading up to the attic where the observatory was housed. She almost bumped into Devin as she rounded the final bend on the stairs.

"Ouch, who's that?" Devin turned, "Sherri!" He looked over her shoulder expecting to see his brother. When Jack did not appear, Devin's face fell. Briefly Sherri gave him the news, in turn Devin informed her, "It's Grandfather. He's locked himself in. He's incoherent. I'm so worried about him, Sherri!" He didn't say it, didn't need to, the alarm in his eyes told her he believed his Grandfather had had a heart attack.

"I've found this. Stand back." Sherri turned to see Glen coming from behind with a large baseball bat in his hand. It was obvious by the way he wielded it, as to his intentions. She and Devin stood aside as the first thwack hit the locked door. Again Glen hit it, and again...from inside the observatory came movement, then a voice, croaky at first rising to crescendo.

"Leave me alone! Go away!"

"Grandfather!" Devin yelled relieved to hear the old man speak, "let me in!"

"You alone?"

Devin motioned to his companions for silence. "Yes, Grandfather. Let me in."

"Where's Jack?"

Devin paused unsure of what to reveal. All kinds of thoughts rushed through his mind. If he said, 'downstairs,' Grandfather would want Jack to come up. If he said 'outside,' Grandfather would want Devin to go get him. If he said 'in hospital,' there might just be a chance that his Grandfather would come out of the room and ask to be taken to him. That chance was slim, as Grandfather hated strangers. There would be hundreds in a hospital.

Still it was a chance he had to take. "Jack's in the hospital, Grandfather."

"In hospital!" His Grandfather shrieked, "what happened to him?" Chas Baxter's face rose to mind.

"He fell off his horse." Devin didn't feel it was appropriate to reveal all that had befallen Jack.

"Oh, that's good then." The Grandfather sighed raggedly.

"Good?" Devin didn't follow. "How can it be good?" His Grandfather was pretty weird sometimes.

"Not that." Grandfather replied, "just good that Chas Baxter hasn't hurt him."

Sherri gasped, stifling the sound with a hand to her mouth. Her eyes asked questions her lips could not.

"Grandfather…Chas Baxter is miles away…" Devin began only to be shouted down by his Grandfather yelling, "No! He's not! He's not! He's outside…he's watching the house!"

Sherri was stunned.

Pitifully, Devin shook his head. "No, Grandfather…you're wrong. Baxter didn't follow us here…"

"Not Baxter! I said Chas Baxter! He did! I tell you. I've seen him! He's hiding in a hedge outside."

Devin frowned, "That doesn't make sense Granddad. Either it is or it isn't Baxter."

"Oh, come see for yourself!" The Grandfather replied irritably.

When Devin heard the key in the lock, he motioned for his friends to duck out of sight. Pushing open the door, Devin stepped inside. He was not surprised to hear his Grandfather lock it behind them.

"There." The Grandfather pointed indicating the telescope. "Look through that. Don't move it. Can you see him?" Devin peered into the telescope. He saw nothing at first, just a bush. He didn't really expect to see anything other than that. When he did, he too stumbled backward.

"It's not Baxter." He told his Grandfather.

"Of course not! It's Chas, his son. Anyway how would you know, you've never seen either of them!" The Grandfather cried accusingly.

'Either of them?' Now Devin knew his Grandfather had lost it. He was seeing his enemy in plural.

"Grandfather, it's decades since you've seen him. Photo fits don't come into it." Grandfather was about to argue, when Devin told him, "Besides, I know it isn't Baxter. It's someone else. Someone I know." Someone he'd rather not know. More to the point someone he'd rather Cheryl had never met.

"His name is James Sullivan. He's Cheryl's husband."

"Cheryl?"

"Sit down, Grandfather. There's something I need to tell you." Briefly he garbled the story of James, and Cheryl the woman he loved. Clearly, Grandfather was shocked. "You're having an affair with a married woman?"

"It's not like that, Grandfather…listen…I can't discuss this with you now. I have to warn Cheryl and call the police. James tried to kill Sherri last night."

"One less reporter in the world is no loss!" Grandfather spat. He followed Devin to the door intending to lock it behind his grandson before anyone else could intrude. Devin thought of that. As he turned the key in the lock he extracted it and placed it in his pocket. Grandfather's angry shout bellowed down the stairs, Devin ignored it.

Chapter Thirty-four

Letting the dust settle, Sherri waited till Devin, Cheryl and Glen had gone downstairs, before she turned the handle of the observatory door and opening it, she slipped inside. The Grandfather turned, his face ashen when he caught sight of who had entered the room.

"Get the hell out of here!" He launched striding purposefully toward her. For a split second Sherri felt afraid, then she stood her ground. "Grandfather, listen to me!" He stopped, his hand raised above her intending to strike. Slowly it fell to his side. Something in her eyes soothed him.

Turning his back on her he walked to the window. "Nothing you can say will make me change my mind about reporters, young lady." His voice sounded strained...weary.

"I'm not expecting it to." Sherri told him walking into the room. She motioned to the telescope, "Can I take a look?"

When he said nothing she placed her eye to the lens and after a few moments was able to distinguish the face in the bush. "Mm, I can see how you were fooled into thinking that was Chas Baxter."

The Grandfather looked stunned, "You know him?"

Sherri nodded, "Me and a whole lot of other unfortunates around New York." She paused thinking of something then began, "Grandfather…"

"No!"

"Grandfather, please?"

"No!"

"Please?"

"No, no, no!"

"Will you God damn let me speak!" Staring at Sherri, Grandfather placed his hands over his ears as she started to yell at him, "GRANDFATHER, LIKE IT OR NOT YOU HAVE TO KNOW THIS! IF CHAS BAXTER WAS INVOLVED IN THE HOMOCIDE YOU AND HORACE WITNESSED, YOU COULD HELP TO PUT HIM AWAY FOR A LONG, LONG TIME."

"THERE'S NO NEED TO SHOUT. I'M NOT DEAF!"

Sherri smiled. She hadn't stopped shouting when she'd noticed that the Grandfather had taken his hands from his ears.

"Grandfather, please. So many people are afraid of this man. The police have been trying to convict him for years. He always has an alibi. He's getting away with murder. Grandfather, you might be the only person who has ever witnessed that. You could be the only man to stop it happening to someone else."

Grandfather was shaking his head.

"Please!"

Still the Grandfather shook his head.

"Why not? I promise you'd get protection, your family also. All you have to do is pick him out in an identity parade. These days he doesn't even have to see you."

"It's not that."

"Then what is it?"

What he said stunned her. It also made a whole lot of sense. "We didn't see Chas Baxter kill anyone. It was his father that shot that poor man. Like two peas in a pod them two were… like twins. I've never seen Raymond since that day, but that's how they get away with everything in the city. They work together."

What a story! If only Sherri could dig it out. Of course, no wonder Chas had an alibi for every death in the city. Every death that lead back to him. They'd been fingering the wrong man. Chas was acting as a decoy. Their partnership was watertight. Everyone believed that Raymond Baxter had been dead for forty years. Long before the murder Grandfather had witnessed. So then if all those unfortunate deaths had been down to Raymond, who was supposed to be dead, then Chas would have an alibi, simply because he was where he said he was at any given time.

Foolproof…

Almost…

Suddenly Sherri realized the enormity of what she faced. Grandfather really was the only one that knew the truth. Why then, had Raymond Baxter spared Grandfather his life? Surely, the death of one more old man wouldn't weigh too heavily on his conscience?

As if he followed her train of thought Grandfather provided the answer. "It happened years ago…long before Chas was born…" Sherri turned and faced the old man wondering what more he was about to reveal. When he began to speak it was as if he was dredging up thoughts from long, long ago…

"I didn't always live in England. From time to time my mother sent me out here, to stay with my uncle. I found out years later that he was my father, my real father. They'd met when my father went to England on vacation." Grandfather's eyes glazed over, in remembrance. "When I left school my uncle…that is my father found me a job painting verandas. One of the houses belonged to a teacher, Ms Lucas she taught music, the piano. I used to stand under her window and listen when she gave private lessons before and after school. One night as I was listening to her play I heard a strange sound, and looking up I saw Baxter a young kid from the neighborhood leaving her house. I was surprised—he didn't seem the musical type. Then I saw him drop something, a purse. I knew then that he'd been stealing from the house. I gave chase, but lost him. Later the police arrested me for the theft. I'd been seen running from the house.

I tried telling them it wasn't me. But when they asked whom I couldn't say. As young as he was, Baxter was a bully, and I was frightened of him, I didn't dare tell.

Next day Baxter took me aside, he thanked me for saying nothing said I was a true friend. I didn't tell him that wasn't why I'd done it. Couldn't tell him he scared the hell out of me. I let him believe I'd saved his ass as a true friend would. He swore that day he owed me one. Promised on his life that at any time in the future if he could repay the gesture he would. I guess that day came the day I saw him kill a man. Though I'm not sure that he recognized me, how else do you explain why he spared my life? He took Horace's life, and ever since, his son has threatened me annually to remain silent."

"Then it's about time you stood up to him, Grandfather. If only for Horace's sake." What Sherri expected she didn't know, a fight perhaps, certainly not a slow nod of his head, his eyes clearing as understanding dawned. "Maybe you're right. A lot of people have died. And his son is a thug." Sherri noticed his gaze wasn't on her as he spoke, it had settled upon the photograph of his wife as though speaking to her.

"I saw something earlier…" The Grandfather surprised Sherri as he turned his gaze from the photo toward her. "You know Jack and I are alike, I take it?"

"The premonitions?" Sherri ventured.

The Grandfather nodded. "Yes. I saw something…"

"What?"

"It doesn't matter. Just know I saw the light…" His words trailed away and Sherri felt infinitely relieved that he would testify. The streets of New York City would be a safer place with Raymond Baxter and his son behind bars, "however…" He fell silent and attempting to prompt him Sherri felt sad when he flinched away from her touch, "it doesn't change the way I feel about reporters…nor the fact that you deceived me, young lady…it may take me a long, long time to forgive you for that, if ever."

238

Sherri smiled, "That's okay, Grandfather plenty of time. I plan on sticking around for a good few years yet."

"Well as long as you are, you can help me downstairs. And don't go getting any ideas, just you remember, any port in a storm will do...just because I need your help doesn't mean I like you." He told her gruffly.

Sherri smiled, any port in a storm? Yeah, right...

* * *

The soft sound of nickering caught Glen's attention as he walked through the grounds, searching for the horses. There they were, they'd seen him first and came trotting toward him. Glen spoke to them tenderly, reassuring them, as they rubbed their foreheads against his arm. They were skittish, any little sound causing them to look around wildly...Glen was aware these mares would need a long rest to recuperate from their ordeal before they could be hired out again. Maybe never...one rule of Star Spangles, all mares had to be placid of nature...well schooled...it were possible these three mares would never make the grade again...they would have to be sold or used for breeding.

It was a shame, and Glen cursed the fact that Devin should have known better than risk riding with reports of thunderstorms...still he reasoned, the man hadn't been around horses all his life and had a lot to learn. Glen decided he would need to educate Devin about horses.

Still, he should be thankful for small mercies. The mares though stressed, were unharmed, the same couldn't be said about Jack Richardson. Poor bugger would be in bed for weeks. He may walk again, but he'd never ride...the risk was too great...one more fall...and he may never walk again.

"Come ladies..." Glen took up the reins, turned and tugged. The mares followed meekly behind. They trusted him...but still they kept a wary eye on their surroundings...it would be a long time before they forgot what had happened to them and every time the wind blew they'd be off...running for their lives...

A sad fact but true...those mares would never be the same again.

Chapter Thirty-five

Four Months Later

Cheryl looked around her, as though seeing everything for the first time, "I never believed I would ever live here." She told the man at her side who still clutched the suitcases, one in either hand as he collected them out of the truck.

Cheryl reached for one. "Here let me help you, darling, I'll take these inside, and make us a cup of coffee."

Her husband's eyes twinkled. "Forget the coffee, Cheryl. My thirst is for other things." Cheryl's tinkling laughter echoed across the grounds, "Oh, Devin, really! Is that all you ever think about?"

"As it happens…" He laughed, dropping the cases, to sweep his wife up into his arms, "I love you Cheryl Richardson, and I shall never tire of making love to you." He cried loudly not caring if his Grandfather heard him.

Cheryl laughed some more, "Well, you had better get used to the consequences then, hadn't you?" she teased with a knowing smile.

"Cheryl!" he cried, swinging her around, "what already! We've not been married two months!"

"It only takes a second, Devin. And there have been an awful lot of seconds since we married that we have participated in those sort of things, you know?"

"I know. I was there, and I loved every second of it," Devin remarked, "but a baby! I can't believe it!" He shook his head with disbelief. "How long have you known?"

"A while. I wanted to wait until we moved back in here before telling you because it seemed appropriate. Are you happy, Devin?"

"Happy! It's marvelous. Oh Cheryl, I can't tell you how happy this makes me feel. Does any one else know?"

"Yes." She admitted guiltily, "I wanted you to be the first to know, but your Grandfather noticed I was being sick in the mornings and it was he that suspected what it was. A pregnancy test confirmed it."

"My Grandfather!" To say Devin was surprised was an understatement.

Cheryl nodded, "Don't be a goldfish Devin," she laughed as his mouth dropped open, "aren't you going to carry me over the threshold?" she teased him, "that's if you can still lift me."

"That depends," he grinned.

"On what?"

"How far along are you?"

"Happened the day of our marriage, darling. This is a wedding night baby."

Devin groaned, "That's heavy!" He teased, yet without further ado, he swept his wife up into his arms, and kicking open the door carried her straight inside, his words echoing behind him. "Now Mrs. Richardson are you going to let me have my wicked way with you or not?" He asked with a gleam in his eye.

"Oh, it's already way too late for that, my darling."

* * *

A kilometer or so further away, Sherri helped Jack out of the truck outside Devin's old cabin on the mountain. He halted her as she made to step inside.

"What?" Sherri looked up and saw nothing out of the ordinary. "Something wrong, Jack?"

"Sherri…" Jack stared at her his eyes wide and incredulous, "I've dreamed this moment a thousand times. I've seen all of this before." He laughed.

"Well that doesn't surprise me. You often 'see' things before they happen. So tell me what have you seen regarding this place?"

"That we're going to be happy here, Sherri." He told her tenderly.

She leaned forward and kissed him. "I didn't need a premonition to tell me that, Jack. It's so beautiful here." Sherri turned around and around, trying to take in all the dancing facets at once, an intermingling panorama of sunlight and dazzling sundogs that sparkled amid the rain notorious along the Appalachian Trail. "How can we not be happy?"

Jack came to stand behind her, his arms enveloping her, drawing her up against him. "You know I've said this before Sherri, but I'll say it again, nothing is more beautiful than you."

Sherri shivered she loved it when he said that. "What you see is how you make me feel, Jack. I'm beautiful when I am with you."

Overwhelmed by her words Jack made his own assessment, "Then my darling you will be beautiful always, for I plan never to leave your side." His voice was husky and quivering and with raw desire. His emotions swept over him as he drew her into his arms. Her mouth was soft and pliant, warm and welcoming when he kissed her.

On this, the first night of their marriage all boundaries were gone and they entered the cottage… kissing and laughing… looking forward to their future.

* * *

Devin stretched and yawned, rolling over to look at Cheryl as she slept soundly at his side. He loved her so much. He could not believe that they were married, that they were expecting a baby and his hand strayed to just beneath her navel, awed by the thought that his child lay there. Its tiny heart beating, its trust placed into the hands of those who had created it. "I will love you till my dying breath and beyond." Devin leaned forward and kissed his wife's belly, bestowing the vow on his unborn child.

Cheryl stirred but did not wake, and Devin cuddled her close, thanking God for the fates that had brought her to him. Laying there dreaming of the future it was expected that he should think of the past...and his thoughts turned inward to the last time they had stayed at the estate...the weekend of the storm...when all their dreams had come true thanks to a nightmare...and a literal one at that.

Fortunately, Jack, having sustained broken vertebrae and slipped discs did eventually recover, even though he'd needed two whole months of bed-rest, before he was able to walk unaided again.

Devin giggled, huh bed-rest! It's a wonder he got any at all, Sherri stayed with him the whole time, refusing to leave his side much to Grandfather's chagrin and Jack's discomfort, as like he and Cheryl in his old room, the two had squeezed into Jack's single bedroom together.

Devin smiled, Jack's power of resistance was incredible, but then his back injury did have a lot to do with that. No wonder the poor guy had insisted that they be married as soon as he was well enough. Devin chuckled, wondering if his brother's first night of wedded bliss had been as wonderful as his had been.

Roused by his laughter, Cheryl stirred, and opening her eyes, she smiled as her stomach rumbled. "I can see now why you are always eating these days," Devin laughed, "and you shouldn't be drinking coffee you know?"

"I know. I guess it will have to go. Besides, it does make me feel a bit cranky these days. Shall I make you some? How long have you been awake?"

"No, to the first and not long to the second. I was thinking about the last weekend we were here."

Cheryl hesitated. "Oh don't remind me. I've been trying to forget about that. Although in many respects it was the beginning of my new life."

Devin nodded, placing his arm around her shoulders, helping her to sit up. "Yes, but James' body came as a great shock, I don't think you ever truly accepted that. It wasn't a pretty sight to identify him. I think it would do you good to talk about it."

"Maybe." Cheryl replied staring wide-eyed into space, her thoughts inward.

Devin let her be, waiting until she came back to him. She needed to face the horrors that haunted her. Some nights she woke screaming and now that he knew she was pregnant, he worried about the stress to the baby.

Cheryl knew she had to face it sometime, put it behind her and get on with her life. Now might be as good a time as any to put the past well and truly behind her.

James was dead, he would never hurt her again, "Okay." She told her husband with a wan smile. "We'll talk about it."

Devin held her close as she drew in a deep breath…and began to relate the horror of that day…

Chapter Thirty-six

"The worst of it was after the police had arrived." Cheryl told Devin as they discussed their last fateful day at the estate. "You took the officers up to the attic, and when they looked through the telescope, James still hadn't moved from that spot. That was creepy. He must have seen the police arrive. I was so scared then, Devin. If the police could not frighten James, what could?"

Devin said nothing, just squeezed his wife's shoulder encouraging her to continue. She had to do this by herself. All he had to do was be there for her, with the appropriate comments when needed.

"When they asked us to stay at the house, I'd never been so frightened. I had a terrible feeling that James was too clever for them. That he had anticipated this and while they were out there, he would come here. He'd come here and finish the job he set out to do, and by the time the police came back, they'd find you and me dead and James long gone.

That was why I ran outside, Devin. I wasn't running away from you, I just knew that I had to take the danger from this place. If James saw me, he'd come after me and leave you alone. He didn't know who you were after all. You could have been one of many at the house that day." Cheryl smiled, "Though what he would have thought to me, if he'd assumed Grandfather was my boyfriend, I'll never know."

Devin chuckled.

"He might have assumed Glen to be you though. He'd already seen Glen going after Sherri, so it was possible. We know he'd already made one mistake in identity, so if he could assume Sherri were me, how much more easily could he have assumed Glen was the man I'd left him for?" Cheryl raced on, "once outside though, I was uncertain what to do. I didn't really want to challenge James. To be honest, I'd thought no further than to lead him away from the house. I should have known better really, James wouldn't have stopped until he'd found out whom I'd come here to see. But you don't think of things like that at the time, Devin. I just saw that I'd brought James here, so I had to get him away from here, simple as that.

I think I had decided to hurry down the drive up to the gates. If James were watching the house, he'd surely see me leave it. But that's when I heard that terrible scream. I forgot everything after that.

When I glanced back I saw three of the five police officers come stumbling through the underbrush, hands held to their mouths. One was vomiting openly…I knew then that something terrible had happened.

When they saw me, they tried to usher me back to the house. Their eyes were wild, Devin. I was so afraid for what they had seen."

Her voice slowing now, Cheryl stared straight ahead, remembering the grisly sight that had met her eyes not long afterward. Devin prompted her to continue, and the eyes that she turned to him were wide and fearful. The pulse in her throat thumped erratically. It was hard for her to continue.

She stared at him a long moment, and her lips began to tremble as she continued "I never want to see anything like that again in all my life, Devin. Promise me, you'll take those wires down?"

"Already done, my love. Had them removed last month." He was taking no chances of another tornado sweeping in and doing that again.

Relieved, Cheryl sighed, "Good. Oh God, Devin…what a way to die!"

"He deserved it!"

To Devin's surprise Cheryl shook her head. "Oh, don't get me wrong, he was a bastard, deserved all he got but, Devin, think of it… Imagine dying like that!"

"He can't have known much about it, Cheryl."

"I believe he did. Sherri heard him scream remember? She also heard those wires snapping, said it sounded like a ricochet. Not just once either, but several times. No telling which ones cut through him first."

Realizing, Devin nodded. "Hadn't thought of that."

"When those police came up to me and said I should go back to the house, my first question was, 'had they seen him' and they started throwing up again. I was bewildered by their behavior. Oh God, Devin, then when you came outside it was to ask the police what they were doing back at the house."

"I remember. I said to them, 'he's still watching the house. Why aren't you doing something about that?'" Cheryl shook from the memory. Devin hugged her closer to his side.

"They said, they knew he was still watching the house, but there was a reason for that." Cheryl shuddered, "they said the reason he was still looking up at the house was because his head was stuck in the bush, but the rest of him was all over the place."

Remembering, Devin felt the same wash of nausea drift over him as he had back then.

"We had to identify him." Cheryl whispered. "Why did they make us do that, Devin? We'd already told them it was him."

"Everyone has to make a formal identification, Cherie. It's the law."

"Then someone should change it. God, Devin, when we saw his face close up, you wondered why on earth you hadn't noticed the truth via the telescope."

"Yes. I remember. I thought the blood on his face had been caused by the thorn bush, what a shock it was to find that the wires had decapitated him."

Cheryl shuddered. "Yes, and then there came the rest…bits of him everywhere." Cheryl placed her hands over her face…"God, it was awful." She whispered, "Awful. No one deserves that kind of death, Devin. Not even James. It was as though he'd been put through a meat slice, or as Jack aptly put it a giant cheese cutter. Did you know he had a premonition about that?"

"Yes. He told me." Devin replied gravely.

Weakly, Cheryl smiled, "You were right, Devin. I did need to talk about this. But I don't ever want to talk about it again, do you understand?"

"Just as long as all your dreams are sweet from now on, Mrs. Richardson, that's alright with me."

"Oh my love, how can they not be?"

Devin said nothing, just looked at her expecting she would elaborate. She did.

"I have everything now, Devin. I'm so happy and we have a baby on the way. Life will be sweet from now on. I'm sure of it."

"I'm sure of it too. We came through a long dark tunnel, didn't we? That is, all of us. Grandfather, his tunnel was the longest, took him almost thirty years to get through. I guess it was the same for Jack and I…then there was Sherri and her six year problem with Jack… and you with James…and look…" Devin shrugged, "in one weekend, as nightmarish as it was at the time, everything was solved. Incredible when you think of it huh?" He grinned sheepishly, "so my brilliant idea of the star dappled night mare that became a real nightmare made all our dreams come true."

Cheryl nodded, and snuggling closer to her husband laughingly whispered, "And now that Star Spangles have made you a partner we'll have horses to ride any time we want here on the estate and it's not that I'm complaining…but you know what Devin…"

"What?"

"Next time you tell a brilliant joke…make sure you get the punch line right, okay?"

"Can't do that honey, I'm notorious for forgetting the punch line."

"Then you'll have to stop telling jokes."

"Then how will I make you laugh?" Devin raised his eyebrows up and down suggestively, "I know." And he proceeded to tickle her. Cheryl laughed till breathless when she begged him to stop.

"Only if you say you'll love me forever." He continued tickling her.

"I'll love you forever! Stop, stop!" Cheryl squealed.

"Only if you say I can have my wicked way with you whenever I want."

"Okay, okay, anything." Cheryl laughed and squirmed beneath his questing fingers.

"Anything?"

"I...just...said that didn't I?" Tears of laughter were running down Cheryl's cheeks. "Just give me time off for labor."

"No chance!"

"Devin!" Wide eyed, Cheryl stared at him.

Devin chuckled and ceased his tickling as Cheryl's face registered disbelief.

"You wouldn't?" she asked.

"Wouldn't what?"

"You wouldn't try to make love to me while I'm in labor."

"Why not?" Devin asked her innocently. "I've heard that semen helps to open the cervix at that time."

Cheryl stared at him open mouthed. "You wouldn't?"

Unable to kid her any longer Devin started to laugh then he threw back the covers and started kissing her all over.

"You were kidding right?" Cheryl hoped.

Devin laughed.

"God, Devin you almost had me there!"

"There was no almost about it."

They kissed and caressed until desire washed over them...

"Good joke though, wasn't it?" Devin asked as he snuggled alongside her.

With his kisses making her dizzy, Cheryl muttered an incoherent reply...

"What was that?" Devin chuckled.

A second later neither spoke again for the rest of the morning.

Chapter Thirty-seven

Up early, Grandfather whistled to the dogs and began walking down the drive.

He'd always wanted a dog, more especially since meeting Simba, and now he had three of them, puppies, two Golden Retrievers one white, one sandy, and a tan and black German Shepherd. Grandfather fondled their ears as they raced to meet him jumping up trying to lick his face.

"Steady, steady," he laughed, "you'll have me over. Or is that your plan, huh? Get me down on the ground and lick me to death?" Grandfather laughed merrily. "Now let me tell you what we are going to do. We're going to walk right around this place, that okay with you?" Three pairs of bright eyes told him it was. Three tails wagging frantically expressed their delight at having him with them.

"I've never seen the place properly." Grandfather told them, "you saw it last night, so care to show me around?" Barking, the dogs circled him happy to oblige. Together the man and dogs walked across the lawn toward the estate gates.

"We'll start here." Grandfather told the dogs, "and we'll finish back here, then we know we've seen it all." Tongues lolling in eager expectation the puppies' bright eyes amused him. "Just want to do something first." Walking up to the gates Grandfather traced his hands over the molded ironwork grapes. "Always wanted to do this." He told the dogs, "ever since I first came here. Nice workmanship this. See the detail? Those grapes look real." The dogs wagged their tails.

"Well come on then." Grandfather laughed, "I can see you are eager to be off. Wolf, come on, Boy." Grandfather stopped and turned back, "Wolf?" He walked over to where the German Shepherd had his nose squeezed through the bars of the gate looking at something in the distance. For a moment a shiver ran the length of Grandfather's spine. "What is it, Boy?" He asked anxiously trying to see whatever it was that the dog could see.

Suddenly a rabbit broke its cover and tore down the road disappearing under a bush. Wolf barked frantically. Grandfather sighed with relief. "A rabbit...phew...for a minute there..." He left the sentence unfinished, peering around him. He knew it would take longer than four months to stop feeling uneasy but he was trying.

"There were these men see? Raymond and Chas Baxter and a few of their family I'd known nothing about...anyway they're firmly behind bars now. Raymond got life. And I know it's likely that they might try to send someone after me...but we left no trace. Poof...gone...we left in the night...straight after the trial... sort of witness protection. Couldn't tell the cops I had a vision of a happy future for us all...they'd think I was a basket case...so we have to pacify them and change our names ...eventually...in the meantime...that's why we got you guys...and you're supposed to bite strangers okay...not lick them to death." Grandfather chuckled.

Deep down he hoped the Baxter's would bear him no further threat, but maybe that was wishful thinking. A good deal of people had thanked him for his courage to speak out, even though it had taken him so long. They'd understood, and had not accused him of cowardice, but he didn't feel very brave. Still here...in the mountains...with all this security and his dogs…maybe…hopefully…as hard as it was to believe life would be sweet from now on…he had to have faith in what he had seen in the vision.

Strange really, how easy it had been to give evidence, to stand in court and do so, and he'd wished he'd done it years before. The look of pride on his grandson's faces, on Philippa's, Sherri's and Cheryl's had been more than enough to erase the threatening glares Baxter and his tribe had issued his way.

He'd been afraid true, but Grandfather had seen a glimpse of the future and that had helped him hold his course.

"Thank God for premonitions. That's what I say. Otherwise I might still be holed up in my cottage afraid of anything and everything. And thank God for Sherri, too."

Grandfather had soon realized how wrong he'd been about her…in fact about all reporters. It hadn't been the fault of a journalist that had gotten Horace killed. Why he had ever assumed it had been…Grandfather could no longer fathom. "A case of not being able to see the wood for the trees." He supposed speaking his thoughts aloud.

"Talking of which…" Ahead of him the wide expanse of clearing stood empty and open, "we have to do something about that clearing don't we, Boys?" Grandfather told the dogs, "you've nowhere to cock a leg have you? Good job I've bought lots of saplings, be nice to have some trees around here again." he laughed and began visualizing where he would plant them. "I've bought oaks and apple trees and cherry trees, and native British trees to remind me of home. Home? What am I saying?" Grandfather spoke aloud, "I am home." For the first time he realized that, and he was happy, truly happy.

"Wolf…Ice… Fritz…Come on, Boys. Let's go." Bounding around him the three young dogs were eager to be off, and Grandfather threw sticks for them to chase and chew.

Yes he would be happy. Devin had been right. There was so much to do at the Estate, and everyone he loved was there with him… Grandfather smiled…even Philippa.

"Never thought I'd marry again." Grandfather chuckled, as he gazed across the grounds at Philippa pegging a few bits of washing out.

"Pity you couldn't have been there, Boys. Yesterday we had a double wedding with two times Jack Richardson's getting married on the same day, at the same church at the same time. It caused quite a stir I can tell you. Best day of my life in decades." Grandfather's smile faded as he told the dogs, "felt sorry for Sherri though. Her parents are another story and her brother Ethan is in Brazil on business and she wasn't able to invite her city friends. No sense in looking for trouble..." Grandfather told the dogs. "Baxter and son may be behind bars, but you can bet your bottom dollar...they'd love to know where we've gone."

Wolf barked loudly.

"What's that you say, Boy? You'll see them off if ever they come here?" Grandfather smiled. "I'm sure you will, Boy. I'm sure you will. You'll just have to grow a bit first, just so your bite is worse than your bark, you understand?"

Wagging tails...mountain trails... looking all around him Grandfather breathed easily...

"Well guys... let's take that walk. The past is over... today is the first day of the rest of my life...and I plan to enjoy it. You coming?" he spoke brightly, walking with a spring in his step, while the three dogs bounded around him, "it's time I let the future begin."

END

Printed in the United States
46301LVS00004B/235-237

9 781424 108411

66602493R00057

Printed in Dunstable, United Kingdom